The Wrath of the Marquess

BARBARA RUSSELL

OLIVER HEBER BOOKS

Cover art by Dar Albert at Wicked Smart Designs

Published by Oliver-Heber Books

0 9 8 7 6 5 4 3 2 1

AFTER HAVING BEEN assaulted by a horde of famished ants, swarms of wasps, and even a giant lizard that had no business living in the current geological era, and in England of all places, Cora understood why her late mother had always said that picnics were for reckless people. She admitted defeat to Mother Nature and stood up from the blanket under the tree, brushing breadcrumbs and ants from her skirt. Enough wilderness for today. She needed a bit of civilisation.

"Do you want to leave already, Mama?" Although almost ten, David stammered and still had problems speaking fluently, courtesy of his father's cruel behaviour.

She caressed his unruly auburn curls. "You stay here with Mrs. Marshall and have fun. I'll take a tour of the church over there where hopefully there are no wild creatures." She pointed at the mediaeval church rising from the middle of a meadow with a tall bell tower. "Unless you want to come with me."

David scrunched up his face, wrinkling the freckles over his nose. "No, thank you."

She kissed the top of his head. "I'll be right back."

"Your ladyship." Mrs. Marshall nodded as she kept playing cards with David.

Cora inhaled the sweet scent of wildflowers and pine resin, wondering when the last time she'd been so calm and free had been. Perhaps before her marriage or immediately after it, which was unfair to her son. David was one of the best things— no, the only good thing her wretched marriage gave her. She would go through her ordeal with Jacob ten times over only to have David.

The sudden darkness in the church blinded her for a moment. When her sight adjusted, she made out the tall oval windows and the dark wooden pews carrying the scars of thousands of supplicants. Simple yet warm and welcoming.

It was odd to feel at home in an old church she'd never been to before. Although the tension usually tightening her chest left her whenever she stepped out of her house. Not really her house. Her husband's house. And she didn't consider Jacob her husband either. A husband was supposed to cherish and protect his wife and son. From that point of view, she and Jacob were strangers, sharing the same accommodation.

Her footsteps echoed off the high-vaulted ceiling, and the flames from the candles trembled as she walked past them down the aisle. The cold air sent a chill down her spine, but she didn't mind it. Jacob's house in London had many stoves and fireplaces, yet her heart never warmed there.

She stopped in front of a stained-glass window depicting a blooming lily. The sunlight filtering through the glass cast a riot of colours on her dull grey dress. She played with the elusive patches of light that danced over her skirt as if the universe itself tried to cheer her up. The church tilted for a split second, and she put a hand on a Grecian column for support. Dash it. Had the ground quaked, or was she dizzy? She couldn't tell. The constant tension at home, the arguments with Jacob, and her worries for David's safety made her feel disconnected from the world, numb. Only her love for David pushed her through her bleak days that had no promising future. A door shut, and she held her breath, searching the dark corners.

"Is anyone there?" Her voice resounded through the church.

A large shadow came out of a dimly lit nook, and a tall man wrapped in a cloak swept into view, jolting her. What if Jacob had come to Colchester to force her to come back to London?

She couldn't help but cry out and step back. Her legs hit a pew, and she lost her balance. The man lunged. Lord, he was going to hit her. Her pulse spiked, but her legs locked. She covered her neck with her hands and screamed, mentally bracing herself for the pain to come. But none came. Strong fingers closed around her shoulder and steadied her with a kindness she'd rarely met. Controlling her breathing, she dared to gaze up.

"Madam?" The man's deep baritone matched what little she'd seen of him. "I'm sorry I gave you a fright." He released her shoulder and moved back.

She straightened and found herself staring at a pair of intense emerald eyes. Everything about the man was intense from his impressive build to his thick, curly black hair forming a curtain over strong eyebrows.

Goodness, she'd screamed in his face. "I didn't see you. That's all."

"I saw you tottering, and you dropped this." He handed her a woollen glove, staring at her as if worried she might bite him.

"Thank you." She snatched the glove from his hand with a gesture harsher than she meant.

The folds of his cloak drew apart, revealing the clothes underneath. He wore the madder red uniform of the army, but that was where her military knowledge ended. He could be a general, a private, or belong to any given rank, and she wouldn't distinguish one from another. But she was alone with him. Not even the vicar was present. A cold sensation coiled around her neck, but her anxiety had nothing to do with propriety. He was a good foot taller than she and twice her size, with hands that could squeeze her throat without effort. He could easily overpower her, drag her to a dark corner, and do as he pleased with her. No. Not every man was like Jacob; she ought to remember that.

"Are you all right, madam?" He stepped further back, but if he thought he looked less menacing, he was sorely mistaken.

"I'd better leave." She dropped a quick curtsy. "Good day, sir. Thank you for the glove."

"Don't leave on my account. I disturbed you. Please stay. I was about to leave anyway to catch the next train. I must return to my garrison in London." He bowed, hat under his arm. "Madam."

"Sir." She stepped aside to let him pass.

As he brushed past her, she caught a whiff of his spicy, clean musk, so refreshing compared to Jacob's smell of tobacco and cruelty. He glanced at her from over his shoulder. Maybe she imagined things, but she could swear his stare meant to say she was an odd woman. Well, screaming for no reason while stumbling over her own feet surely hadn't made her appear sane. Despite his build, he was light on his feet, which made no sound in the empty church.

The man had barely time to take a few steps away from her before the ground quaked hard enough to make her wobble again. No, this time it wasn't her dizziness. The ground lurched like an untamed horse. The walls groaned and cracked in a grinding of stone against stone that shot a shiver down her neck. Debris rained from the ceiling, and dust obscured the sunlight as the beautiful stained-glass window shattered. Her mind lagged behind, not quick enough to realise that the earthquake was real.

"Madam." The man wrapped himself around her and dragged her under the marble altar in one smooth move. His hard body smashed against hers, and she raised her arms instinctively against the assault.

David. She struggled, wrestling against the man's strong arms. "Let me go. My son."

The crashes from the crumbling church covered her words.

She couldn't see anything aside from his dark cloak and red jacket. The shaking seemed to go on for hours as the church disintegrated around them. The deafening chime of a church bell, followed by a thundering, metallic sound, meant the bell tower had collapsed. Dust thickened the air, suffocating her. The man never let her go, pulling her against his chest. Surprise more than fear caused her breath to hitch, but the protective way he held her slowed her pulse.

He let her go when the world stopped shaking. She coughed as the air turned heavier than a blanket over her nose. Dust covered her lips, and only a few rays of sunlight filtered through the rubble piled around them. She and the stranger exchanged a terrified glance. He breathed hard, and his eyes were impossibly wide. Fine particles, like talc, whitened the top of his head and his eyelashes.

"Are you hurt?" He checked her face with clinical intent.

She passed a hand over her cheeks and chin, feeling the dust stuck on her skin. "I don't think so. You?"

"All in one piece. Just scared." He crawled out from under the altar although there wasn't anywhere to go. The debris covering his cloak slid down when he moved. "Don't move for now."

She curled up in a corner and hugged her bent knees as he explored the narrow space around their shelter. Pieces of broken Grecian columns, statues, and masonry formed an enclosing cave around them with fissures and cracks from which sunlight filtered through. The man didn't go far, only a couple of feet, and he couldn't stand up so cramped the space was.

He wiped the dirt from his face. A shallow cut on his cheek bled. "We're sealed here. I don't want to move anything. The entire structure might collapse. There isn't much we can do but wait for someone to remove the rubble." He plopped himself down next to her with a loud exhale.

"I can't stay here. My son was right outside the church when the earthquake started. I must see how he's faring." Her breath came out in quick pants. "What if he needs help? What if he's injured?" She started to crawl out of the altar, but he stopped her, holding her by her waist.

"We must wait." Reasonable words, but her heart ordered her to run.

"I can't." She gripped his arm. "My son is out there."

He gently pulled her back. "You're going to hurt yourself. I don't have the strength to move these large boulders. Someone will come soon."

"But David..." A lump swelled in her throat, cracking her voice at the thought of David lying under the rubble.

He closed his big, rough hands around hers. "If he was outside in the open, then he's likely faring better than we are. Where was he exactly?"

She let him hold her hands, needing this stranger's comfort. "He was under the old oak tree close to the river, playing cards with his governess."

"I'm sure he's all right. That tree is strong and steady. During an earthquake, it's better to be under a tree than in a house or an old church." He sat next to her, releasing her hands.

She rubbed her aching forehead, controlling her breathing. The man was right. David would be fine.

He watched her as if worried she might rush to remove the rubble and kill them both. "It's hardly appropriate, but given the circumstances, I'm going to introduce myself. I'm Ethan Hertford, Lord Captain in the Seventh Royal Fusiliers." He bowed his head. "What's your name, madam?"

The name stunned her. Not that she knew what a captain was or did compared to a commander, but Hertford was a family name she recognised. He was the son of the Marquess of Stark. "I'm Cora Hadder... I mean Wiley. Hadder is my maiden name. My husband is Lord Jacob Wiley, Earl of Roxbury."

At the mention of her husband, he narrowed his eyes to slits. "It's a shame we met in such an unfortunate situation, Lady Roxbury."

Despite all those years, the title 'Lady Roxbury' didn't sound as if it belonged to her. "Please call me Cora, my lord. The circumstances are rather informal."

"Then please call me Ethan." He flashed a grin she might have found charming if it weren't for her worry about David.

She cleared her throat and swallowed a lump of dust. " You're the son of the Marquess of Stark. I met your father, Lord Stark. You look like him."

He ran a hand through his thick curls. Dust rained from them. "Yes, the marquess is my father."

She couldn't ignore the way his voice softened. "Do you know my husband?"

He stretched out his long legs as much as the confined space allowed. "A bowing acquaintance. I can't say I know the earl well."

Cora wished she could say the same.

His jaw clenched. "Is your husband in Colchester as well?"

Heavens, that would be a nightmare worse than an earthquake. "No. I'm here with my son David to visit the country and take a moment of rest from London's busy life and coal smell. Children need to spend time outdoors and breathe some fresh air."

"I have to take your word for it. I'm afraid I haven't spent a lot of time with children, thank goodness," he whispered the last two words.

"You don't like children." She couldn't completely remove the hint of disapproval from her voice.

He scrubbed the back of his neck. "No, it's that they're often loud and full of energy, and I don't have patience for them."

Jacob had a similar opinion, only ten times worse. "David is special, and I'm not saying that because he's my son. He's almost ten, but he's very mature for his age." Thanks to the fact he hadn't had a normal childhood, despite her best efforts. "He must be worried about me. I hope he stays with his governess and doesn't search around for me."

Ethan stroked her hand with the rough pads of his fingers. "Do not worry. You'll see David soon." He'd misinterpreted her emotions.

She was worried about David, but the reason her voice cracked was because Jacob didn't love his own son. Worthless boy was his best term of endearment. Likely, he wouldn't care if David got injured. The worst thing was that David believed every insult his father spat out. She stared at the dirty floor, collecting herself before Ethan saw the deep hurt in her eyes. That was hardly the right moment to discuss her family's problems with a stranger.

"Are you going to be deployed somewhere?" she asked to change the subject.

He left his hand on top of hers, and she didn't mind. The near-death experience was to blame for her lack of judgement. But on second thought, who cared?

"Yes, I'm about to leave," he said, "for Lias, an island in the middle of the Indian Ocean. I haven't been deployed actually. I volunteered."

She stiffened. She didn't want the man, who had saved her from being crushed under the rubble, to be one of those gentlemen who believed that brutal force had to be employed to conquer and dominate other people. He was a future marquess. No one had forced him to become a soldier. Less fortunate men didn't have a choice but to enlist to save their families from starvation.

"May I ask for what reason you volunteered?" Gold, diamonds, spices, everything?

If he noticed her challenging tone, he didn't show it. "I was deployed to Lias years ago. There's a group of pirates, the Thorne Pirates they're called, who keep attacking and terrorising the people on the island. They come and pilfer as they please." He stroked his cleft chin, lost in his thoughts.

"I see. They're competing with the empire." She arched her brow.

Instead of reproaching her for her sarcastic comment, he let out a bitter chuckle. "Alas, I wish the pirates cared only about silk and spices." He turned towards her, emerald eyes going hard and cold like the gems they resembled. "The Thorne Pirates trade in slaves. They take everyone they can snatch, making no distinction between women, old people, or children. Their victims are never seen again. In fact, the pirates ignore offers of gold or jewels in exchange for the kidnapped. It seems that slaves are more valuable."

She held her breath for a moment. "That's awful, but why do you want to help? What motivates you?" She dispensed with sarcasm, genuinely wanting to know the answer.

"I hate injustice. My grandfather fought in the Napoleonic Wars. He said Napoleon was a tyrant who didn't care about how many of his men died as long as he could get what he wanted. That was what motivated my grandfather to go to war. He wanted to stop Napoleon from conquering all of Europe, an endless blood-bath. My father shares the same sentiment. I want to fight for a purpose, to protect those who can't protect themselves, not to let powerful people become even more powerful."

She sagged against the leg of the altar in relief. At least he wasn't one of those men who enjoyed violence for its own sake. "I'd be terrified to face slave traders. Aren't you afraid?"

He reclined his head, exposing his strong neck and Adam's apple. "Yes, I am. That's why I came here." He pointed in the direction of where the beautiful stained-glass window had been. "My mother is buried in the church's graveyard. She was born in Colchester. I came to tell her I was leaving and that I might meet her soon." A corner of his mouth quirked up. "One way or another."

"I hope you return home safe and victorious." She tentatively closed her hand around his, putting all her admiration for him into the gesture.

He whipped his head towards her, his lips parting in surprise.

She removed her hand. "Apologies."

"Don't. I appreciate your concern. I'm ready to die, but I don't want to." He chuckled nervously. "We came quite close to dying today. I wonder if it's a sign that I should stay here or a good omen since we survived."

"I'd take it as a good omen. I think your cause is a noble one. Not many people care about the lives of distant inhabitants of the empire."

"It's a pity." He winced as he stretched his legs again and shifted his position. "The other reason why I want to go is because of the colours, the food, and the nature." His smile was broad and genuine now. "When I served in Lias, I made many friends. If you open yourself to the islanders' culture, they'll welcome you with all their hearts. The first time, I stayed in a magnificent room with red stucco parrots in relief on the walls. They were coloured so vividly I could believe they were real. I expected them to fly away. When the weather became too hot, I would press my cheek against the cool wall." He spoke with such passion she couldn't help but wish to see those distant places too. "And the music there is booming with a quick tempo. I love it—"

Loud voices came from the other side of the wall of rubble, cutting him off.

"Is there anyone here?" a man shouted. "Anyone?"

"Yes. Help!" she said at the same time as Ethan said, "We're under the altar."

"How many of you? Are you injured?" The man's voice came muffled through the masonry.

"Two people. No injuries," Ethan said.

"Stay still," another man said. "We'll take you out in a moment."

The man's prediction turned out to be rather optimistic.

The moment became a few stifling hours of fear of being squashed by a loose piece of marble. But with each stone and wooden log removed, a slice of the sky came into view. She leant against Ethan, resting her head on his shoulder, too scared and tired to think about propriety. He covered her with his cloak and held her hand, shielding her every time a brick or a piece of masonry rolled too dangerously close to them. She clamped a hand over her nose and mouth as dust lifted into the air. The men's voices and the grinding stones were the only sounds.

Cora and Ethan didn't talk, but with her cheek against his chest, the steady beat of his heart reassured her. When the rubble was removed to form a passage wide enough to reveal a group of tired men, she sobbed in relief.

"Sir, madam, you may come through." One of the men waved Cora and Ethan out through the opening.

She breathed in the fresh air, her chest tightening.

"My lady." Ethan helped her up.

Her legs quivered after the cramped position she'd stayed in for hours, but he steadied her as if he didn't suffer from her same predicament. She squeezed herself through the passage, helped by a group of strangers with grim faces and caked blood on their hands. Ethan crawled out of the opening after her.

"Thank you." She sobbed, gazing around at her rescuers. "Thank you." She sobbed harder when Mrs. Marshall rushed towards her in a flutter of dark clothes.

"Your ladyship." The older woman held Cora in a strong hug. "We were so worried."

"David. Where is he?"

"Safe. Not a scratch. Do not fear." Mrs. Marshall patted Cora's cheek. "He's waiting for you with the nuns who organised a camp by the river. Everyone is there. Many houses have been damaged or are unsafe so tents have been pitched. They're the safest option for now. I came here to see if you were all right."

Cora shivered from relief, sagging against the governess. "Thank goodness."

Ethan shook hands with the people of the rescue party, thanking each one of them.

From his calm composure and steady voice, it was hard to

believe he'd been trapped with her under the rubble. Only the scratches and the dust belied his ordeal.

Cora accepted a flask of water from Mrs. Marshall and gazed around the town. Goodness. The ground itself had cracked. What once had been houses, now were piles of rubble. An eerie silence lingered. Not even the birds sang.

"My lady," Ethan said. "Where may I escort you?"

He had to be exhausted. She should refuse his offer of help for his own sake after he'd taken care of her, but she didn't want to. "The camp, please?"

Cora, Ethan, and Mrs. Marshall walked down to the river through piles of broken bricks, masonry, and disturbing stains of blood.

"We were very lucky," she said.

"When David and I saw the church collapse, we were distraught." Mrs. Marshall hid her face in her handkerchief. "I mean, after everything you've been through with his lordship, it wouldn't be fair for you to—" She fell silent as Ethan angled towards her.

Cora held her hand. "It's all right." She wasn't talking about the collapsed church, but the fact Mrs. Marshall had almost spilt Cora's personal problems.

She sped up when the camp came into view. White tents stretched along the river bank. Some people cried. Others showed blood-stained bandages. Ethan walked next to her, silent and protective. She skidded to a stop at the entrance of the camp, searching for David through the crowd of children.

"This way." Mrs. Marshall led her to the edge of the camp.

Men with bandaged heads and torn clothes lay on cots in the open tents. The gruesome view didn't have time to upset her too much because she spotted a familiar mop of auburn hair.

"Mama." David threw himself in her arms.

"My angel." She hugged him, inhaling his clean, soapy scent. Tears burned her cheeks as she scattered kisses on his face.

"I thought I lost you," he whispered, resting his head on her chest.

"Never." Still holding him, she turned towards Ethan.

He stood at attention, his expression unyielding as he watched her and David. "I had no doubt your son would be safe."

"Thank you, Captain." She held David more tightly, wiping her tears.

David stared at Ethan with suspicion.

Ethan bowed. "At your service. Now that you're safe, I'd better leave and see if my room at the inn is still available. I guess I missed my train to London."

A sudden, irrational fear took hold of her as he spun around to go away. "Will I see you again?" she nearly yelled.

His hard features softened. "I will seek you before leaving for London for a proper farewell."

Farewell. How sad. But he was a stranger. She shouldn't feel shattered by his departure. Yet as he raised a hand in goodbye, heading for the town, she couldn't deny the sense of loss gripping her.

two

THE INN ON the outskirts of the town where Ethan had booked a room was still standing, but the innkeeper wouldn't allow anyone to enter. A crack had ripped through the wall like a bolt of lightning, and the roof was set askew. Unless Ethan wanted to risk being buried under the rubble again, his only chance was to spend the night in the camp and leave for London the next day. He'd hoped the inn would have been undamaged since it wasn't in the town centre. No such luck.

If he were honest, he didn't mind the idea of staying. He'd have the opportunity to see how Cora and her son were faring one last time. Hard to believe such a sweet woman was Lord Roxbury's wife. He hadn't told Cora the complete truth. He knew her husband better than he'd let her believe. Lord Roxbury had been at the military academy with Ethan. When the order to join the British army on a real battlefield had arrived, Roxbury had quietly been dismissed after his father had pulled all possible strings to keep his precious son safe. Not that Ethan could blame a parent for wanting to protect his child, but while Roxbury was a formidable fighter, he didn't shine for bravery, humility, or kindness.

If Roxbury had been a common man and not a titled one, he

would have been dishonourably discharged for his outbursts about refusing to go to battle, his arrogance, and his insults against fellow cadets. Cora might not be aware of her husband's shameful cowardice, or maybe she didn't care. Or perhaps Roxbury had grown to be a wise man. Whatever the truth was, informing her of how Roxbury had begged his father to be removed from the academy was none of Ethan's business. Many men didn't possess the courage to march to the battlefield, but Roxbury had retired from the army right after receiving the order to leave for Lias. He was nothing more than a deserter.

The closer Ethan walked to the camp, the faster he went. He changed his mind about talking to Cora when he spotted her out of her tent, hugging her son and laughing softly with him. Mother and son shared the same auburn hair and eyes the colour of warm whiskey. When she laughed as heartily as she did now, her whole face brightened, and the scatter of freckles on her pert nose became more evident. No, he shouldn't disturb her. She was happy and safe. That was all that mattered. Somehow, leaving her started an ache in his chest, but he was about to sail to the Indian Ocean on a dangerous mission. He needed to focus.

He turned around when she called him.

"Ethan. It's me."

The amount of happiness surging inside him at hearing his name on her lips was ridiculous. "My lady." He faced her and bowed.

She brushed a curl from her face. "You really don't like children. Is this why you were leaving without saying a word?" Her light tone tore a smile from him.

"I didn't want to disturb you."

"Not at all. I was telling David how brave you were in the church while I was terrified."

He shifted his weight, not sure why the compliment started an odd flutter in his belly. "Hardly brave. I'm afraid I can't do anything about earthquakes. We were lucky."

"You're being modest." She positively glowed when David shuffled closer to hold his mother's hand.

"Evening, my lord." David stared up at him with large eyes before averting his gaze.

"Lord Stark, this is my son, David." She caressed his curls with a tender gesture.

"Thank you for saving my mama." David offered Ethan a small, shaking hand.

The boy had courage. Ethan had to give him that. David looked terrified but was ready to shake the hand of the man who intimidated him.

Ethan obliged. "It was an honour."

He closed his hand around David's tiny one, and an odd sense of responsibility weighed on him, which didn't make sense. He would soon leave for the other side of the world. Why would he feel responsible for a child he barely knew and who had a loving mother?

David flashed a smile before putting some distance between them.

"We were going to the canteen to help with the dishes since many people were wounded. Would you like to join us?" Cora said.

David nodded, half-hiding behind his mother.

"I would," Ethan said. Why not be useful?

As they walked along the path between two rows of tents, David threw curious glances at him. The child had none of his father's features. Hopefully, his character was different.

Ethan's military training proved useful in the canteen. He set up a chain of work to wash, rinse, and dry the dishes as Cora and David worked next to him. The boy tried many times to say something, but he always stopped before talking.

"Is there something you want to tell me, lad?" Ethan tried not to sound too serious.

Cora gave David an encouraging nod.

"What's the name of your regiment, sir? Mama couldn't remember," David finally asked in a whisper.

So that was the question he'd been eager to ask. His speech was troubled. The boy stammered and drawled as if he were scared of being punished.

Ethan set aside a pile of clean dishes. "I'm a captain in the Seventh Royal Fusiliers."

Cora slanted him a fleeting, warning glance.

David stopped drying a pot. "Royal Fusi... Fusiy..." He shook his head. "Difficult to say. I speak funny, don't I?" He frowned, resuming his work.

Ethan took the dry pot and placed it on a shelf. "No, you don't. I reckon that once your facial muscles become stronger, you'll feel more confident. I couldn't pronounce my 'r's when I was eight. The physician said I had to strengthen my throat muscles. He was right."

David showed his wide smile, and two dimples appeared on his cheeks. Ethan couldn't help but smile back. Cora instead found the soapy water suddenly fascinating, her lips pressed tightly in a flat line. What did he say wrong?

When darkness crept across the camp, Ethan escorted Cora and David to their tent. David kept yawning, slogging behind. His eyelids drooped, and his head nodded off.

"You're going straight to bed." Cora held his hand.

"I don't want to go to sleep right now. I want to walk to the river and see the stars..." He didn't finish the sentence as his eyes fluttered.

Cora stumbled when her son could barely stand so tired he was.

"Another day, laddie." Ethan scooped him up in his arms without thinking.

The gesture came naturally. David sagged against his chest, breathing softly, his body limp.

"He's asleep already."

"He does that," Cora said. "The first time it happened, I was worried, but it seems normal for him."

"It's a gift. I wish I could do the same."

"You said you didn't like children."

"I don't. But you said David was special, and I agree." Ethan put a hand on David's back. The child's breath feathered on Ethan's neck.

"Thank you," she whispered.

"I don't mind carrying him."

"No, I mean, for not making fun of him." She caressed David's head. "You know his muscles aren't the problem, don't you?"

"I do." He doubted David's problem was physical.

"I always tell him he'll speak flawlessly soon, but other people laugh and make fun of him. It's hard for him. He's afraid to speak in front of strangers."

Yes, Ethan reckoned David had gathered all his courage to talk to him. "Children can be cruel to other children. They say what they want without thinking about the consequences."

She shook her head. "I wasn't talking about children."

"Adults can be cruel too."

Her eyebrows knitted together. "Indeed."

Something cracked in his chest when he laid David down on the bed. He tucked the blanket around the boy, and after that, he didn't have any excuses to stay in that tent. David stirred in his sleep, muttering something. It was odd to think Ethan wouldn't see him again soon. Or never.

Cora shifted her weight when he closed the flap of the tent. "I guess you're leaving tomorrow," she said.

"At dawn. London then Southampton."

She wrapped her arms around herself. "We'll stay here. Our cottage doesn't have any apparent damage, and as soon as the town council declares it safe, we'll leave the camp."

"Aren't you going back to London?"

"Not for now." She gazed up at the stars.

Ethan followed her gaze. London's smoke and lights covered the starlight. Here it shone in all its silver beauty on Cora's delicate profile and her porcelain skin. David was right about wanting to see the stars.

"I admire your courage to risk your life to protect others," Cora said still looking up at the sky, but her tone held a gravity that hinted that something deeper was going on in her thoughts.

"I've been trained to fight and kill when necessary. I don't want to use those skills for the wrong causes. It's not about courage," he said. "The decisions we make are always about pain versus pain."

She tilted her head, and a long curl caressed the gentle line of her jaw. He had to fight the impulse to tuck the wayward curl behind her ear. How curious.

"What do you mean? Pain versus pain?" she asked.

"Staying here and doing nothing is more painful than leaving and facing death. It's always a matter of choosing what's less painful."

"You're right. The choice always leans towards what causes less pain. The lesser evil." She shivered although the night was warm.

He dipped his head to see her amber gaze. "What pains you, my lady?"

A flush crept over her cheeks, but it wasn't a good type of flush. She opened and closed her mouth.

"Apologies," he said. "I didn't mean to be so bold."

"Not at all." She tugged the shawl around her shoulders. "You gave me a reason to ponder my decisions. I have only to find the courage to do the right thing and ask myself what is less painful."

"I'm sure you will find your courage." Whatever decision she talked about.

Her smile didn't reach her eyes. "Your faith in me motivates me, and your courage inspires me. What happened today, feeling death so close..." She trembled again. "It makes me think about my future and especially David's future."

He had to ask. Besides, he would leave soon and not see her

again, or for a very long time at the very least. "When we were in the church, I gave you a fright, and you reacted in a certain way."

"What way?" She lost the colour in her face.

"Reflexively. As someone who's used to being hit." There. He'd said it. He'd seen many soldiers returned from the battlefield reacting in a similar fashion, curling over themselves, trying to hide, too used to receiving pain. "And Mrs. Marshall hinted at a difficult situation for you."

She trapped her bottom lip between her teeth, her lovely features tightening. If she slapped him, he wouldn't blame her. "I don't always react like that. It happens, not often, but my situation is complicated."

Anger tasted bitter in his mouth. He clenched his fists. Roxbury. Not only an arrogant coward but a swine as well.

In for a penny, in for a pound. "Even David?" The question came out like a low growl.

"No." There was fire in her gaze and ice in her voice. "Never. I've never let him touch my son. He'll never touch him. No matter what I have to do."

That was a relief of sorts.

"And..." She swallowed. "He doesn't hit me. Not really. He's brusque though."

"But he frightens you." That would be enough for Ethan to kill Roxbury.

"Yes, he does." Her voice was barely above a whisper.

Frightening her was the same thing as hitting her. The result was the same. She didn't live a full, happy life because of her husband.

He inched closer and lowered his voice. "There' is a lady in Marylebone. Her name is Mrs. Sterling. She's the wife of one of my men. She helps women who might be in need of protection and succour. She manages a centre close to her house where she welcomes women who want to leave the past behind. If you need help, please consider that option. Mrs. Sterling is a trustworthy person."

She nodded. "Thank you."

"Tell her I sent you. She'll help both you and David."

Mrs. Marshall stuck out her head from her tent. She didn't say anything, but her questioning expression was a reminder that Cora was a married woman whose reputation he ought to consider.

He stepped back from Cora. "Lady Roxbury, I regret the circumstances in which we were introduced, but it was a pleasure to meet you. I hope we'll meet again."

A sudden choking sensation caught him. He might never see her again. He shouldn't be upset about not seeing a stranger again, but for the first time, from the moment he'd volunteered to leave for Lias, he hoped to return home safe.

She grabbed his hand with surprising energy, clinging to him with desperation. "Please come back. We need brave men like you." Her auburn eyelashes fluttered down in a sad gesture that tore at his heart.

"I wish you only happiness." He slid his hand out of hers. "We aren't all monsters."

"I know." Her smile didn't light her eyes. "Be safe."

"Farewell." He bowed from the waist before leaving a little piece of his heart in her elegant hands.

three
Four Years Later

As CORA SAT in the carriage with her husband, she rubbed the back of her stiff neck. Her muscles throbbed even though Jacob had hurt her several days ago. The attack had been swift but had caught her off guard.

She wondered if the pain came from her body or her mind. Sometimes it was difficult to distinguish between the two. At least the violence didn't happen often and didn't leave bruises if that was any consolation. She had only to learn to keep her distance from his mercurial moods and avoid angering him until she put aside enough money for David and her to leave. The sum she'd squirrelled with careful patience over months would barely cover the trip to Calais for David and herself. She needed thrice that amount to start a new life in France, away from Jacob and his cruelty.

He sat in front of her, his icy blue eyes regarding her with contempt. And to think there had been a time when she'd found his eyes warm and charming, caring and compassionate. How wrong she'd been. They had the colour of an ancient glacier and were just as hard and cold. Oh, he was handsome. She couldn't deny that. He was the most handsome man she'd ever seen. Fine features, a straight nose, and bouncy golden hair that framed a perfect jaw. But if there was a person who embodied the old saying 'looks are deceiving,' it was him. And she'd been deceived. Deeply so.

"Why do you keep touching your neck?" Even his voice sounded misleadingly tender and caring as if he were genuinely worried about her.

"It's sore, and you know why." She hoped to give him back some of his uncaring attitude.

He arched a perfect eyebrow. "Stop this fuss. I barely touched you. You simply love playing the victim and trying to make me feel guilty for something I didn't do. You know I care about your well-being."

Did she imagine the sarcasm in his voice? She couldn't tell anymore.

She didn't say anything because he wasn't expecting an answer and he wouldn't care anyway. Besides, arguments with him tended to end with him dismissing her feelings as hysterical or imaginary, and with her growing frustrated.

He'd touched her. He'd closed his elegant but very strong hands around her neck and squeezed just because he enjoyed controlling the life flowing in and out of her while she remained petrified.

He opened *The Times* and hid behind the ironed pages. So much for caring about her.

The title on the front page caught her attention. Lord Commander Stark and his division, after having returned to London from Lias Island, had made a speech about the importance of protecting every corner of the empire from looters and slave traders. The complete defeat of the Thorne Pirates had brought him fame, not always of the good kind.

Ethan. The relief of learning he was safe in London had been overwhelming. Not a day had gone by in the past years without her thinking about him. Also because his name appeared in *The Times* every other day, especially after his father had died.

Jacob folded the newspaper, and she couldn't read more. "Stark does nothing but preach about equality, freedom, and brotherhood these days, like a damn Frenchman," he said, drumming his fingers on his knee. "He thinks he's morally superior to anyone who didn't fight in a battle."

She remained quiet and let him talk. It was the best strategy to avoid an argument.

News about the gruesome battles to crush the pirates' trade had circulated for weeks. Many soldiers had died. Others had lost their limbs or mental sanity. But the island was thriving now that the menace had been vanquished. Ethan had been awarded with the Victoria Cross for bravery. A war hero. Not that his bravery pleased London's peers.

Jacob huffed. "No one can endure his holier-than-thou attitude anymore. It's a matter of days before he's kicked out of the gentlemen's club. Arrogant prick."

Surely, Jacob would play a role in Ethan's being dismissed.

She hadn't seen or communicated with Ethan since the Colchester earthquake. He might have forgotten her, but a warm flutter started in her chest at the possibility of meeting him again before she left London. He was here.

Would he be disappointed to learn her situation hadn't changed much from the last time they'd seen each other? Would he think less of her? Had he changed and become arrogant as Jacob said? No, that wasn't possible simply because everything that came out of Jacob's mouth was a lie.

The carriage rolling to a stop forced her back to reality. The footman opened the door and pulled out the steps.

Jacob tossed the newspaper on the seat and blew out a breath. "Let the farce begin."

"Farce?" she asked, climbing out of the carriage without his help. Not that she needed it or wanted it, but there had been a time when he'd behaved like a gentleman to her.

"What else would you call this?" He waved dismissively at the rest home of the Royal Veterans' Society.

She tilted her head back to take the building in. One of the best structures in town, in one of the growing areas of London, the place had the air of a great palace with its large bay windows, portico, and wide front gate. The bright white walls reminded her of the aristocratic houses in Belgravia.

What the rest home symbolised stood tall and proud; it was the only place in London where war veterans, who didn't have a family, could stay and recover from their ordeal before finding some accommodation or a job. If the soldiers were unable to work, the Royal Veterans' Society took care of them.

Jacob didn't offer her his arm as they entered the rest home. "I don't understand what the purpose of such a structure is. It should be a profitable building. We should split it in new town-houses for respectable, paying families."

She had to bite her tongue not to reply. The soldiers in the rest home were more than respectable.

Helping soldiers who had seen too much war recover and find happiness again wasn't a farce but a noble pursuit. Definitely more noble than Jacob's passion for immediate pleasures, his three favourite 'D's as he called them— drinks, drugs, and damsels.

She couldn't voice such a thought. He would yell at her and then pretend nothing had happened, that she was overreacting and playing the victim. One day, he'd wake up and wouldn't find David and her in his house, and although she wouldn't be able to see his face, it would be the best day of her life.

The polished floor and gleaming benches in the entrance hall matched the posh façade. Jacob crossed the room with long strides while she took her time to gaze at the clean walls tinted in soothing shades of blue.

A few men sat on the wooden benches. Some of them smoked

cigarettes. Others stared at the walls. Missing limbs and scars were a testament to the brutality of the wars they'd fought around the world. The men didn't talk, nor did they wail in pain. Yet their agony was palpable. Pebbles grew on her skin at their quiet suffering. They cast disinterested glances towards Cora and Jacob as they walked down the long corridor towards somewhere.

Jacob clicked his tongue. "And they want me to approve and spend my money in this place." He set his blue eyes on the patients with disdain.

"Spend?" she asked. Finally, she might understand what they were doing at the rest home.

He stopped in the middle of the corridor and exhaled as if he needed to collect his patience after an idiotic question. "It's a complicated story. I won't waste my time trying to explain it to you, but the rest home is built on a piece of land that belongs to three different people. I'm one of those."

"You own a part of this rest home?"

He lowered his eyebrows. "You've never been particularly bright."

Swallowing her next comment required all her concentration. Years ago, his insults would have shaken her deeply and reduced her to tears, making her wonder if she truly was an idiot. She was ashamed to admit in those days, she would have felt worthless and begged for his forgiveness. Now his barbs left behind a trail of anger and resentment but not self-loathing. He couldn't hurt her as he'd done in the past. She'd been poisoned so many times by his venom she'd grown immune to it. Not without pain.

To calm herself, she mentally counted all the pounds she'd set aside so far. Every time she stored half a shilling away, the fear of being caught chilled her because he counted every last coin he gave her and that she spent. Her maid was no better, too scared of Jacob to help her mistress. But the discomfort was worth every penny. Literally.

"This place is filled with dim-witted idiots," he said, not caring about keeping his voice low. "David would fit here nicely." He sniggered at his own joke.

Enough. Insulting her was one thing. But David had to be left out of his parents' endless arguments.

"Jacob," she said through clenched teeth. It was her turn to come to an abrupt stop in the hallway. "Don't you dare."

"What?" He turned towards her with a menacing, quick move. He was a formidable pugilist after all, light on his feet and strong with his fists. His chest rose, stretching the fine fabric of his waistcoat. "Stop defending that spineless boy. He's stupid and lazy. As soon as he turns fourteen, he'll leave for the Royal Military College, and if those tutors can't turn him into a man with their whips and rods, then he can go and live wherever he wants as long as it's far away from my money and me."

Over her dead body. Anger flamed her cheeks. If her plan went well, she and David would be far from London and Jacob in a matter of months. Sometimes she wondered how Jacob would pass the time without harassing his wife and son.

Freedom was her goal. Although obsession was a more appropriate term.

It was hard to believe the evil creature in front of her was the same man who had wooed her and conquered her heart with poems, tears, and flowers. He'd been pure charm, caring and loving. He'd promised— no, sworn to respect and cherish her, telling her over and over how deeply he loved her. She'd believed his every word. What a fool she'd been.

"David doesn't need your money," she said.

He jabbed a finger at her. "You should be grateful that I'm in a good mood today." He shook his head, resuming walking towards the end of the hallway. "This place needs to be cleared, and to hell with this rabble."

That rabble he so despised included soldiers who had been deployed to every corner of the empire to fight for queen and country, and Jacob had built his fortune on the blood of those soldiers. The deeper they walked down the corridor, the more men they passed. While those in the entrance hall had been quiet, these others shivered, their teeth chattering as if the temperature were freezing. Some muttered under their breath. Her chest tightened for a man who tried and failed to button his cufflinks with a trembling hand. The more he tried, the more his hand trembled.

She couldn't ignore him. "Do you need help, sir?" she asked, stopping in front of him.

The man blinked fast before nodding. "Thank you."

"What the hell are you doing?" Jacob hissed.

"It'll take a moment." She made short work of buttoning the cufflinks before Jacob seized her arm and yanked her away.

"Stay away from these crazies, or I swear I'll have you locked up here too."

She shrugged herself free. "Don't touch me."

The quick contact with his hand had her breathing hard, mostly in fear. She put on a brave face and was aware of how manipulative he was, but the fear always lingered. She hated how he could still frighten her deeply.

He pinned her with a scorching glare that promised retribution in the privacy of his house. "I can touch you whenever I want." He was about to say something else, but a shout coming from the other side of the corridor cut him off.

They both remained still, but there was no other sound.

Jacob's sculpted lips twisted in a cruel snarl, ruining his perfect beauty. "If that idiot Stark thinks he can buy my share of this place from me, he's mistaken. I'll drag him to court. This whole thing was his father's idea."

At hearing that name, she stifled a gasp. Ethan. It wasn't surprising that he was involved in the Royal Veterans' Society, which meant she might meet him now. Her pulse sped up. She wasn't ready to meet him, especially since she was with Jacob. Ethan would see how Jacob behaved towards her. He would wonder why she hadn't left her husband. But she was going to. She had a plan.

"Do you really want a legal battle?" She stopped, not wanting to provoke Jacob further if only for Ethan's sake.

"I'm not afraid of a confrontation. I won't bother to explain to you all the legal intricacies of land law or how this place ended up with three owners. David must have taken after someone after all." A corner of his mouth quirked up in a smirk as he stared at her, waiting for her to talk back.

She wouldn't give him the satisfaction of offering him another reason to disparage her. With Jacob, who demanded constant attention from everyone, indifference was the best weapon against his attacks.

"To keep this horrible place up" —he waved a hand around— "Stark and Lady Kingsley need my approval as well, or these filthy soldiers will find another place to grovel. My father might have indulged in the late Lord Stark's fantasies of charity. Not me."

Yes, the late Earl of Roxbury had been a sweet man. How such a gentleman had produced someone like Jacob was a mystery.

"Sir." Another man reached out and grabbed Jacob's hand. His gaze was lost in a horror only he could see. "There were cannons. The ground exploded..."

"Get off me." Jacob snatched his hand out of the man's and closed a fist. "You filthy—" He raised his hand, ready to punch him.

"Don't." She shoved Jacob hard. Heaven help her.

The moment he staggered back, nearly losing his balance, and stared at her in shock was both exhilarating and terrifying. He wouldn't let the affront pass. He wouldn't wait this time. She'd stood up against him, but her defiance would cost her another sleepless night of pain and fear, or worse, he would vent his anger on David, punishing him by forcing him to sleep on the floor or eat only kitchen scraps for a week.

Jacob's cold fury reached her heart with the precision of a stiletto and caused her blood to chill.

"How dare you," he said in a low tone that was ten times more frightening than a shout. He stretched out his hand, his anger directed towards her this time.

He was going to grab her by the throat— his favourite punishment.

She stepped back and braced herself for the attack, ready to shove him again, but the blow never arrived. She chanced a look at the beast who was her husband only on paper.

A tall, broad man had blocked Jacob's arm and held it in a firm grip. "You touch her, and I'll kill you." It wasn't a threat but a solemn oath.

She would recognise that deep, calm baritone everywhere even after years. Even though she'd spoken with him for less than a day.

"Ethan," she whispered, but it sounded loud enough for him to hear her.

He turned towards her, pushing Jacob out of the way with a careless gesture. "Cora."

The rest of the world vanished. Her gaze locked with his, stopping time.

Only a few years had passed, but he'd changed. His hair was long, reaching his shoulders in thick curls. The style suited him. His features had hardened, his gaze had lost the hopeful light she remembered, and his body had broadened further. The dark suit he wore enhanced his powerful body, adding a layer of menace to his build. The backs of his hands were lined with thin scars, a testament to the violence he'd encountered, and his biceps bunched underneath the fabric of his sleeves. But no shiver of fear went through her. Quite the opposite.

"I heard you returned." She couldn't avert her eyes from his face. Familiar but new at the same time.

Jacob said something she didn't care to understand or acknowledge.

The sweet sensation warming her wasn't new though. She and Ethan had shared only a few hours together, but while she didn't remember every word they'd exchanged, she did remember how he'd made her feel.

Taken care of. Important. Worthy of love. The most wonderful feelings.

His expression softened. "My return home has been chaotic. I trust you and David are well."

"We are, my lord." She fiddled with her hands, bobbing a quick curtsy. He was a marquess now.

His tone held a strained note she couldn't ignore. He had to be surprised to find her still trapped in her loveless marriage with Jacob. She was surprised as well. But things out of her control had happened in a situation where she already had very little control. She had the urge to explain herself to him as guilt gnawed at her, to tell him she wasn't weak.

I didn't mean to stay with Jacob. I need money. Jacob controls every penny I spend. I have to cheat and lie to set aside a shilling with the constant fear of being caught. I walk the streets only to pick up coins.

"You know this man?" Jacob asked, adjusting his cravat and stepping in front of Ethan.

"This man is His Lordship Ethan Hertford, the Marquess of Stark," Cora said, shocked by Jacob's lack of respect. Ethan was a marquess.

"I know who he is, you idiot." Jacob bared his teeth.

Emerald flames lit Ethan's gaze in a moment. "I will not tolerate that language, Roxbury. I heartily discourage you from disparaging Lady Roxbury in front of me." The 'or else I'll rip your limbs off their sockets' was left hanging between them.

A vein in Jacob's temple beat a quick tempo. He wouldn't be stupid enough to confront a marquess who was also highly decorated on top of being a proclaimed war hero.

Jacob turned towards her. "In which circumstances did you

meet the marquess?" The last word sounded like the hiss of a snake.

Cora feared the moment she would be in the carriage alone with him. "Lord Stark helped me during the Colchester earthquake. We were trapped in the church together."

"You never told me," Jacob said.

"I knew you wouldn't care."

She and Ethan exchanged a long stare. An entire conversation was shared between them. He remembered everything about her. The softening of his features and the way his eyelids drooped a little told her that.

"I would have cared to know you'd met Stark," Jacob said.

Ethan tensed as if ready to punch Jacob. "Why are you here, Roxbury? I told you I'd meet you next Tuesday. I do not appreciate you coming here and disturbing the guests, and I certainly would never allow you to hit a lady in front of me."

"I own this building—"

"Only a share."

"Still a share. And the lady is my wife. What I do with her is none of your business." Jacob moved to grab her arm, but Ethan was faster and blocked him again.

"I meant what I said." Ethan's wrath thickened the air. "You will not hurt her. You will not touch her. You will not insult her."

As much as Cora appreciated Ethan's standing up for her, his involvement would only anger Jacob further. She only had to endure Jacob's presence a little longer, for her son. If Jacob caught a hint of her plan to escape, he would take David away from her and lock her up.

"Why would I listen to you?" Jacob used his charming, deceiving voice, seemingly not angry.

"Because if you hurt her, Roxbury, I'll personally talk with the queen. A marquess who has recently been awarded with the Victoria Cross can be very persuasive. And the queen is particularly sensitive to women's situations."

That got Jacob's attention. No better argument than the queen to force him to listen. Her power could destroy him, strip him of his status, of his wealth.

Squandering money wasn't among his many vices, and he did have a talent for business. As a man without scruples, he didn't care about the nature of the business. He understood money and status better than he understood humans.

Jacob took a step back. "Why do you care?"

Ethan stalked him, radiating fury. "I care about men with no honour because, without honour, there's no respect. And I care about how men with no honour treat their wives. And I mean it. If you hurt Cora, the queen will be informed."

Jacob pointed a finger at him. "You'd better be careful, Stark, because I can bring this place down brick by brick. I own the land where this damn building stands . You need me if you want to keep this bunch of lunatics under this roof."

"You aren't going to come here again unless I've been informed. Now leave before I remove you myself." Ethan stretched out an arm towards the exit. "Needless to say, our meeting next week is cancelled."

"Cora, come," Jacob tossed over his shoulder as he marched towards the entrance hall.

Cora didn't follow him. She rubbed her forehead. "I'm so sorry. There's no excuse for his behaviour."

"Cora," Jacob yelled.

She curtsied. "I'm sorry." She went to leave, but Ethan caught her hand gently.

"Forgive my boldness. How are you, my lady?" Ethan's presence overwhelmed her, and she wasn't sure if it was in a good or bad way.

"It's complicated. Please, I have to leave before he grows angrier." Goodness. She wished she'd sounded more confident. She wasn't Jacob's slave, but that was the picture she painted for Ethan.

"I don't want Jacob to vent his frustration on David." She'd talked too much.

He didn't say anything for a long second before releasing her hand slowly, making her feel the callouses on the pads of his fingers. "You will always find a friend in me. If he hurts you, send for me. I'll be with you in a moment."

He probably had no idea how much his words meant to her. How wonderful was the feeling of being cared for?

"Thank you." Her voice cracked. Without looking at him, she hurried down the corridor to catch up with Jacob.

With no honour, there's no respect, Ethan had said.

She feared the warning concerned her as well.

four

ETHAN PUSHED AWAY the account books of the rest home. After the unpleasant encounter with Roxbury and the pleasant one with Cora, he found it hard to concentrate on numbers. Not even his warm, comfortable office could help him collect his thoughts. He scratched his ear, or rather, the place where his right ear had once been. From the moment a pirate had sliced it off, the skin itched sometimes, and his hair tickled it.

Great. Another distraction from the bills and papers.]

The bills to pay weren't the problem. The rest home's endless legal quagmire was. He had enough money to pay for the food, coal, and medical supplies for the centre, and Lady Kingsley, the third owner of the building, sometimes offered small donations.

Luckily, he'd become a surgeon in the army, which allowed him to apply his medical knowledge to the centre. But that bastard Roxbury had a point when he'd said he could bring down the rest home. Ethan had behaved cockily in front of the earl, his temper fuelled by Roxbury's aggressive manner towards Cora, but the earl had the law on his side. Also, Ethan might have exaggerated his influence on the queen.

Roxbury owned the largest share of the land where the rest home sat, but that wasn't the only worry Ethan had to face.

The building had been turned into a recovery centre for veterans by his late father, while according to the law, it was designed to be a residential area. An oversight on the part of Ethan's father, who had founded the Royal Veterans' Society site years ago without proper consultation. The late Lord Roxbury had been a caring gentleman, who had given Ethan's father the freedom to do whatever he'd wanted. A judge might rescind the use of the building as a rest home if he wanted to, considering the place was halfway between an asylum and a boarding house, hosting a higher number of people than it should, and operating in a residential area.

Roxbury had only to ask his solicitor to take a closer look at some very old land registry documents. The only good thing was that the obnoxious earl had no idea that the tiny, restrictive clause existed, for which Ethan was grateful. He suspected the late Lord Roxbury might have had a role in that.

Likely, Roxbury had never checked or cared for the documents of the formerly decrepit building he shared with two other peers. The area of London where it stood had never been profitable until now. With the city expanding at an alarmingly quick rate and the people of all classes growing wealthier, that anonymous part of London was becoming fashionable, and Roxbury would soon see the value of that land.

Yes, Ethan might find another place although time was slipping away. He'd searched for another suitable building and owned other houses, but having a place up and ready to accommodate around one hundred and twenty soldiers, whom society did its level best to forget, required time and preparation. A few of them needed peace and quiet and to stay away from others.

These men wouldn't survive if they found themselves in the streets even for a few weeks, not with their broken bodies and troubled minds. Unscrupulous people would take advantage of their precarious conditions in the best of cases. Some of them couldn't provide for themselves and needed constant assistance. Ethan would never, ever leave them to their own devices.

"Ethan?" A knock sounded from the door. "It's me. I know my voice is music to your *ear*."

Ethan shot his gaze up. "Come in."

Grinning after his daft pun, Finn limped inside. His wooden leg thudded against the floor at each step.

"I hope you came with important news and not to make silly jokes." Ethan scratched his missing ear again.

"My jokes are very clever. You lack sense of humour." He plonked down onto the chair in front of the desk. "I visited the old St. George Hospital as you asked me to do. The place is rotting to its core as we suspected. It'll need at least a year of solid work before anyone can spend a day there without catching consumption. Not to mention the road needs new cobbles and pavements. And street lamps. And a new sewer. Shall I continue?"

"Damn." Ethan tossed the pen on the desk. "How can it be so difficult?"

"Simple. The best buildings in London have been taken to become fancy houses, hotels, and gentlemen's clubs. The worst ones are those left for the poor or are classified as non-residential, and with the speed at which London is growing, it'll be increasingly difficult to find a place for our soldiers. No one wants a centre with veterans in their quarter. Can you imagine a place like the Royal Veterans' Society in Belgravia?" He leant closer. "It doesn't help the fact half of the peerage considers you an ass."

"I will quarrel with anyone who insults my soldiers. No exception." Sod London. Sod the peerage. Sod Roxbury. Ethan almost wished the man would provoke him again. He would have the perfect excuse to challenge him. "What options are left?"

Finn sighed, drumming his fingers on the armrest. He was

missing two in his right hand, courtesy of the same explosion that had claimed his leg. "We need more time. Or we can convince Roxbury to sell us his share and politely tell him to sod off and rot in hell."

"I like the last part of the second option the most."

"Are you coming to the evening auction?" Finn rubbed his knee.

"Would it be wise?" He rearranged his papers just to have something to do. "My last few interactions with London's peers have been abysmal."

"Mrs. Sterling will be there." Finn gave Ethan a pointed look.

"That would be a further reason not to go." Ethan signed the last cheque for the payments. "I don't want to upset her."

"Clarify your position, perhaps?"

"I tried, and she called me a coward, then a murderer. She needs someone to blame for her husband's death, and I was his commander."

"James's death isn't your fault." Finn touched his wooden leg. "War is a messy affair. You can't control everything. Besides, he disobeyed your orders."

"Still, a commander is responsible for his men, and I have no intention of informing James's widow that her beloved husband behaved like a spoiled child when it came to obeying reasonable orders." He massaged his forehead, pushing that last heated conversation with his lieutenant out of his head. "Who else will be at the auction?"

"Lady Kingsley. She showed interest in selling you her share of the building, but she has concerns about the arguments between you and Roxbury, who's pushing her to sell him her share. It would be great if you could meet her during an informal event like tonight. She invited all your men, after all. Just control your temper and lend your remaining ear to me, and everything will be all right."

"Naturally." He scraped his chair back, getting mentally ready for a night of forced smiles and dull chatter.

Although every support, monetary or otherwise, was essential to helping the veterans. Especially if litigation was going to start over the land.

"Ethan." Finn stood up as well. "May I suggest caution with Roxbury?"

"He's vile and a coward. I won't tolerate his arrogant behaviour."

"I agree with your assessment, but we don't want to push him too hard. The last thing we need is Roxbury getting a closer look at the legal situation of the centre." Finn clasped Ethan's shoulder. "Control your temper."

Ethan would. If Roxbury would control his.

EVERY TIME CORA HUGGED DAVID, the worries and sorrows of her day lifted from her heart as if by magic.

She kissed his cheek and tucked him into bed. "Don't stay up waiting for me. I might be late."

"Are you going to be alone with Lord Roxbury again?" His young face was wrinkled with too many worry lines. But then again, a child whose father forbade him from calling him papa had reasons to worry.

"Don't worry. I think he'll behave." For now.

Ethan's threat had silenced Jacob during the trip back home from the veterans' centre. She wasn't deluded. His revenge would arrive, but at the moment, she enjoyed the truce. She pulled down the hem of her dress, making sure the fabric left her throat free.

"Good night." She rose in a swish of silk, but David grabbed her hand.

"Will you come here when you return?" he asked. "I don't care if it's late."

"Absolutely, my angel." She took a deep breath and left the lamp on the nightstand lit as he liked it. "Don't worry about anything."

Anxiety coiled in her belly when she left David's room. Her maid waited for her in the corridor, pale and tense as usual.

"Does your ladyship need anything else?" she asked.

"No, Cooper. You may retire for now."

"My lady." The maid scurried away like a frightened mouse.

Cora could relate. The closer she walked to the hallway, the harder her body quivered. Thank goodness Jacob wasn't ready yet. He would complain endlessly if she caused him to leave late. She waited for him, pacing.

"There you are." Jacob came down the stairs, elegant in his dark evening suit. "Come here and let's be quick."

She walked over to him and stretched out her arm.

He seized it and latched a golden bracelet around her wrist. "Don't try anything stupid. You'll return it to me when we are back home." He closed the latch with a snap. "Your reticule?"

She handed it to him, pressing her lips together.

He rummaged through it, not caring about ruining the delicate silk. "Good."

Yes, she didn't carry any coins or anything valuable.

"Show me." He stepped closer, hounding her.

A flare of panic caught her. "Is it really necessary?" She hated the quiver in her voice.

"Don't question me," he gritted out. "Not after the manner with which you behaved in front of Stark."

She glanced at the corridor. "Can we at least go to the parlour?"

"No."

"But—"

"I said to be quick." He forced her to step back.

She went to the quietest corner the hallway had to offer

although a footman or her maid might come at any second. With trembling hands, she grabbed fistfuls of her skirts and lifted them, revealing her stockings and garters. Her breath came out in quick pants as he patted her down, shoving his rough hands under her petticoats. He touched her inner thighs and slid his fingers under the garters.

"How can I hide anything there?" she snapped and regretted it.

His grip on her thighs became painful, tearing a whimper out of her.

"Shut up," he said. "Or I'll squeeze your throat."

The thought of his rough hands around her neck was strong enough she nearly believed he was already choking her. She swallowed hard, tasting the bitterness of her fear.

He searched her drawers with harshness through the slit between her legs. "Shall I make you wet for me? If I rub you long enough, you'll moan for me."

"I might cast up my accounts on your silk suit." She grimaced as he gave her one last harsh stroke.

"I might use my belt on your son's back," he spat.

If he followed through on his threat, she'd stab him.

He ran his hands up her body. "Turn around."

Her blood boiling, she did as told.

He unbuttoned her dress with speed and efficiency before tugging the bodice down. She winced and closed her eyes as he checked her back and corset, shoving aside the chemise without worrying about ripping it, and kneaded her breasts with too much energy.

"You're hurting me." Where her voice lacked confidence, it made up for it with anger.

"So you learn to respect me." He squeezed her breasts hard until she cried out in pain.

There had been a time when she'd loved the feeling of his hands on her body, but that time was long gone.

"Cover yourself," he ordered, releasing her.

She tugged at her skirts and fixed her bodice, gazing down while he buttoned her dress. Endurance was her best defence. She wouldn't suffer this humiliation once she left him.

He grabbed her chin and forced her to stare at him. "Don't try to deceive me, Cora. There won't be any marquess's threat to protect you."

She shrugged herself free. "I hate you." She infused as much loathing as she could into her words. It was odd how saying 'I hate you' was as powerful and liberating as saying 'I love you.'

"That makes everything better."

A footman seemingly appeared out of nowhere to open the door. How embarrassing. Likely, the man had seen the whole scene. Jacob headed towards the carriage, tossing orders over his shoulder to the footman.

She took a moment to calm her erratic heartbeat. The bracelet caught the light, shining with pretty glimmers. If she could sell it, she would have more than enough for her escape. Except that Jacob never let her keep any jewels. He was careful with the silver, too. Even her wedding ring was stashed in a strongbox in his room, and the household was too terrified of him to help her. Never mind that she'd found a way to stash aside money, to steal from him right under his nose. There was a disturbing pleasure in knowing she tricked him.

They didn't exchange any words in the carriage, and thank heaven for that. She had nothing to say to him. The reason he took her with him was only because avoiding gossip was paramount. If she disappeared entirely from society, people would talk. God forbid someone might imply she had an affair. Oh, she'd like to see how he dealt with the gossip when she was gone.

He grabbed her arm again when she was about to climb out of the carriage.

"Don't think Stark scared me," he said in a low tone. His

breath stroked her cheek. "It would be unwise of you to believe so."

"Trust me, I know the depths of your cruelty. It's hard to forget." She headed for the entrance of the museum before he could say anything. A small victory. A short respite. For his revenge would hurt her ten times more. Her sore breasts were proof of that.

five

A FTER THE SEMIDARKNESS in the carriage, the bright lights of the museum glared at Cora, and for a moment a tall marble statue of Zeus seemed to move towards her as if to admonish her behaviour towards her husband.

Well, go away, Zeus.

Jacob took her arm from behind her. "You aren't in the position to upset me."

"All I ask is for you to leave David and me alone."

He tightened his grip on her arm, sinking his fingers into her flesh. "You and that rat depend on me. I pay for the food you two eat, the clothes you wear, and the rat's tutors. You'd be nothing without me."

"We'd be free without you." She tried to yank her arm free, wincing as his fingers didn't yield. She would get bruised. "You are nothing."

For a split second, his features contracted in an ugly mask as if the evil underneath his angelic beauty had come to the surface. Was she a horrible person for feeling pleasure in hurting him? She hated how he'd changed her through the years. He'd brought out her dark side. A side she needed to survive.

"Lord Roxbury." Lady Kingsley sauntered towards them, smiling fondly at her. "Lady Roxbury."

Cora curtsied, taking the opportunity to remove her arm from Jacob's bruising grip. "My lady."

Jacob's face transformed in the span of a second. The hard lines of his features softened into those of a man with sweet charm. From devil to angel faster than she could blink. She recognised the signs of his manipulation because many times his calculated charm had fooled her. Judging by how Lady Kingsley flushed and batted her eyelashes, Jacob fooled her too.

"My lady." He took the lady's hand and kissed it with a perfect bow straight out of the gentleman's manual. "It's always a pleasure to see you." The warm, caring way he said it made it sound genuine.

Lady Kingsley blushed like a debutante, falling prey to his charm.

Heaven. Cora wanted to scream that he was a fraud and a deceiver. If she could, she would shake Lady Kingsley's shoulders and tell her to run because he was a master of deceit and never meant what he said unless it was a threat.

Lady Kingsley's smile never faded as she stared at Jacob as one would stare at a saint. She couldn't be more wrong. "I'm glad you decided to attend tonight's auction, Roxbury."

Jacob gracefully bowed. "May I ask what the purpose of tonight's event is? Your invitation didn't mention it."

Lady Kingsley fanned herself. "We're raising funds for the establishment of a women's house in Whitechapel."

"Is Mrs. Sterling starting her endeavour again?" Cora asked before she could stop herself.

One of the reasons she hadn't left Jacob was because Mrs. Sterling's women's shelter had been closed and dismantled at the request of a group of lords and ladies, on the grounds that the shelter caused disruption. Another slap in the face to those women in need of protection and compassion. Cora hadn't known where to go. With no money or friends, she'd stayed.

Lady Kingsley shook her head. "Not Mrs. Sterling. Since her husband died and the shelter was closed, Mrs. Sterling withdrew from her charity work. These funds are for a new, better shelter built in a more suitable area where no one will be upset."

Oh, great. How sensible.

"A noble cause." Jacob held Cora's hand with a devotion that would strike as genuine to the untrained eye. "Every woman should feel safe in our civilised city. Although I shall remind you that Mrs. Sterling didn't run a women's shelter but a kidnapping organisation."

The flare of burning anger caused Cora to bristle. How dare he?

"A kidnapping organisation?" Lady Kingsley echoed.

Jacob nodded solemnly. "Mrs. Sterling made women disappear, taking them away from their families, children, and husbands. Forged documents, quiet escapes from England, and other illegal activities. Allegedly."

Lady Kingsley muttered her surprise. "I had no idea."

Jacob continued. "Mrs. Sterling never stopped to ponder if those women wanted to leave their husbands or not, or if the women she helped were criminals or not. The women, who asked for Mrs. Sterling's help, vanished into of thin air. That's the reason her establishment was closed after she refused to tell where the missing women ended up."

"Because Mrs. Sterling was protecting those women," Cora said. "She helped women, who were abused by their husbands, to leave."

"Leave?" He narrowed his gaze to a slit. "Marriages are sacred. Mrs. Sterling had no authority to break the holy unions between two people."

Cora glared at him, her body a bundle of repressed anger.

"Today, our morals are disappearing. I wish there were more gentlemen like you, Roxbury," Lady Kingsley said.

I wish not. Cora removed her hand from her husband's grip as quickly as she could. "Yes, Jacob is quite a rare gentleman." And she used the term 'gentleman' with sarcasm. "Perhaps that's why he's special. We don't want to have too many men with his talent, otherwise he'd become one of the many."

The lady frowned. "I'm afraid I'm not following, Lady Roxbury."

But Jacob was. He shot Cora a glare of pure hatred, and once again, she marvelled at the fact he could manipulate his expressions and hide his true emotions so well.

"Nothing of importance, my lady," Jacob said. "My wife likes to jest."

"Well." Lady Kingsley tugged at her velvet sash. "We should go to the great hall for the auction to begin. We have some wonderful paintings to show and sell to the highest bidder." She fell silent as footsteps approached.

Jacob's charming features transformed again when he glanced behind him. Cora turned around and exhaled in relief. Wrapped in a tailored dark coat, Ethan entered the museum, followed by a small group of men.

"Lord Stark." Lady Kingsley gave a polite bow of her head. "Thank you for coming."

Ethan focused his emerald gaze on Cora as he turned to Lady Kingsley. Even after his gaze left her, she felt his intense stare straight into her heart. He bared her soul with one look, and the sensation wasn't exactly pleasant because she didn't want him to see the ugly parts of her.

"Lady Kingsley, Lady Roxbury." Ethan bowed, removing his tall hat and freeing his thick black hair. He took a moment before acknowledging Jacob's presence with a brusque nod and an arched eyebrow. "Roxbury." He did nothing to hide the hostility in his tone.

Jacob instead offered a deep bow in submission and cowering a little as if Ethan had been hostile to him for no reason. "Stark, what a pleasure to see you here."

"Please introduce me to your friends, Lord Stark," Lady Kingsley said, glancing behind the marquess.

"My lady, this is my dear friend, Mr. Finn Purnell, detective at Scotland Yard." Ethan stretched out an arm towards a dark-haired man.

Mr. Purnell limped forwards. A thud resounded when his right leg hit the floor, and he missed two fingers in one hand. "Lady Kingsley, Lady Roxbury." He hesitated before addressing Jacob. "Lord Roxbury."

There was another man with a scar crossing his face and splitting his nose in two, and another had a black eye patch strapped to his face.

Ethan gestured at the man without an eye. "And my lady, may I present Mr. Fraser—"

"Oh, please, Stark," Jacob said, flourishing a hand. "Do you really expect us to welcome such an odd party?"

"What do you mean?" Ethan said at the same time as Lady Kingsley said, "What's your objection, Roxbury?"

"My lady." Jacob turned towards Lady Kingsley all sweetness and smiles. Cora might vomit. "You invited the most prominent ladies and lords to tonight's auction, and Lord Stark had the audacity to come here with common soldiers who seem straight out of a circus."

Cora gasped, touching her chest. "Jacob, please," she muttered, her request honest. "These soldiers fought for the empire."

"No offence, gentlemen." Jacob sounded genuinely apologetic, but she knew better. "We're raising money for a noble cause, and I'm afraid your presence here might discourage some of our most sensitive guests from taking part in the fundraising, which would undermine the purpose of tonight's event. Many ladies would find your presence disturbing."

"Disturbing?" Ethan's jaw clenched tightly.

Jacob waved a hand to encompass Ethan's party. "Scars, missing limbs, lack of other body parts. Surely, you must consider the ladies' delicate feelings. They wouldn't appreciate being exposed to such a crude reality. You and your men might be used to seeing such disfigurements, but the ladies are not."

Lady Kingsley gripped her sash, glancing from Jacob to Ethan. "But Lord Commander Stark is a war hero. The queen herself presented him with a Victoria Cross."

Jacob sighed. "Alas, the commander was disfigured himself, wasn't he?"

Really? Cora studied Ethan. She couldn't see any scars or missing limbs.

"I..." Lady Kingsley stammered, fiddling with her sash again.

Jacob leant closer to the lady and lowered his voice. "His right ear was chopped off."

Lady Kingsley turned to Ethan. "Good gracious."

"I didn't know," Cora said, feeling guilty for not having inquired about Ethan's health as he'd done about hers.

"Why would you?" Jacob pinned her with another burning glare for her only. "Lord Stark doesn't mention his infirmity, and rightfully so. What sort of gentleman would let the world know he's disfigured?"

"My lady?" Cora angled towards Lady Kingsley.

"Well..." Lady Kingsley tormented her poor sash again.

Ethan tensed, causing his cloak to stretch across his broad chest. "I think that Lord Roxbury can—" He fell silent when Mr. Purnell coughed in his fist politely. Ethan blew out a breath. "My lady, thank you for your invitation, but we don't want to upset any of your guests and ruin the evening. Thus, we're leaving."

"You can't!" The protest rushed out of Cora's mouth before she could think about her words.

Every head turned towards her. Great. She'd yelled and ordered a marquess to stay.

"You shouldn't leave," she said in a lower tone. "It's unfair."

"I will not stay where I'm not wanted, or worse, I won't cause any disruption to an important charity event." Ethan put his hat back on. "And I won't let my friends be ridiculed for showing the marks of their bravery and duty." His expression turned glacial when he slanted towards Jacob. "Appearances are deceiving, Roxbury. We might look like circus freaks, but we aren't different from any other person."

Jacob remained deadpan. Not an ounce of sympathy flickered across his face.

Lady Kingsley wrung her hands. "But... Lord Stark, if you and your friends take the last row of seats where the other guests won't pay you any attention, perhaps..."

Cora parted her lips in horror. "My lady."

Lady Kingsley had the decency to blush. "It was only an idea."

"We won't disturb you any further, madam." With an elegant bow, Ethan dismissed himself.

The others copied him. He walked with his friends towards the set of double doors.

"Really, Roxbury," Lady Kingsley said, flustering. "I fear your concerns are rather unfounded. My guests won't be horrified by a group of loyal servants of the queen."

"What would you do if the ladies walked out of the auction or worse, fainted because of those men?" Jacob asked. "We want to end up on the front page of *The Times* for the right reasons, madam. Our wish to help those poor women should be our main concern."

"I guess you're right," Lady Kingsley said without confidence.

"That's why I offered to buy your share of the veterans' rest home." Jacob blocked the lady's view of the leaving men. "If you sell me your share, you won't have to deal with Lord Stark and his questionable friends. You're too precious and kind to be involved with those rowdy soldiers."

Cora released a sharp breath as Lady Kingsley lacked the strength to tell Jacob to leave her alone. "My lady, you shouldn't—"

"Besides," he said, cutting her off. "Lord Stark isn't welcome in some circles due to his aggressive refusal to accept other people's opinions on military matters."

"Such as?" Cora asked, balling her fists.

"Such as calling a duke an idiot because he said a soldier's duty is to die when the queen says so."

Lady Kingsley shifted her weight and opened her mouth, but whatever she had to say, Cora didn't hear.

Cora had had enough. "If you'll excuse me. I need some fresh air." She hurried after Ethan before Jacob could say anything.

Ethan shouldn't leave. None of his friends should.

"Lord Stark." She rushed down the marble stairs, catching up with him on the pavement.

"Lady Roxbury." He removed his hat again.

In the gesture, his hair parted, revealing his missing ear. She hadn't noticed it before. His smile had nothing of the carefully constructed charm Jacob's possessed. It was ten times more charming for that reason.

"I apologise," she said to the others as well. "What my husband said is inexcusable."

Mr. Purnell shrugged. "Thank you for your concern, my lady, but we're used to this treatment."

"That makes the situation even worse," she said.

"I'm sure we'll close our eyes to the insult," Fraser, the man with a missing eye, said, provoking a round of laughter among his friends.

Cora didn't even chuckle. What was so funny?

Mr. Purnell clicked his tongue. "Also, the evening included a piano concert at the end. I'm afraid Ethan doesn't have the ear for music."

Another round of laughter burst out, but she didn't join them. Ethan laughed louder than everyone.

"Everyone has their talent," Ethan said to Mr. Purnell. "But you certainly don't have a green thumb."

And more laughter. Cora pressed her lips hard. What in the blazes was happening? What were they doing?

"Gentlemen." She raised her voice to overcome the chatter and chuckles. "I'm sorry, but you aren't taking the situation seriously. You said you shouldn't be mocked for your scars, and I agree, but why are you laughing?"

Ethan stopped laughing. "We always make jokes, my lady. But that's the difference."

"We can," Mr. Purnell said. "And we do."

She wasn't convinced, and she didn't agree. They'd fought for their country and returned home to be shunned and made fun of by people who had never been in a battle. There was nothing to laugh about. It was a tragedy. She closed her fists, digging her fingers into her gloved palms.

"Cora." Ethan stepped closer. The intimacy of using her Christian name stunned her. "Thank you for your kindness. We aren't taking what happened lightly, but we've learnt that forcing our way into society isn't the right approach. We wait and move at the right time, when people are ready to accept us. This is how we win our battles."

"But it's not fair." She fought a sob of frustration. "The people who shun you are the same who benefit from the service you and your fellow soldiers provide. The least they can do is to be kind." Why wasn't he as mad as she was? Why didn't he march back inside and demand to take part in the auction?

He gently took her hand and brought it up to his mouth for a kiss. His warmth reached her through the fabric of her glove. "Good night, my lady. Your kindness won't be forgotten."

He slowly released her hand, leaving a warm trail on her fingers. He and his friends resumed walking down the pavement, laughing and jostling each other. She waited until the shadows swallowed them.

She didn't understand Ethan's behaviour, but she understood honour, and Lord Ethan Stark was the most honourable man she'd ever met.

She decided then and there that she wanted to volunteer at the rest home.

Maybe her decision came from a sense of shame for what Jacob had said. But she wanted to do something for Ethan and his kind heart.

six

ETHAN READ AGAIN the list of patients and residents in the centre, trying to find those soldiers who could be dismissed. With the precarious legal status of the building, he had to think about reducing the number of occupants. An impossible task.

A few of the veterans lodged there didn't have anywhere to go. No families, no money, and no home. Others were still too troubled by the shock of the battlefield to face the real world and didn't have anyone who could take care of them. The Royal Veterans' Society was their only chance at a normal life. They needed time and care to recover, and he would do anything to help them, including avoiding angering Lord Roxbury.

Next to him, Finn rubbed his forehead as he read the list as well. "I can't find anyone who could be relocated."

"Neither can I."

"Those who are physically and mentally fit don't have anything outside of here. We need more time. We have too many delicate cases." Finn sagged in the chair and stared at Ethan.

"What?" he grumbled.

"I don't blame you, but last night was a complete disaster. The auction was our opportunity to attract interest in our work, restore your reputation, and meet Lady Kingsley. And the situation ended up harming us."

"I agree, but if we had forced our presence upon Lady Kingsley's guests, we would have lost her favour. She was conflicted. I'm sure she's thinking about last night with regret. Let Roxbury pick up the mantle of the victorious villain. He fits it well." Too well. Ethan was eager to see Cora soon and offer his help.

"Yes, but the number of patients and lodgers is increasing, and there are men who can't share a room with others due to their mental states. We need Lady Kingsley's support to expand the centre and force Roxbury to sell his share. We need more space, supplies, and nurses. Once he's out of the picture, we can quietly fix the legal problem of the building."

Shouts resounded from the corridor as if to prove Finn's point about the increasingly tense cohabitation of the guests.

Ethan pushed aside the list and pressed a finger to his temple. "I don't want to refuse help to anyone in need."

"That's decent of you, but we need to do something after last night."

Ethan leant back on his chair. "What do you suggest?"

Finn shrugged. "Talk with Lady Kingsley. Let her see who Roxbury really is. Tell her everything you know about him."

"She seems under a spell when he's around, and I don't have any evidence of his foul behaviour."

The door was flung open. Ethan shot up on pure instinct but softened when Mrs. Sterling strode into the room. She didn't greet him or smile. She didn't acknowledge Finn's presence. She came to an abrupt stop in front of his desk.

"Mrs. Sterling—" He bowed.

She slammed an envelope on his desk. "I don't want your charity."

Finn exchanged a terrified glance with Ethan.

"It's not charity," Ethan said, keeping his voice calm. "I'm aware that your husband's pension isn't enough to cover your expenses. The sum I offer will allow you and your daughter to live decently."

"It's not a shame to accept the money, madam," Finn said. "James wanted to take care of you."

She whipped her head towards him like a bloodhound who caught the trail of prey. "James wanted to return home to his family, and you failed to protect him."

Ethan held up his hands, biting down a comment about his late lieutenant being a reckless, ill-tempered man who couldn't follow orders. "James was very brave and an excellent fighter" — that was true— "but no one can fight against an explosion." Especially when James shouldn't have been in the warehouse the pirates had blown up.

She pointed a finger at him, her black eyes turning darker. "Keeping your men safe was your duty, and you failed. As I said, I don't want your charity." She stomped out of the study, leaving behind a trail of anger and Ethan's offer of money.

Finn shut the door. "You should tell her the truth."

"For what purpose? Torturing her?"

"She might accept the money."

"She's a proud woman. She won't believe me and will hate me more than she does now." He glanced at the window, catching a glimpse of the angry widow striding down the pavement. "I prefer she hates me than taint her husband's memory."

"James's death wasn't your fault." Finn must have repeated that a dozen times, but Ethan didn't fully embrace the truth.

Guilt piled up on top of his other worries. Unbidden, his thoughts drifted towards Cora again. The way she'd voiced his dissent and almost ordered him to stay had left a mark in his mind. She was a fierce protector of what she thought to be right, and he could do nothing but admire her for her courage and compassion. Her passion and determination were both refreshing and enticing. When she became angry, her amber eyes were set on fire. He couldn't help but find her strong spirit attractive. Every encounter with her left him in turmoil; his thoughts were scattered, and he kept thinking about what he should have said and done to impress her.

"What are you thinking about?" Finn asked, sitting down again.

He gazed up as another knock came, sparing him from giving an answer. "Come in."

The door inched inwards. As if conjured up by his thoughts, Cora came into view. A large hat covered her glorious auburn hair, and for some stupid reason, a sting of disappointment bothered him. He wanted to see her glossy, flaming curls fall over her shoulders and frame her high cheekbones.

He shot up to his feet quickly enough to shove his chair back and regretted his speed when she recoiled.

"Lady Roxbury." He bowed.

Finn stood up as well and bowed, leaning on his walking stick. "My lady."

"My lord, Mr. Purnell." She dropped a curtsy. "Forgive my intrusion. The nurse was busy, and I came here directly."

"How can I help you?" Ethan asked.

Her cheeks flamed, and he was sure he'd never seen a more beautiful colour. "Actually, I came here to ask you if you needed help."

"Help?" He tilted his head.

She waved in the direction of the hallway. "I would like to volunteer here."

Not what Ethan had expected to hear, and if he was going to be honest, he wasn't completely happy. "Does your decision have something to do with last night's incident?"

If misplaced guilt had brought her here, he wouldn't let her suffer for something she didn't do.

"Yes and no. As I told you, I don't approve of my husband's

behaviour, but I'm here because I believe in your work and what you're doing to help the soldiers."

He arched an eyebrow. "Are you aware that our guests and patients here have stories and scars that might upset you?"

She jutted out her chin. "I'm aware, and not at all frightened."

Finn nodded towards the door. "Ethan, I'll stay here and finish the paperwork. You'll show Lady Roxbury around to help her decide what she wants to do."

Actually, Ethan wasn't sure Cora should spend time at the centre. It was hypocritical of him, especially after last night, but he worried about what she might see and hear. Once one heard and saw certain things, there was no going back. The horrors of the battlefield would stay with her forever. She should keep herself away from the gruesome darkness of war. He didn't want her anywhere near the dark reality of a soldier's life.

"I won't faint, Lord Stark." She gave him the same determined attitude as last night.

"I'm not concerned about your fainting. I'm concerned about your mind." Nevertheless, he left the documents on the desk for Finn. "Some men are still in a delicate phase of their recovery, and they might have outbursts or crises that are hard to witness. I'm sorry to say that some men might be rather violent on certain occasions."

"I won't disturb those patients who need to recover. I'm happy to do whatever you think it's appropriate for my skills. And I trust you to keep me safe."

Bloody hell. Ethan's chest rose with a riot of emotions. She had no idea how important her trust was to him. Of course he'd keep her safe. Her safety would be his personal mission.

Finn tilted his chin in a 'go on' gesture. Ethan couldn't refuse her offer. Besides, he needed every help he could get, and from a selfish point of view, he was eager to spend more time with her.

He held the door open for her. "Let's start our tour then."

Her smile lasted a second. "There's something I must tell you."

"Yes?"

She hesitated, glancing at Finn. "My husband doesn't know I'm here. Not even my maid knows, and I'd like to keep it that way," she whispered.

He wasn't surprised Roxbury didn't approve, but he didn't like the idea of her needing to lie to do what she wanted. "He won't hear a word from me."

"Ethan never turns a deaf ear to a lady's request," Finn said.

"Shut up." Ethan chuckled, but Cora didn't crack a smile.

Finn held up a hand. "Anyway, Lord Roxbury won't hear anything from me, my lady. In fact, I don't plan to talk to Lord Roxbury at all."

She gave him a nod. "Thank you."

Ethan held the door open for her. When she brushed past him, her arm touched his chest, and he ignored the quick shot of energy going through him. Her presence here only increased his respect for her.

He headed towards the common room where those guests who suffered from mild conditions gathered.

"You did an excellent job here," she said.

He got lost in admiring her freckles. They formed a heart-shaped pattern across her nose. Why hadn't he noticed that before? "I can't take credit for it. My father opened the centre with the help of the late Lord Kingsley and the late Lord Roxbury. The idea came when my father realised too many soldiers returned injured and shocked from the front only to receive neither warmth nor succour from their own country. Many of them had lost a limb and couldn't find a job. Others carried the war with them and couldn't let it go. Former soldiers die in solitude every day. The empire uses them and discards them when they aren't needed as if they were an embarrassment. All of them need our help, not our scorn."

The sunlight danced on her eyelashes, setting them on fire. "Do the soldiers you accommodate live here permanently?"

"For as long as they need it. We help them find a job and encourage them to regain their independence, but some of them need more time." He paused before entering the hall. "Many members of the House of Lords think the government shouldn't help them. The soldiers shouldn't live on charity, the lords say. But my goal here is to allow these men to heal from whatever malady of the mind or body they suffer from and be themselves again. If they feel useless or hopeless, they'll never improve."

She nodded solemnly. "What can I do?"

The way she sounded determined to help gave him a ridiculous amount of joy. He wasn't sure why. While he despised some members of the *ton* for their disdain for the veterans, he also met many generous souls. Cora wasn't the first woman to offer her help. Yet a word from her started a deep turmoil inside him.

"We have doctors and nurses who take care of the guests with physical impairments, helping them to walk or use their hands again, but what they miss is someone to talk to." He entered the hall where sofas and armchairs were scattered around.

Bookshelves and a large fireplace gave the room a cosy appearance, and its secluded position away from the main road guaranteed peace and quiet, exactly what these men needed.

"These soldiers won't need stitches or fresh bandages," he said, "but don't underestimate the effect their invisible injuries can have on your mind as well. The scars of the soul are contagious."

A shadow crossed her face. "I understand, my lord."

"Ethan, please." The constant back and forth on the use of his Christian name and title confused him. He'd better be clear. "I thought we agreed to use each other's names."

She bowed her head. "We did. Ethan."

He liked the sound of his name on her lips. "Is there anything else you need to know?"

"I understand you need Jacob's legal support to keep this centre open."

"I do." Unfortunately.

"I'll do whatever I can to help you, but Jacob doesn't really take my thoughts into consideration." Bitterness dripped from her voice.

He'd been around too many soul-scarred people not to recognise one immediately.

"I remember asking you if he hurt you years ago. You don't have to say anything you don't want to," he hurried to say when she opened her mouth. "But I have a new question for you."

"Yes?" She paused in the middle of the room, her chest rising as she held her breath.

"Why didn't you ask Mrs. Sterling for help?" He tried not to let his concern slip into his words. Mrs. Sterling had helped dozens of women successfully. If Cora had asked for her help, she and her son would live far from Roxbury.

Her bottom lip quivered, and he wanted to kick his own arse for having upset her. Or better yet, to kick Roxbury's arse.

"You don't have to answer," he whispered.

"I want to. In fact, I've wanted to talk to you about that for a while. After you left Colchester, I stayed there for the rest of the spring and the beginning of the summer." A corner of her mouth curled up. "Those were peaceful months I spent with Mrs. Marshall and David. When it was time to return to London, bad weather kept us in Colchester for a few more weeks, delaying my meeting with Mrs. Sterling. When I sought her help, her husband was dead, and she didn't accept any visitors, understandably so."

Ethan worked his jaw. James's death had caused a rift between Ethan and Mrs. Sterling and had forced Cora to stay with her husband.

"Mrs. Sterling was grieving," Cora said. "She disappeared from society. I didn't have the chance to meet her, and then her centre was dismantled soon after the tragedy because of people's complaints, and I missed the opportunity to leave. But I have a plan. It's slow progress, but I will get what I want." She lowered her voice. "I will leave Jacob and start afresh. Believe me."

"Is there anything I can do to help you?" He meant it although aside from killing Roxbury, other possibilities failed him. Hiding the wife and heir of an earl had unpleasant legal ramifications he couldn't ignore. The rest home didn't need more troubles.

"No, thank you." She brought a hand to her neck and paled. "I appreciate your interest though."

"You can tell me anything. You can ask me anything," he said. "Anything you need."

He didn't have Mrs. Sterling's connections or an understanding of her work. He couldn't provide forged documents and safe passages to other countries, and Cora had to leave London, and England, if she wanted to start a new life. The law was on Roxbury's side. If she left with his heir, the future Earl of Roxbury, the police would chase her and David. Besides, she wouldn't leave without David, and the child posed a new series of difficulties Ethan wouldn't know how to solve. Not to mention his relationship with Mrs. Sterling was too strained to ask her help.

"If you need money," he said when she didn't talk. "I can provide for you and David."

She flushed but not in a good way. "Thank you. I... I'll let you know how much I need."

That was a start. She didn't react as Mrs. Sterling had done, although by the way she lowered her gaze and voice, she found asking for money embarrassing.

"I hope that your husband has behaved." Or he would seek Roxbury right in that moment.

"He did. Thank you."

He loitered in case she added something else. Since she didn't want to tell him more, they'd better start to work. "Let me show you what your work here might be."

seven

ORA'S WORK AT the centre wasn't exhausting or difficult, but when she finished her shift, she exhaled in relief. She'd underestimated the gravity of dealing with people who had gone through a war. She'd played whist, chatted, and taken tea with a few of Ethan's guests. Nothing too complicated. Yet a heaviness set on her chest. Maybe the conversation she'd had with Ethan was partly to blame for her fatigue. She would accept his offer, take the money, and leave. She could be in France in a couple of weeks. Her dream would come true. She had only to write to her contact in Paris and arrange her stay. Mrs. Delois wasn't a friend, a mere acquaintance, but the woman had promised to help Cora if she decided to go to France granted Cora had the money to pay Mrs. Delois.

She left the main hall and headed to Ethan's study. If she wrote to Mrs. Delois that night and Ethan gave her some money, she and David would leave as soon as Mrs. Delois replied with a suitable date.

She knocked on the door. "Ethan? It's me, Cora."

"Come in." Not Ethan's voice.

"Mr. Purnell." She searched the small room, but only Ethan's friend was present.

"Lady Roxbury." Mr. Purnell staggered to his feet.

"Don't stand up on my account."

He did all the same. "A lady deserves respect. How do you find your work here, my lady?"

"I enjoyed it, thank you."

The sound of wood against wood came when he shifted his weight. "Then I hope we'll see you again."

"I played whist with Mr. Jackson."

Mr. Purnell leant against the desk. "Did he upset you? He usually doesn't talk much. In the months I've been here, I haven't heard more than a handful of words from him. I'm not sure what troubles him."

"It's what he doesn't say that speaks louder." She sat on the chair to allow him to sit as well. "He has a lost, empty stare and a constant tremor in his hands. It's heartbreaking."

"You're quite perceptive, madam." He sat down with a clunky noise.

"I tried to engage him in conversation, but I think he isn't ready yet."

"I think you'll do an excellent job here. After I returned from Lias Island, I didn't necessarily need to speak every day." He lifted the hand with the missing fingers. "One doesn't realise how important the thumb is for every hand movement until it's gone. Well, unless you are a violinist." He laughed, but she didn't return the laughter. "Losing my thumb bothered me more than losing my leg, and some days the loss bothered me so much I refused to talk."

"The accident must have been horrible for you."

"Blissfully, I don't remember much of it. Ethan and I were charging against the pirates along one of the narrow streets in Lias." He closed his fists and imitated a charge. "Then there was an explosion. The Thorne Pirates had an obsession with explosives. The next thing I remember is waking up in a hospital bed, minus my leg and fingers. I'm grateful for not remembering. Then Ethan ordered me to return home. Unfortunately, I had to leave Lias two years before he did."

She wasn't sure she would be grateful if she were in his position. "You're very brave."

"Not really. I have to thank my wife and son for putting me back on my feet." He laughed. "As a manner of speaking. And Ethan, of course. He helped me find a job at Scotland Yard."

She couldn't laugh. Her chest tightened for him.

"Have I upset you?" He scrubbed the back of his neck. "Please be honest."

"I still don't understand how you gentlemen can joke about your tragedies."

"It helps, I guess, as long as it's done with the right intention. We aim to lighten up the situation. It's not appropriate for everyone, and we would never make fun of someone who doesn't appreciate that. But for those of us who do, it's a relief and the best cure." He paused, drumming his fingers on the desk. "The only problem is that I've exhausted all the possible jokes about ears for Ethan. Ears are difficult subjects to make jokes with. If you have any suggestions, I'm all ears." He tapped his forehead. "Why, I'm a genius."

This time, she laughed. "Oh, Mr. Purnell, you're incorrigible." She rose but waved him down when he tried to stand up. "Please stay seated. Thank you for the chat."

"You're welcome," he said. "But you were looking for Ethan, I guess."

"Is he here?" She hoped she didn't sound too eager, but she'd rather talk to him sooner rather than later. She regretted not having discussed the details of his offer immediately. He'd caught her off guard with his bluntness.

Mr. Purnell consulted a logbook. "Ethan should be in Long Mary's Brothel on Tottenham Street. Usual visit. He's going there more often as of late."

Cora leant closer. A brothel? "I beg your pardon."

He pointed in the direction of Tottenham Street. "The brothel."

Yes, she knew what a brothel was, but why was Ethan there? "I wonder—"

The door swung inwards, cutting her off. "I'm sorry for the intrusion, Mr. Purnell." A very agitated woman strode in. "Your ladyship." She curtsied.

"Mrs. Parker." Mr. Purnell staggered to his feet. "What is it? Mr. Brown again?"

The woman breathed hard. "'Fraid so, sir. He's upsetting the others."

"Can I help?" Cora asked.

"No, do not worry." Mr. Purnell hurried towards the door. "Everything is under control. You may go home and rest. Sorry for the abrupt goodbye, my lady."

"My lady." Mrs. Parker urged Mr. Purnell out.

He and Mrs. Parker disappeared in the hallway, leaving Cora alone with her shock.

She loitered on the pavement outside the centre. Jacob wouldn't be home for another few hours, and David was busy with his riding lesson for another hour at least. On the other hand, Tottenham Street was just around the corner.

As she started walking, she found a penny on the pavement and snatched it, considering it a good omen. A quick detour to Tottenham Street wouldn't be a problem.

It wasn't that she meant to spy on Ethan, but... All right. She burned to know if he was one of those men who paid for a tumble, and she needed to talk to him anyway.

The thought of Ethan enjoying himself in a brothel left a bitter taste in her mouth. He didn't strike her as the type of man who took advantage of unfortunate girls. Girls who didn't have other means to sustain themselves. It was sad. Those women worked in a brothel not because it was their choice.

She would take a walk around the area and then head to the park where David was taking a riding lesson. Along the way, she changed her mind with each step. Right or wrong, Ethan was entitled to his privacy. What he did in his spare time was none of her business. But she would be lying if she said her esteem and respect for him wouldn't waver. She slowed her pace close to Tottenham Street and came to a stop in front of the infamous building.

Long Mary's Brothel had seen better days. The walls contained more mould than bricks, and red paint flaked from the front door as if the building were bleeding. Goodness. As brothels went, this one was decrepit. Who knew what diseases those girls risked catching in such a place? The smell wasn't the best either, a combination of rotten eggs and putrid fish. She should leave. She would talk to Ethan another day. A day or two wouldn't make much difference.

Cora didn't mean to stay, but right then, Ethan came out of the brothel. In his dark coat and bowler hat, he was easily recognisable. He adjusted his jacket and the collar of his shirt. A girl threw herself at him, wrapping her thin arms around his neck, and he held her with one arm since his other hand held a heavy-looking leather bag. They chatted while holding each other before he kissed her forehead and released her. Heaven. The girl was so young she could be his daughter.

Not Cora's business. She'd seen enough. She shouldn't judge. He had several qualities and was a decorated soldier. No one was perfect. The end.

She spun on her heels and headed to the park. She'd said she shouldn't judge but... Ethan's behaviour was a disappointment. She'd thought he was a man of integrity. But to each their own. Although why did he need to visit a brothel? She kept going in circles with her thoughts. She wouldn't be surprised if she burst a blood vessel in her brain.

"Cora." His voice startled her.

Dash it all. She definitely should have been faster. She turned towards him inch by inch. "Ethan. Fancy that." Her voice sounded strangled to her own ears.

He gave her a charming smile, walking towards her. His coat-tails flapped around his long, strong legs. "What are you doing here?"

"I had some errands." She moved a hand around. "What about you?"

He jabbed a thumb in the general direction of the brothel. "A patient. More than one actually."

Annoyance left a bitter taste in her mouth. He lied on her face.

"A patient? Why, are you a physician?" she asked.

"A surgeon more than a physician. I practised in the army." He patted his leather bag. "I worked with the army surgeons until I learnt the trade. I don't have a certificate though, but I'm thinking about getting a proper degree."

And she was supposed to believe that? "You'd excuse me if I doubt your word. I saw you coming out of the brothel with a slip of a girl clinging to you like an extra limb." She didn't mean to sound so angry, but she wouldn't apologise for her tone.

His eyebrows drew together. "I was—"

Once she started talking, she couldn't stop her tongue. "Don't you know those poor girls were likely forced into that life by sad circumstances? Taking advantage of their misfortune is appalling."

He held up a hand. "Yes, but—"

"The fact you pay them for their services doesn't make it all right," she went on. "They don't want to have a tumble, but they must in order to survive. Not to mention they won't probably see more than a farthing since they have to hand their earnings to the madam of the brothel. This is hardly a fair trade. I thought you were different."

"Cora!" His commanding tone shut her up. She had more to say but held her tongue. "I didn't visit the brothel to pay for a tumble. I went there to visit a few girls who needed help. They can't afford to pay for a physician, and unfortunately, many respectable doctors prefer not to call on a brothel for fear that their reputation might be damaged. I'm the only option for them, and I don't mind. If you don't believe me, you may go inside and ask." His tone was polite but firm.

"Oh." She shuffled her feet, wishing that a natural event, like a dinosaur suddenly returning from extinction, saved her from the embarrassing moment. "It's that I saw that girl hugging you."

"Jane?" He huffed. "She's a child, barely eighteen. I could be her father."

"Yes, that's what I— oh, bother." She rubbed the space between her eyebrows. "I apologise for jumping to conclusions. I meant no offence."

"You did."

"Yes, I did. But I regret it. Apologies."

He scowled. "Accepted."

"Great."

"Great."

They stood in the middle of the pavement, and she found it difficult to meet his gaze. Or to ask him about his offer of money. How annoying.

"I really am sorry," she said. "I haven't met many remarkable examples of gentlemen. You truly are honourable."

"I appreciate your courage to confront me." He offered her his arm. "May I escort you wherever you are going?"

She didn't take it. "David is having a riding lesson at the park. I was going there."

"Excellent. I love horses. And I haven't seen David in years. He must be twelve now."

She slid her arm through his. "Thirteen."

"A young man then. How's he faring?"

She found herself leaning against his solid shoulder. "He's so handsome and clever. He can speak without problems. He's still hesitant but much better."

"I had no doubt." His muscles stiffened under her arm. "And is his father equally fond of him?"

She'd been wrong. The most embarrassing moment in her life was right now when she had to confess that David's father disliked his own child so much he didn't even call him by his name. "Not really."

His muscles stiffened further. "What is Roxbury complaining about?"

"Everything."

"For example?"

She stared at the tips of her boots appearing and disappearing from underneath the hem of her skirt. Jacob had never kissed, hugged, or praised David. His behaviour hurt her deeply and was devastating for David.

"I don't wish to talk about that further. Please understand. It's very difficult for me to..." A traitorous sob broke her voice.

The wave of sadness caught her off guard. Maybe it overwhelmed her because Ethan had proven to her once again he was an honourable man while she'd doubted him. Being close to him only showed her how different he was from Jacob. Obviously, she was a terrible judge of men. Or maybe it was because Jacob couldn't be more different from Ethan, and she was reminded of her husband's senseless brutality. Whatever the reason, the more she cried, the more uncomfortable she felt. She hated crying because she wasn't a victim; she fought back. But sometimes being strong meant to cry.

She slid her arm out of his and sped up. "I'm sorry."

"Cora, please." He caught up with her and took her hand gently. "I must apologise. I didn't mean to upset you with my questions."

She wiped her tears quickly. "No, it's not you. You did nothing wrong."

"Cora." He tugged at her hand. "Look at me."

No, she didn't want to. He would see how fragile she was at

that moment, how angry. Because she should have understood a long time ago who Jacob was. Instead, she had let herself be deceived by his sweet words and handsome looks.

She slipped her hand from his grip. "I have to go. I'm sorry."

"Cora."

"Please. I need to be alone." She hurried along the pavement, and he didn't follow her.

eight

CORA WAS GLAD Jacob had ignored her for the whole day. After she'd returned from the park with David and her maid, Jacob had been nowhere to be seen. The butler had informed her his lordship would dine out and return late. A blessing. She could have a nice and quiet dinner with David in the small dining room overlooking the garden.

"And now Lord Stark is a commander?" David asked, cutting a large piece of his steak.

"I believe so. He was awarded the prestigious Victoria Cross for bravery," Cora said with no small amount of pride.

"Capital."

She was about to say Ethan had asked about him when the sound of quick footfalls cut her off. She would recognise the sound of those steps anywhere.

"There's nothing capital about receiving a piece of rusted metal for having crawled through a muddy jungle." Jacob strode inside and scraped a chair back. "Stark is nothing but an idiot."

David straightened up and stared at his plate. Cora stiffened. What was Jacob doing here?

The footman hurried to bring a bowl of hot soup, bread, and

cheese to his master. Jacob dismissed him and the butler with an impatient wave afterwards.

"A Victoria Cross is not just a piece of metal," Cora said. "The crosses are made from the cannons taken by our troops in Sebastopol during the Crimean—"

"Did I ask for a history lesson?" The way Jacob wielded the cheese knife made the blunt blade look dangerous. "Stark is no one." He put all his hatred in the last two words. "A crippled, mutilated, deluded man."

David flinched at each word.

Jacob slammed his hand on the table, causing the glasses to shake. "Stop being so damn weak, rat. If you have something to say, then say it."

Wincing, David muttered something she didn't understand.

"Louder," Jacob said, slicing a piece of bread.

"Leave him be. You're frightening him." Cora squeezed David's hand, but he didn't gaze up at her.

Jacob pointed the knife at her. "You turned him into a spine-less worm. You do nothing but defend him and justify his every weakness. Look at him. He can't answer a question without trembling."

"Because you're yelling at him," Cora said.

Jacob snatched David's unfinished steak and cut a piece for himself. "See? I can take his food, and all he does is whimper."

"That's his dinner." Cora grabbed David's plate, pushing it closer to David.

Jacob did the same, dragging the plate towards him in a messy tug-of-war. The situation would be laughable if not for Jacob's absolute seriousness. It certainly was ridiculous.

Jacob cut another piece of meat. "If the rat wants his dinner, he'll have to take it from me like a man."

David shivered, staring at his hands on his lap.

"Stop hiding behind your mother's skirts." Jacob tossed the

steak to David, hitting his face and spraying drops of juice everywhere.

David groaned when the steak slapped his cheek.

"Jacob." Cora shoved to her feet.

David ran away from the room as his father laughed.

"Shut up," Jacob said among bursts of laughter.

"David." She started to follow him, but Jacob yanked her back.

"See what he has become?" There wasn't a trace of his beauty left. He was all demon.

"You terrorise him instead of nurturing him and loving him as he deserves."

Jacob gripped her wrist hard enough to make her whimper. "I swear I'll turn him into a man, or I'll kill him."

She cried out when she wrestled her wrist out of his steely fingers. They would leave her bruised. Not that it would be the first time. She rushed to follow David, anger bringing hot tears to her eyes.

"Darling." She barged into his room and hugged him, kissing the top of his head.

He clung to her like a vine, shivering. But he didn't say anything.

"Forget what he said. He doesn't know you." She scattered kisses on his face, tasting the steak. "My angel."

He took in a shaky breath, and she waited for him to say something, yell, or insult his father. But nothing came. He didn't rant or vent his frustration at his father. She wished for a reaction, an outburst, or a cry. His calm meant he believed what Jacob said.

"You aren't weak." She hugged him harder before wiping his face with a handkerchief. "You aren't weak. You're a brave, beautiful boy."

Again silence. She held him until his shivers died down. No matter how many times she told him he wasn't weak, he didn't say anything.

"Talk to me," she whispered.

He curled up on the bed and pulled up the cover to his head. She sat next to him, stroking his hair and growing angrier with Jacob.

After David refused dinner and fell asleep, she tucked him into bed.

As she dragged herself to her bedroom, her temper boiled. Her only solace was the money she'd put aside and Ethan's promise for more. She locked the door and waited for any sounds that might inform her Jacob was coming. No noise came. Hopefully, he'd gone to his study. She opened the wooden box hidden underneath a loose floorboard and watched the coins she'd so arduously collected, just watched them. She added the penny she'd found and enjoyed the clinking noise it made when it tumbled over the other coins. Two hundred pounds. If Ethan could lend her another couple of hundred pounds, she and David would leave immediately.

She sat at her writing desk and started to write to Mrs. Delois. Tears welled in her eyes, but she wiped them mercilessly. She refused to consider herself a victim.

She was fighting back, one pound at a time.

ETHAN GROANED and bent forwards when Fraser punched him in the stomach. The blow emptied his lungs of air and shot pain into his head. He held up a hand to signal he needed a breather. Likely, a week of rest. Bloody hell. Sparring was becoming increasingly difficult for him. Every time he fought, pain burned his shoulder, distracting him. The blade that had cut his ear had slashed his shoulder as well. A sloppy stitching job done under a rain of bullets and the lack of carbolic acid had done the rest. It was a miracle he hadn't died of blood poisoning.

But he needed the exercise and to think about what had

happened with Cora, about why she'd left so abruptly. Hadn't he proven to her she could trust him?

On the other side of the fighting ring, Fraser jumped from one foot to another, light and quick. Sweat glistened over his skin. Considering he had only one eye, his speed and precision were impressive.

"Too much, Commander?" Fraser asked without amusement. Another sparring companion might have gloated on his victory, but Fraser knew his commander fought ghosts as well.

The other gentlemen and eager boxers of the club urged Ethan to carry on.

"Come on, Ethan," Finn said from behind him. "You think too much, and I bet five pounds on you." He shoved Ethan none-too-gently towards the middle of the ring.

"Five pounds!" Fraser yelled, offended.

Ethan rubbed his shoulder. "It's not that I think too much. My shoulder bloody hurts."

"Oh, you poor thing." Finn patted his back.

"Shut it, Finn." He raised his fists and braced himself for Fraser's second assault. "I'm ready."

"We can stop, Commander." Fraser wiped the sweat from his chin.

"No. Do your worst." He would regret his words.

Ethan parried a blow and dodged another. But when Fraser threw an uppercut, another shot of sheer agony went through Ethan's body, and he recoiled. He replied with a hook, but his shoulder throbbed. The pain lasted a second, enough to cause him to pause. The hesitation cost him another punch in the stomach. Bugger. Ethan bent over and gasped. He was too old for this stunt.

"Commander." Fraser touched Ethan's back.

"I'm all right." He wasn't. "The match is yours."

Finn, acting as the referee, raised Fraser's arm. "One-Eye Fraser is the winner, and Ethan owes me five pounds."

Ethan clapped his friend's back among the cheers of his fellow fighters. "Well done."

"I'm sorry." Fraser shook Ethan's hand.

"Don't worry." Ethan recognised his limits. A deep wound that had got infected and healed badly was a problem he'd carry forever.

"Who challenges the winner?" Finn asked the small crowd of boxers.

"I do." A voice thundered from the other side of the hall. Roxbury made his way to the ring.

"Very well," Finn said.

Ethan stiffened, and Fraser stopped wiping the sweat from his face. Roxbury lifted the ropes and walked underneath them, gazing around as if waiting for someone to stop him. He removed his shirt, showing well-shaped muscles that warranted some respect. Reluctantly, Ethan left the ring. Fraser was an expert boxer. No need to worry. And the gentlemen's club had strict rules when it came to boxing.

Roxbury slid on his gloves while Fraser threw shadow punches.

"Gentlemen, you know the rules." Finn exchanged a glance with Ethan. "May the best boxer win."

The moment the fight began, Roxbury stalked Fraser like a bloodhound. Not even Fraser's quick footwork saved him from a series of hooks and uppercuts that caused his body to shake. Roxbury was quick and precise; a coward, yes, but the bastard could fight. He shifted to the left towards Fraser's blind side and hit him in the small of his back.

Unfair.

Roxbury moved so quickly he broke through Fraser's guard more than once and hit Fraser's head a few times, taking advantage of his reduced field of vision.

Groaning and gasping, Fraser doubled over.

"Enough, Roxbury." Ethan jumped in the ring.

Fraser winced, a hand on his ribs. "It's all right, Commander."

"No, it's not. Roxbury is taking advantage of your limited field of vision."

Roxbury spread his arms. "So what? He's missing an eye. His problem. Not mine."

"Taking advantage of someone else's physical condition is against the rules, my lord," Finn said.

Ethan stepped between them. "What do you expect from a coward? From someone who asked his dear papa to be relieved from his military duty out of fear."

Silence dropped. Only Fraser's laboured breathing could be heard. A few gentlemen muttered their disagreements. Finn shook his head in disapproval at Ethan. In retrospect, Ethan should have stayed quiet.

"You have no proof of that, Stark," someone said.

"It's your word against Roxbury's," another shouted.

"You soldiers have become too arrogant." That was Lord Ashby, another peer who had never seen a military academy. "Just do your duty and shut up."

"You're a bloody idiot, Ashby," Ethan shouted. Not his best comeback. But anger and pain were never a good combination for clever responses.

Finn shook his head again and mouthed, "Calm down."

"How dare you." Ashby turned red in the face. "Don't you know who my father is?"

"Do you?" Ethan shot back.

"Oh, boy." Finn hid his face behind his hand.

"Hit him, Roxbury!" Ashby raised a fist, because of course he wouldn't jump into the ring and fight Ethan himself.

Loud voices and yells echoed in the training room.

"I'll take advantage of whatever I *see* fit. Pun intended, Fraser," Roxbury said over the din. "Tell me, Stark, do you believe yourself clever for having gone to war and returned without an ear? I'd say you are the bloody idiot."

Anger burst into Ethan's brain. He moved before he could think and tried to smash his fist against Roxbury's jaw. But he was faster. He sidestepped Ethan and hit his bad shoulder with surgical precision. Instant, cosmic pain; it was so excruciating that Ethan couldn't even shout. All the air was punched out of his lungs as he dropped to his knees.

Roxbury seized his hair and yanked his head up. "Stay away from my wife, Stark, or the pain you feel now will be only a taste of what I'm going to do to you."

That was the last thing Ethan heard before Roxbury smashed another fist into his throbbing shoulder, and the pain caused him to pass out.

nine

YEARS SPENT AMONG soldiers and battles had scarred Ethan's mind, damaged his shoulder, and taken one of his ears, but they had also honed his senses. He paused in the middle of the gravel path in his garden and tilted his head to direct his good ear towards a subtle noise. What was it? A body dropping to the ground? Feet shuffling?

The loud thud coming from a corner of his garden hinted that something heavier than a cat had landed on his property. If it was a thief, it had to be the worst criminal in history since Ethan's bad ear could detect the noises. Anyone could attempt to trespass into his house in search of loot. Today was the wrong day to challenge him. After his abysmal performance in the ring and the shame of fainting in front of his friends, he didn't feel inclined to forgive. Finn and Fraser had told him his fainting was justifiable. He disagreed. Whole-heartedly.

His ego still bruised by Roxbury, he marched towards the other side of the garden, fists clenched, ready to drag the thief out of his hiding place. The bushes swayed as something large moved behind them.

He raised his fist and lunged. "What are you doing here?" he roared.

A boy cried out and scurried towards the wall on his feet and hands. His terrified amber eyes looked larger in his small face framed by auburn curls.

"I'm not a thief, sir." The boy held up his hands.

Ethan had seen David for a handful of hours years ago, but the shivering boy had to be him. Besides, the resemblance to Cora was extraordinary.

The boy remained petrified. His fine jacket was torn in a few spots, and his shiny leather boots had scratches. Definitely, he wasn't a street urchin.

Ethan crouched and cleared his throat. "I mistook you for a thief. I won't hurt you. Are you David Wiley?"

The boy hugged his knees. A scatter of freckles lay across his nose, just like Cora's. "I am he, sir. Do you remember me?"

"I do, and you look exactly like your mother."

David's face brightened, but he didn't stop shivering. "I remember you as well. Very well."

"Does your mother know you're here? Did she tell you to come here?"

David shook his head. "Mama doesn't know. I was with Lord Roxbury."

Lord Roxbury, not Papa. That was confusing.

"Do you mean your father?" Was there something Ethan didn't know?

The brightness vanished from David's face. "Lord Roxbury doesn't want me to call him father."

"Why?" he couldn't help but ask.

"Lord Roxbury says I'm too worthless to be his son."

Instant anger flared in Ethan's chest and shot up to his brain. A ringing noise buzzed in his ears. How dared that pathetic excuse of a man to say that to his own son?

"Lord Roxbury can go to—" He had to refrain himself. "What

happened? Why did you climb the wall to my house?" He hoped he didn't sound too menacing.

David hugged his knees harder and hunched his shoulders. "You'll be angry with me."

"No. I promise you on my honour I won't be angry." Not with David anyway. His father was another matter. Ethan sat on the ground, legs crossed, and waited for David to speak.

David swallowed hard. "I was in the carriage with Lord Roxbury when he made us stop right in front of your house."

Each word came out slowly. David didn't stammer but was hesitant when speaking. Ethan had seen the same behaviour in many shocked soldiers who found it difficult to talk about their experiences on the battlefield. Patience was the key. He didn't prompt David to talk but waited.

"I'm hiding." David rested his chin on his knees.

"From your father?"

David nodded. "He wanted me to throw a stone through your window. I refused. He became angry." He shivered again. "I ran away."

Hell. Ethan raked a hand through his hair, not sure what the best strategy would be. Take the boy home? Keep him hidden? "Why did he want to break my window?"

David shrugged. "I don't know, sir."

Ethan had a hunch actually.

"He..." David took a few deep breaths. "He said I had to prove to him I was a man. That I had to do what he said and break your window, but it was wrong. Mama wouldn't approve."

Ethan suppressed the urge to take David's hand in case the boy recoiled. "You did the right thing, and I thank you for being brave enough to refuse to obey your father."

David released his grip on his legs, his face suddenly happy. "Was I brave? Really?"

"Incredibly brave. Not many men would have the courage to

refuse a stupid order." Ethan stretched out his hand towards the boy. "I'm in your debt, Mr. Wiley."

"Just David, please." He shook Ethan's hand with surprising strength.

"David it is then. Would you care for a cup of tea?" He rose slowly not to frighten the boy.

David curved his back over his knees. "I should leave. Lord Roxbury is looking for me, and he must be furious."

Ethan longed to measure his own fury against Roxbury. "You're safe here. You can come and stay here whenever you need a place to hide. My door is always open for you, and you don't have to leave unless you want to."

"Do you mean it, sir?" David narrowed his eyes in the same fashion as Cora would.

"Every word. I won't let your father hurt you when you are here with me. You're under my protection."

The boy sprang up to his feet, showing his teeth with a wide smile. "Then I'd much appreciate a nice cup."

"This way." Ethan barely took a step inside before Mrs. Parker rushed towards him.

"My lord, there's a man at the door, who demands to see you. He claims to be Lord Roxbury." Mrs. Parker frowned at David. "And where did this boy come from?"

David released a shaky breath at the mention of his father, his brightness gone.

"This is David, my guest, and he's welcome here any time he wants." Ethan put a hand on David's shoulder, feeling the boy's muscles tense.

"Very well, your lordship." Mrs. Parker wrung her hands. "What about our other guest?"

"I'll deal with him myself." Ethan gave a reassuring squeeze to David's shoulder, but the boy didn't relax. "Follow Mrs. Parker to the sitting room, and she'll give you a cup of tea and some biscuits."

Mrs. Parker glanced from Ethan to David but didn't ask any questions. "We have some freshly baked almond biscuits I'm sure you'll find delicious. Follow me, David."

"Are you sure, sir?" David whispered.

Ethan nodded. "I'll deal with Lord Roxbury. Go."

David did as told reluctantly, shuffling behind the housekeeper. Once he disappeared behind a corner, Ethan strode to the hallway. Anger caused black spots to throb in his vision. He hadn't experienced such scorching fury since Lias Island.

In a fine afternoon suit, Roxbury paced and smacked his walking stick against the marble floor. The rhythmic click-clack itched along Ethan's skin while the butler stood in a corner, seemingly stunned.

"You may leave, Dawson," Ethan said to the butler. "What do you want, Roxbury?" he asked once alone with the earl.

Roxbury came to an abrupt halt. Harsh lines etched his face. "Have you recovered well from your fainting?"

Bugger off. "I won't repeat my question."

"That witless boy. I believe he's hiding here."

"I don't know what you're talking about." He opened the front door himself. "Now remove yourself from my property before I remove you."

Roxbury tapped the pommel of his walking stick against Ethan's chest. "You should be nicer to me, Stark, unless you want your lunatics in the streets. I reckon they'll be arrested in a matter of minutes if they spend a day among civilised people."

Ethan moved before he could think. Anger had replaced his brain. He grabbed the walking stick and Roxbury's hand and pulled towards him until Roxbury's angry face was an inch from his nose. "You should be nicer to your own blood, or you might find yourself in the streets after I kicked your sorry arse."

Roxbury didn't flinch. "Should I be worried? Forgive me if I'm not after you fainted like a frail damsel."

"You cheated."

Roxbury smirked. "Do I look like I care? For the last time, I know the rat is here. You keeping him in your house is kidnapping."

Ethan let him go but not without effort. He bit down a comment about David being there of his own free will.

He straightened his jacket and brushed an invisible speck of dust from his sleeve. "You don't understand. The boy needs a firm hand. He'll never be ready to carry my family's name if he keeps snivelling and whining about how hard his life is. Pathetic."

"He's thirteen," Ethan said.

"He isn't a child, and I decide how to raise him."

"Leave." He opened the door fully. "Or I'll call Scotland Yard."

Roxbury paused on the threshold. "You're making a big mistake, Stark. Don't cross me. I've been patient with you and your bunch of lunatics. If I apply enough pressure, your centre will be closed tonight." He moved to leave but paused again. "That doesn't mean I'll let your centre stay open. I want that building to be profitable and make money. It's a matter of time before Lady Kingsley agrees with me. With each passing day, she sees you for who you are, a mentally insane man. Then we'll kick you and your freaks out." He touched the brim of his hat before finally leaving.

Ethan regretted his temper the moment Roxbury left the house. After the night at the museum, Lady Kingsley didn't favour him. He slammed a hand on the closed door. What was the point of holding a title that outranked an earl if he couldn't keep the men in his centre safe? Only because Roxbury held a larger share of land than Ethan did and could charm Lady Kingsley. He shouldn't let his anger rule him, not as long as he needed Roxbury. But hell, he couldn't allow Roxbury to mistreat David and Cora.

He took his time to go to the sitting room, needing to push down his temper before seeing David.

The boy stood up from his chair when Ethan entered. "Sir."

"Stay seated." Ethan sat in front of him.

A steaming cup of tea and a plate of almond biscuits lay on the polished table.

David closed his trembling hands around the cup. "Did he leave?"

"Yes."

"Was he angry?"

"Yes."

David's breathing sped up. His cheeks paled. "I must leave. The longer I stay here, the angrier he'll be."

Ethan touched David's arm. "Wait. Where's your mother?"

David stared at his cup for a long minute before answering. "She should be at the Royal Veterans' Society."

"Let me send for her. We'll wait for her here together. Don't leave until she's here."

Ethan made short work of sending an urgent message to Cora via his footman. He could go to the centre with David, but it wasn't a place for a child who already suffered from an overload of worries.

"Your mother will be here soon." Ethan poured himself a cup of tea. He needed it.

David ignored the tea and the biscuits. His knuckles showed a few scratches, likely from when he'd climbed the wall to Ethan's garden. Drops of blood trickled down his fingers.

"You're hurt," Ethan said.

"It's nothing."

"Let me take care of those cuts." Ethan took a clean cloth and a bottle of carbolic acid.

David didn't protest when Ethan dabbed the cuts. He didn't make a noise even though the disinfectant had to sting.

"I worked with the surgeons in the army," Ethan said. "I don't have a degree in medicine, but I learnt on the field."

David raised his gaze. "Did you see many wounded, sir?"

"Many. Pirates don't have mercy. The army surgeon couldn't

keep up with the wounded, who never stopped arriving. That's how I started helping him."

"I wouldn't be able to do it." David winced but didn't complain.

Ethan wrapped a light bandage around David's hand. "Sometimes the circumstances decide for us. You're brave. I don't doubt you would find the courage to face blood if needed. Not that I ever wish you that." He tied the bandage.

Despite the encouragement, David didn't brighten. Ethan had exhausted his ideas about how to cheer up the boy and acknowledged his failure. He didn't have many opportunities to talk with a child. They sat in silence, sipping their tea. He smiled, but David didn't smile back. Great.

"David." Cora strode inside the sitting room before the maid could announce her, her capelet fluttering behind her. "What happened?"

Ethan stood up as David rushed to hug his mother. Mrs. Parker followed.

"What's this?" Cora held David's bandaged hand. "Are you hurt?"

"Only a scratch," David said. "Lord Stark disinfected it."

"I apologise for not having greeted you properly, my lord." Cora curtsied, her voice trembling.

Ethan bowed. "It doesn't matter."

"My lady." Mrs. Parker seemed at a loss.

"You may leave, Mrs. Parker." He tilted his head towards David, wishing he talked with his mother about what had happened.

"What is it? What are you doing here?" Cora stroked David's hair.

David hesitated, glancing between his mother and Ethan. "Lord Roxbury took me with him in his carriage. He stopped in front of Lord Stark's house and ordered me to break a window with a stone. I refused and escaped here." He stammered throughout his short speech.

Cora pressed her lips in a white slash. "I see." She inhaled a few times. "Lord Stark, thank you for taking care of David. You've been most kind."

"It's a pleasure to have David as my guest," Ethan said.

"He's going to be angry," David whispered.

"He asked you to do something despicable. He has no right to be angry." She cupped her son's cheek. "We'll go home together, and I'll talk to him. You don't have to see him."

"Is there anything I can do?" Ethan asked.

Cora kissed David's cheek. "Go to the hallway and wait for me, all right?"

David nodded. "Thank you, Lord Stark." He waved before walking out of the sitting room.

"Ethan." Cora gazed everywhere but him. "Is your offer of money still up?" She had the same lost expression as the other day in front of the brothel, and Ethan didn't like it.

"Of course. How much do you need?"

She swallowed a few times. "A few hundred pounds. Two hundred."

"I'll give you more than that. When do you need the money?"

"Tonight or tomorrow at the very least."

"Absolutely." He took a step towards her. "I'll have it ready for you. I can talk to your husband if you want." Or punch him.

She avoided his gaze. "I appreciate your help, but I'm worried that your involvement might anger Lord Roxbury further."

"But—"

"Please think about it. The moment he gets a hint of what I'm planning to do, he'll call the police, and your presence will only make him suspicious. Let me deal with him. I'll go home, pack a few things, and be here as soon as possible. He should be at his club anyway." She flushed then paled. "You must know I might not be able to repay the loan."

Seriously? "I don't give a bloody damn," he nearly growled,

and he wasn't going to apologise for his swearing. "I only care about you and David."

She raised her large eyes to him. He wasn't sure if it was gratitude or fear shining in them. "Thank you for your help. Really." She closed her trembling hand around his, sending a jolt of emotion through him.

"You're most welcome."

She withdrew her hand quickly. "I must go." She hurried out of the sitting room with nervous steps.

The sense of injustice gnawed at Ethan's heart, but he had to respect Cora's decision. Besides, what could he do aside from punch Roxbury until some sense penetrated his thick skull?

ten

T HE HOUSE WAS eerily quiet when Cora entered the hallway. Aside from the lamps in the entry hallway, the lights were off, and no footman or maid had opened the front door. Even Cooper, her maid, wasn't there to welcome her. She had used her own key. Odd.

"Where's everyone?" David said.

"I don't know."

The servants never had their free day all together. Jacob must have dismissed them. No matter. Maybe it was better this way. Her escape wouldn't have witnesses.

"I don't like it, Mama."

She stepped closer to the stairs when the sound of Jacob's footsteps reached her from the other side of the door.

After years of living with him— or rather, of sharing the same house as he did, Cora had learnt to sense his mood from the air itself even before he entered a room.

The cadence promised war. Her pulse quickened. David straightened. Not that Jacob's foul mood was a surprise, especially after today's incident. She'd hoped she'd had the time to pack a few things, grab her money, and leave.

"He's coming," David whispered.

"Listen." She took his shoulders. "We must pack our things and leave. I'll keep him busy for as long as I can, but you must be quick."

Jacob pushed the door open and strode inside, his dark coat flapping around him. His cold stare wasn't directed at David though.

Cora shielded David and braced herself for Jacob's fury. "You shouldn't—"

"What is the meaning of this?" He took something out of his pocket and dropped it on the console table.

Cora let out a shuddering breath. Her letter to Mrs. Delois lay crumpled in front of her with the ripped envelope and stamps. "How did you get that?"

"What is it?" he demanded again, ignoring her question.

"It's none of your business."

A muscle in his jaw ticked. "In this letter, you wrote to a French woman that you have enough money to pay for a room. How? You stole from me. So yes, it's my business." He pressed his knuckles against the table. "What did you want to do? Leave me as you said to this Mrs. Delois?"

Cora didn't reply, only to keep David safe. If she provoked Jacob further, David would be involved as well.

"Would you leave me and cover me in shame?" Jacob asked, clenching a fist around the letter. "And who would have you? A disgraced woman without honour. People will think you eloped with a lover."

"David, go to your room." She squeezed his arm when he didn't move. "Go. Let me talk with your father."

David hung his head, and the curtain of his curls fell over his face.

"You aren't going anywhere." Jacob seized David's arm and dragged him closer. "I need a word with you as well."

"Leave him alone." Cora removed Jacob's hand from David

with a shove.

"I knew you would have said that," Jacob hissed. "Always defending him. Always taking care of him. What about me?"

"He didn't do anything wrong. Instead, you should be ashamed of yourself." She pointed a finger at him.

"The rat disobeyed me." Jacob's voice acquired that low, calm tone, hiding his cold fury. "I gave him an order, and he refused to do my bidding before running away from me."

"He did the right thing. The same can't be said about you. Come here, darling." Cora opened her arms, and David ran to her. "Why can't you leave him alone?"

Jacob raked a hand through his hair as if genuinely trying to contain his temper. "Stop defending him. Don't you see you're ruining him? He grew up weak and pathetic because you coddle him constantly."

She pushed David behind her. "Leave, Jacob. You need to calm down."

He didn't have the excuse to be drunk. Even when Jacob drank or indulged himself in opium, he never returned home intoxicated, and drugs didn't affect him as they did other men. She knew of his vices only because he openly spoke about them. He had to exercise huge self-discipline though not to fall into those vices deeply enough to kill himself.

"Don't tell me what I need to do." He rummaged through his pocket again and fished out a gun.

Cora gasped. A gun. Jacob might be vicious, cruel, and violent, but he had never, ever wielded a weapon against David or her.

She stretched out a hand towards him in a pacifying gesture. "Jacob, please. Put that gun down."

"I've had enough of you two defying me." Jacob sounded too steady and determined. She would be less frightened if he'd shown doubt or confusion. "I'm tired. You never listen to me. You don't respect me. But I am the one with the money and title, and you depend on me. I pay for your gowns and food and his education, and you repay me with contempt and disobedience. The little bastard will learn a lesson he won't forget." He cocked the gun.

"Mama." David paled, grabbing her hand.

"This is madness. He's your son." Cora stepped back from Jacob, taking David with her.

"I'm not going to kill him, just a scratch to show him what pain is." Jacob closed an eye and took aim. "He doesn't deserve to be my son. He's too much of a coward. A bullet will strengthen him."

"Stop this madness." Her voice reached a high pitch that sounded unfamiliar to her own ears.

Her pulse spiked. What should she do? Jacob blocked the way to the door. If she managed to grab the heavy vase on the console table and hurl it at him, creating a diversion, David might have enough time to flee.

"Move aside, Cora, or I'll shoot you too."

Cora shielded David, moving closer to the vase. "You're mad."

"See, rat?" Jacob snarled. "Your mama defends you, and you hide behind her skirts like a stupid child. That's what I mean. Stop behaving like a damn coward, boy. Stop hiding behind your mother."

Cora inched her hand towards the vase, but Jacob stared at them too closely for her to act.

David shoved her out of his way strongly enough to send her a few feet away, anger etching his features. "So be it. Leave Mother alone. Here I am. Have it your way then. Shoot me."

Jacob raised his gun. "Finally some sense. Take your punishment, boy."

"No." Cora raced and shielded David.

The gunshot thundered in the entry hallway, and a burning, scorching pain tore at her chest and shoulder. She gasped for air and tried to scream, but only a soft whimper came out. Her muscles contracted so hard her back arched. The room tilted and blurred. Jacob came in and out of focus.

"You silly woman." Jacob marched towards them.

"Mama." David couldn't hold her weight, and they fell to the floor when her knees buckled.

Warm blood soaked her shirt and pooled beneath her. What worried her the most was her head becoming light and the sounds coming muffled as if from a distance. If she fainted, David would be alone with his deranged father. There would be no one to protect him from Jacob. She had to stay conscious.

"I told you to move. Look what you've done." Jacob seized her hair and yanked her head up.

Her scalp burned, but she didn't have time to swat Jacob's hand away.

"Don't touch her." With a mighty roar, David shot up and shoved his father.

Jacob fell over backwards with a loud thud and a sickening noise, like that of broken bones.

David punched him in the nose. "I hate you!"

Jacob let out a muffled groan and then remained still, his head turned towards the wall.

Oh no. Cora crawled towards Jacob. Nausea left a bitter taste in her mouth and her body trembled. Her vision was blurred. She didn't trust her hearing either, so she wouldn't know if David was shouting for help. The important thing was that Jacob was alive because David couldn't have possibly killed him.

Please be alive.

"Mama, we must go." David coiled an arm around her waist and tried to haul her up. "Help!"

"Did you... is he alive?"

"I don't know." His voice broke with a sob that tightened her chest. "Mama. I didn't want to... I wanted him to stop."

"I know, I know." She paused in front of Jacob and moved his head.

A red spot marred his cheek and forehead, and a shallow cut crossed his eyebrow, but aside from that, his chest rose and fell rhythmically, his pulse was strong, and there was no blood under him. She sagged in relief. She couldn't care less about Jacob, but her David shouldn't be the one who killed him.

"He's alive," she said, grabbing the console table to stand up.

"Mama, let's go." David helped her stay up. "We must leave."

She staggered forwards. "Yes, but..." She couldn't finish the sentence.

"You're bleeding."

"My money." She glanced upstairs. The thought of climbing the stairs and taking her money out made her want to cast up her accounts.. The room tilted, and she couldn't think straight.

"Mama—"

Jacob groaned and twitched.

David shook his head. "There's no time. Lord Roxbury is going to wake up soon, and you need a doctor. Let's go, please." He sobbed in earnest now. "I don't want to stay here."

"Yes, let's go." Cora leant against him, trying not to put all her weight on him.

He remained astonishingly strong as they limped towards the front door. Blood soaked her shirt and trickled down her waist. Darkness lurked at the edges of her vision. She couldn't pass out. Not now. The hospital wasn't far, but she wasn't sure she could stay conscious for more than a few minutes.

"We're almost there, Mama." David opened the door.

The gust of cold air helped Cora regain her senses. The pain in her shoulder throbbed and burned every time she breathed, and her stomach churned. Dizziness weakened her. Her eyelids grew heavy while her head became lighter by the minute. David said something she didn't grasp as the glow from the street lamps blurred in and out of focus. He waved his arm. She closed her eyes for a moment. There were voices. Keeping her eyes open required all her strength. Somehow, she was climbing into a cab. David took her face, and his concerned eyes filled her vision.

"Mama," he whispered or maybe shouted. His voice came

hushed as if through the water. And she couldn't fight the darkness any longer.

eleven

ETHAN HATED LAW books. They were Finn's province. He was a man of action, and if he could do what he really wanted, he would simply punch some sense into Roxbury and be done with him. Hell, not even the whiskey helped understand the legal contrivances of the Royal Veterans' Society's complicated status.

Sadly, his late father had done a poor job of fixing it. Ethan suspected his father had simply straight out ignored the law and kept doing what he'd wanted. He was lucky Roxbury hadn't looked too deeply into the legal situation. It was a matter of time before he realised the centre was technically illegal.

Ethan would do anything in his power —legal or otherwise— to free Cora from her husband. Now that was one intricate gordian knot he wouldn't know how to untie. Or if he should. He'd crossed a line more than once when it came to Cora. She had to make her own decisions.

Aside from offering her money, he couldn't do much. If she wanted to get rid of Roxbury, she would need to disappear, and that expertise was Mrs. Sterling's province.

He shoved the glass of whiskey and the books aside and rubbed his aching forehead. His future rested on a bout of good luck and the hope Roxbury wasn't suspicious enough to have his solicitor dig into the documents. Not the best of the situations. In the meantime, he had to find a legal way to force Roxbury to sell his share while keeping the veterans, Cora, and David safe.

"My lord. My lord." Mrs. Parker's high-pitched voice snapped him to attention.

"What is it?" He scraped his chair backwards and shoved himself up.

Mrs. Parker twisted the hem of her apron. "It's that boy again, David. He says he's with his mother, the countess, my lord. He's covered in blood and said his mother is dying. I can't... so much blood."

All the breath rushed out of Ethan's lungs. Dying? He ran out of the room. "Where are they?"

Mrs. Parker went down the stairs on unsteady legs, gripping the bannister for dear life. "The boy came through the back door. He's waiting in the kitchen."

Ethan screeched to a halt upon entering the kitchen. Pale and shaking, David stood on the threshold of the open door. Blood, a lot of blood, stained his shirt, neck, and cheek. Ethan was trans-ported back to the battlefield. The screams of the wounded and the booms of the cannons echoed in his mind. He closed his fists and dug his fingernails into his palms hard enough to hurt himself. He had to focus. David's life was at risk.

"Are you hurt?" Ethan strode to him.

"No, sir." David beckoned for him to follow. He left the kitchen and exited through the back door, heading for the street. "My mother is injured."

"The blood isn't yours?" Ethan asked, following David.

"It's my mother's." David's voice cracked with emotion. At least he wasn't injured. "Lord Roxbury shot her."

The news was like a stab in the stomach. "What?"

"Please help her. She fainted once in the cab. I can't wake her up. I'm worried she's dead. I called for help, but the house was empty." A sob shuddered through him.

"Stay calm. Let me see." Ethan stuck his head inside the cab.

Cora sat in a heap on the seat, slumped against the wall. Her head hung over her chest, and her arms fell limply on her sides. Blood soaked her shirt.

He sagged in relief when he found a pulse, slow but steady. "She's alive."

"Who's going to pay me?" the driver said from the box. "This is most irregular."

Ethan fished out a bunch of coins from his pocket and handed them to the man. "There." He gently gathered Cora in his arms, careful not to move her too much.

"Can you save her?" David walked next to him.

"I'll do my best."

Once inside the kitchen, he laid Cora on the scarred table and lit a few more oil lamps. The bullet had torn the fabric of her shirt, gone through her flesh, and exited from her back, which explained the heavy bleeding.

Mrs. Parker appeared on the threshold, a hand on her belly. "Shall I call the physician, my lord?"

"No time. Bring me my bag, towels, boiling water, and sheets."

She hesitated before obeying.

Ethan ripped Cora's shirt off and took a better look at the wound. The bullet had opened a hole in her breast, missing the heart by inches. He'd need to clamp the bleeding artery and stitch it before repairing the tissue and muscles.

"My lord." Mrs. Parker handed him the bag with a trembling hand.

"Clean the tools and help me with the light." Ethan rolled up the sleeves of his shirt and scrubbed his hands with carbolic acid.

She paled. "But the blood... I really can't. I'll be useless, and the maids have left, my lord." She gripped the back of a chair, clamping a hand over her mouth. Her face turned green.

"Leave then. Don't faint. I have to take care of Cora first." Ethan sounded harsher than he meant.

Mrs. Parker staggered out of the kitchen before he could finish speaking. And now what?

"I'll help you," David said. "I'll do anything you ask me to do. The blood won't bother me."

Damn. Ethan wasn't sure having the boy involved was a good idea. David was a child who had just seen his father shoot his mother. Wasn't that enough? Still, Ethan needed help, and David's determined expression was his best chance.

Ethan nodded. "I need you to hold that lamp over here to light the wound."

David did as told without a word. If the blood upset him, he didn't show it. Ethan worked quickly. Removing her corset required a full minute he hated to waste. He ripped her chemise and bared her chest and the ugly bullet hole fully. He cleaned the wound with carbolic acid until the blood stopped oozing.

"Come over here," he said, waving David closer. Again, the boy didn't flinch, his expression solemn.

With a pair of clean tweezers, Ethan removed bits of fabric from the gash before washing it again. He kept an eye on Cora's face in case she came around, but while her pulse was steady, she remained unconscious.

Then it was a matter of stitching the wound from the inside out. Visions of the surgeries he'd performed on the battlefield flashed across his mind, but he gritted his teeth and shoved them away. No time for distractions. Cora's skin showed a deadly pallor that worried him. She'd lost a lot of blood, and there wasn't anything he could do for that. He had to hope she was strong enough to survive.

"Come here." He instructed David to change position and hold the lamp at different angles. "No fragments. That's good news."

David didn't say a word.

Ethan followed Dr. Lister's instructions religiously, disinfecting and scrubbing every tool before using it. Hopefully, no infection would set in. David never complained as Ethan ordered him around. He remained stoically quiet, moving only when Ethan told him to do so.

"Put the lamp down and help me turn her around." Ethan took Cora by the waist and, with David's help, turned her over to her belly to stitch the exit wound.

So many stitches. She would be in a lot of pain when she woke up. There was more caked blood on her back than on her chest. The bastard could have ripped her heart out of her body with that gunshot. He bandaged the wound tightly, wrapping her chest and back with a clean roll of gauze.

When Ethan finished, bloody rags, strips of fabric, and sheets surrounded Cora. Blood stained his clothes, the floor, the table, and the chairs.

"You may put the lamp down now. Well done."

David shivered when he placed the lamp on the counter. "Is Mama going to be all right?"

Ethan wiped his hands. "I stopped the bleeding and stitched the wound. I'm not going to lie. It's a big wound, and she's a petite woman. She lost a lot of blood."

David's bottom lip quivered. "What are you saying?"

He couldn't lie. "Her life is still at risk. We have to wait and see how she recovers. She'll need to drink a lot of water, tea, and broth to regain her fluids. Rest is vital. She can't move until the wound heals, or the bleeding will start again."

David wiped his face with his shirtsleeve. "She might live then."

"Yes. It all depends on how quickly she'll recover." The thought of Cora dying in his arms, of all places, was a dark blade twisting in his gut.

He'd seen young soldiers die in a matter of hours after a gunshot like that, but the conditions in those hospital tents had been abhorrent. Not enough disinfectant to clean the wounds, not enough chloroform or ether to anaesthetise the patients, and no clean gauze. Here at least he'd scrubbed everything and had enough morphia to keep Cora comfortable.

David started to clean up the mess of bottles, gauze, and blood-stained bandages while Ethan wiped the blood from his tools.

"Can we stay here until Mama is better?" David said in a voice so low Ethan barely heard him.

"Of course. I took that for granted. You can stay here for as long as you and your mother need to." How could David think Ethan would kick Cora and him out of his house after surgery?

"Thank you, sir." David ran a trembling hand over his face and staggered on his feet. The cloth he used to wipe a chair slid out of his hand.

Ethan steadied him, taking him by the shoulders. "Why don't you lie down?"

"No, I want to help."

"You did a great job. I'll clean up and make your mother comfortable. You should wipe the blood from your face as well. Go to Mrs. Parker. You'll find her at the end of the hallway. She'll draw a warm bath for you and give you something clean to wear."

David nodded, avoiding meeting Ethan's gaze. He shuffled out of the room but paused to glance at his mother. Worry creased his young forehead. "Sir... I shouldn't leave her."

"I'll take care of her. Don't worry. When you finish, you'll sleep upstairs in your mother's bedroom."

David chewed his bottom lip but nodded again and left the room. Well, Ethan had no idea what the boy meant to say or what troubled him.

He quickly swept the floor and gathered the dirty rags in a basket. Cora lay with her face tilted to the side, so pale that even her lips were bloodless.

He brushed an auburn curl from her face. "What the hell happened to you?"

He gently gathered her in his arms, careful not to disturb the wound. His bad shoulder throbbed at the sudden exertion, but he ignored the sting. Beneath the coppery smell of blood, her fresh scent of lemons wafted. He went up the stairs one step at a time. Her cheek rested on his chest, and her soft breathing fanned on his skin. What were the odds of a patient recovering from such a gunshot? He couldn't remember. Didn't want to. Blood loss was the enemy, and blood poisoning was always a menace.

"Don't die, Cora," he whispered, holding her closer.

He laid her in his bed and stoked the fire in the stove. Surely, she wouldn't have any legal problems getting rid of Roxbury after the incident. Her husband had attempted to kill her. The law was on her side. It had to be. Now, should he ask Mrs. Parker to undress Cora, or should he do it himself? He'd removed her shirt, corset, and chemise. There was little he hadn't seen of her. Her skirt was stained with blood as well.

He untied her boots and removed her skirt and petticoats, leaving her stockings and drawers on. She wouldn't be happy, but it had to be done. He covered her with heavy blankets and added a hot water bottle to the bed.

Exhaustion caught him by surprise once he finished tucking Cora into the bed and prepared the sofa for David. Her pulse pounded with a steady rhythm, which was comforting, but her pallor didn't bode well. Her skin was barely warm. He held her hand and rubbed it, forcing the blood to circulate. Her toes were cold through the fabric of her stockings. Dark circles rounded her eyes, and her gums and conjunctiva were pale.

He should attempt a blood transfusion. He'd done it several times while in the army. For some reason, his blood had never caused adverse reactions to the recipients' bodies. It seemed to have a universal appeal for other people's blood. Chances were Cora would react well.

Chances. He didn't like the meaning of that word.

He started the whole sterilising process again and set up the needles, armbands, and tubes. It had to work. He sat on the chair next to her and pricked his and her arm with the needles. Then he watched as the tube connecting them turned the colour of rubies with his blood.

"Sir?" David waited at the door. He wore a large shirt likely belonging to one of the footmen. The caked blood had been cleaned from his neck and face. He stared in horror at his mother. "What are you doing?"

"Come in." Ethan waved him inside with his free hand. "I'm giving my blood to your mother."

David's chest rose and fell quickly. "What does it mean? What's this?" His breath became laboured. "She'll die."

"Calm down." Ethan took a deep breath. "I've done it before. It's a medical procedure to replace the blood loss due to a patient's wound."

The boy went straight to his mother, narrowing his gaze at Ethan. "And it won't hurt her?"

"Quite the contrary." He didn't mention that blood transfusions could go horribly wrong and cause the patient's quick death. It had never happened with his blood though, and unless Cora received fresh blood, her chances of surviving were low.

David touched her hand. "She's still asleep."

Unconscious, actually. "It's better that way. The body heals faster during sleep."

David didn't seem relieved. "What happens if Lord Roxbury comes here and finds us?"

Ethan scrubbed the back of his neck. "He meant to kill your mother. He'll probably end up in prison for that. He has no excuses."

David perched on the edge of the bed next to Ethan. "He wanted to kill me." His voice broke. "Mama saved me. She stepped in front of Lord Roxbury and took my bullet. She risked dying to protect me."

Ethan put a hand on David's shoulder. "Your father is the only culprit here. You did nothing wrong."

"But if I..." He buried his face in the crook of his arm and sobbed.

Ethan hesitated before patting David's back. "You did well. You have nothing to be ashamed of."

The boy shook hard as he sobbed, hiding his face.

"Your mother will be all right," Ethan said, feeling the blood flowing away from him. "And you need to sleep. You can take the sofa over there unless you want to sleep in another room."

"No. I want to stay with my mother." David wiped his face, letting his wet curls hide his eyes. He walked over to the sofa without a word and without looking at Ethan, who was at a loss.

Ethan leant back, opening and closing his fist to pump more blood into the tube. The movement bothered his shoulder, but it was nothing he couldn't endure. David curled up in a corner of the sofa, looking small and fragile. His shoulders shook, but not a sound came out of him. Silent tears streamed down his cheeks.

Ethan reclined his head and regarded the boy. David was too young to deal with gunshots and blood. Ethan had been in his twenties when he'd seen his first gunshot wound, and he'd been too young then too. Should he say something? He'd already told David the situation wasn't his fault. What more could he say? David kept crying in silence, curled up in a tight ball, and Ethan's chest tightened.

The only good thing about the awful situation was that now Cora and David would be free.

twelve

NOT A WORD about the Earl of Roxbury having shot his wife was in the newspaper, not even in the *Evening Standard*. Ethan guessed it was a good thing. Likely, Roxbury tried to keep the incident quiet while he searched for his missing wife and son. It wouldn't take long before he realised they were in Ethan's house, but as a precaution, he would allow only Mrs. Parker to enter his bedroom lest gossip spread. For now, Cora and David were safe. More than safe. The blood transfusion had been a success. Cora's body had reacted well to his blood, and while her skin hadn't fully recovered its healthy pink colour, it wasn't deadly pale either.

Cora had slept the whole night and day although Ethan had constantly monitored her pulse and temperature and David had caressed her head. But when Ethan checked on her at dawn, her eyes fluttered open. A flurry of emotion caused him to hitch a breath as her amber gaze set on him.

"Cora, finally." He examined her eyes and skin, finding no sign of fever.

She gazed around from underneath heavy eyelids. "Where am

I? What am I doing here? Where's David?" She raised her voice when she mentioned David.

"He's all right. You're in my house, and David is—"

"Here." David jumped off the sofa to hold his mother's hand. "Mama, I'm here."

"David brought you here last night. He was very brave," Ethan said, stepping aside to give them a bit of privacy.

"Darling." Cora wrapped her good arm around David who buried his face in the crook of her neck.

"I'm all right," David whispered.

They chatted in soft, hushed tones while Ethan added coal to the stove and fetched a fresh pitcher of water. The tender bond between mother and son touched him.

"I was so worried, Mama." David smiled for the first time. "Lord Stark saved you."

Cora touched her bandaged shoulder. "Lord Stark?"

Ethan nodded. "You lost a lot of blood. That was my main concern."

"He gave you his blood," David said.

Cora's eyebrows rose to her hairline. "Really?"

"The transfusion went well. Obviously." Ethan stoked the fire. "But you must not move. It's very important that you rest for a few days. The wound required many stitches. You might start bleeding again if you strain yourself."

"Are you hungry?" David asked.

Cora shook her head. "Not now. Later perhaps. But I'd like a glass of water."

"It's normal to feel nauseous after a blood transfusion." Ethan held her head up and helped her drink in small sips.

Instead, David's stomach roared like a bear after waking up from hibernation. They burst out laughing. The laughter released the tension in Ethan's chest.

"Why don't you go downstairs and ask Cook to have something to eat?" Ethan asked. "I have to check your mother's wound."

"Yes, sir." David kissed his mother's cheek.

She closed her eyes, hugging him again. He waved happily before shutting the door behind him.

"Thank you for taking care of him," Cora said when they were alone.

"He's an independent boy. I didn't have to do anything." He prepared the gauze and bottles of disinfectant, hoping the wound didn't have any signs of infection. He inspected his tools again and scrubbed his hands a second time, stalling.

"I guess Jacob has no idea we're here," she said.

"No, he doesn't, and the newspaper didn't report anything about the shooting." He cleared his throat after he'd exhausted the excuses to start. "I have to remove the bandage." Bandage that wrapped around and covered her chest like a shirt. "If you prefer a nurse, I can find one at the centre. It might take a few hours though."

"No, I don't trust a stranger. A nurse will ask questions and understand I've been shot. I don't want to risk Jacob finding us just yet. I don't want to see him."

"All right. Good point." He hesitated before lowering the bedsheet.

As a former soldier, he'd worked with men and handled male bodies without much thought. It was the first time he'd dealt with a woman. The girls he helped at the brothel hadn't needed anything particular aside from syrups, creams, and potions. Cora was different.

He could only imagine how uncomfortable the situation had to be for her. Meanwhile, he would behave like a gentleman, but the lack of privacy was something both of them had to face. The wound was a few inches over her nipple.

"Changing the bandage will upset the wound, but I'll give you something for the pain after I finish," he said. "For now, I need to know where it hurts to understand if everything is all right."

She gave a quick nod. "I'm ready."

He wasn't.

She tilted her head to the side while he carefully unwrapped the bandages. He tried to preserve her modesty, working under the blanket when he could, but there was little he could do about the brushes of his knuckles against her skin. The more he removed the bandages, the more he bared her until she lay half-naked in his bed.

"I apologise." He pulled the bedsheet up to cover her nipples as much as possible.

"Don't worry," she whispered, turning her head towards the bedpost.

The only good thing about the situation was that her cheeks flushed pink. It meant she didn't have any internal bleeding.

The wound hadn't swollen or reddened at the edges. He touched it gently but detected no suspicious lump that might indicate an infection. The smell of carbolic acid wouldn't cover that of blood poisoning. So far so good.

"No infection or bleeding. How's the pain?" He prepared a fresh set of bandages.

She faced him but avoided his gaze. "My whole arm is sore, and I feel weak."

"It's normal. You must rest until you feel better. No, actually, until I say you can leave my bed." He meant it as a joke, a lame one, but she didn't smile.

"We can't stay here." The cold note in her voice hurt him.

"Yes, you can and must. Your wound will start bleeding again if you move. You and David are more than welcome here. Naturally, discretion is advised. I'll personally speak with my household about the necessity of keeping your presence here a secret. Roxbury must not know you are here. I expect a visit from him any time."

She exhaled a shuddering breath, and the urge to hold her and promise her he would take care of everything was nearly overwhelming. "I doubt Jacob will be here soon. David pushed him."

"What?" He stopped rolling the bandage.

"Jacob must have planned the whole thing. The house was empty. No servants. He must have dismissed them not to have witnesses. Jacob aimed at David. I stepped in front of him and got shot. Then David tackled him. Jacob fell backwards and hit his head on the floor. He was alive when we left him, but—" Her voice broke. "What if he's dead? We left him alone in the house. What will happen to David?" Her chest rose and fell quickly as her breathing sped up, straining the stitches. Not good.

"Calm down." He handed her a glass of water and helped her take a sip. The last thing the boy needed was to have killed his own father. That would be a trauma from which David would never recover. "First, I'll make some inquiries to understand what happened to your husband. Then we'll plan a strategy to keep David safe. Finn, Mr. Purnell, will help us. He's an excellent detective, and you can file a complaint against your husband. Finn will take your statement while protecting your privacy."

She swallowed hard and nodded. Tears hung on her eyelashes like tiny diamonds. "If Jacob is dead, I'll take the blame. I'll do anything to keep David safe." Her breathing quickened again. "I'll face the gallows if I have to."

"Cora, stay calm. Nothing is certain yet. You must stay calm and rest to recover quickly." He gave her a handkerchief.

She wiped away her tears but didn't look less desperate.

When she was calm again, he didn't have any more excuses to postpone bandaging the wound. He made a noise halfway between a cough and a groan. "I have to replace the bandages. It'll hurt a little."

She took a moment to answer. "I'm ready."

"I need to lift you to a sitting position." He waited for her to nod again before slipping an arm under her and pulling her up.

Her skin was soft and thankfully warm. When she sat upright, he released her. The blanket slipped down to her waist, and her skin pebbled with goosebumps.

"I'll be as quick as possible. You must stay warm." He wrapped the bandage around her shoulder and over her breast.

She kept her gaze down as he brushed her skin in the process. He couldn't avoid it.

Her muscles tensed when he passed the bandage behind her neck to secure it. "Not the neck," she said. The tendons in her neck stood out. "I don't want anything around it."

"I have to wrap it around your neck to make the bandage more stable. I didn't do it last night because you were asleep." He was confused.

"No." One firm word that didn't leave room for negotiations.

"As you wish." He unravelled the bandage and wrapped it in another way to avoid her neck.

She flinched when he accidentally touched her again.

"I'm sorry." He had to tug at the bandage to make sure it didn't slip. "Is it too tight?"

"No, it's all right."

When the bandage was secure around her shoulder and her breasts were covered, he exhaled in relief. He hadn't realised how tense he was until the job was done. For today. They would repeat this every day, maybe more than once per day, depending on how the healing progressed. He helped her don a nightshirt and fluffed the cushions for her.

Dark bruises circled her eyes. "I didn't thank you."

"You don't have to." He tucked the covers around her. "You must eat and drink a lot. And you must rest."

"I don't have the energy to do anything." The words were heavy with sadness as if she didn't mean them for the time being only but forever.

He held her hand. "You'll feel better soon."

She raised her large eyes to him as if begging him not to hurt her. He found swallowing difficult.

"I'm not sure," she whispered.

"I have enough hope for both of us." He caressed her cheek.

The knock on the door broke the moment.

He released her immediately. "Come in."

Mrs. Parker entered with a tray loaded with food. A rich broth, soup with mutton, rye bread, and red wine. They said red wine helped produce new blood. He wasn't sure there was enough evidence to support that, but it wouldn't hurt.

Mrs. Parker gave a timid smile and placed the tray on the nightstand. "I hope her ladyship feels better today."

"I do, thank you." Cora winced when she tried to sit upright.

"Let me help." He coiled an arm around her waist once again and pulled her up.

Her lips brushed his jaw by accident, but he couldn't deny the quick shiver slithering down his back. He swiftly suppressed whatever inappropriate sensation or thought his reaction was about to produce.

"There." It was his turn to avoid her gaze. "Drinking is the most important thing."

"I'll help the countess, my lord, with the food and her clothes." Mrs. Parker sat next to Cora. "You need to rest as well, my lord, if you don't mind my saying it."

"No, yes, I mean..." He scrubbed the back of his neck. "I'll go then." He walked backwards and hit the ottoman. A pang went up his calf. "Shit. I mean, sorry."

Mrs. Parker had an expression that told him she would smack him in the head if he weren't a marquess and she weren't his housekeeper. Cora instead seemed to fight a smile.

Hitting his calf was worth it if it meant seeing her smile. "I'll see you later."

He shut the door and leant his back against it, wondering what the hell had just happened.

Cora flipped through the pages of the newspaper after breakfast had left her full and with more energy. There was no article on the sudden death of Lord Roxbury or a search for David and her, but she wasn't sure the lack of news was cause for a celebration.

"Is he searching for us, Mama?" David sat next to her, pale and with shadows under his eyes.

"I don't know. The newspaper doesn't report anything about him. It should be good news." Unless Jacob was still lying unconscious in the hallway.

He lifted a shoulder. The shirt was too big for him. He looked smaller than he was in it. "Lord Stark will protect us. That's what he does. He protects people. He said we can stay here."

Cora lowered the newspaper. "Darling, I'm grateful for what Lord Stark is doing for us. He's an honourable man, but we can't ask him to carry the burden of our situation."

"He saved you and told me we can stay here for as long as we want."

"Yes, but he didn't mean forever." She hated watching David's brightness dim because of her words, but she couldn't lie to him. "He's kind, but we dropped our problems into his lap. We can't drag him into our battle against your father. What will happen when the police are involved? Lord Stark would be forced to be involved as well. He offered his help, but I'm not sure he had surgery and hiding us in mind when he agreed to help us."

David ran a hand through his hair. "And we're eating all his food and taking advantage of his generosity."

"I'm more worried about what your father might do to Lord Stark." She closed her eyes for a moment.

The vision of Jacob's determined face as he'd pointed his gun at David flashed across her mind. Jacob had been ready to shoot David. She didn't trust the police, and Jacob's servants would never testify against him. Besides, they hadn't seen anything. She should make new arrangements to leave as soon as she could travel before Jacob stopped her. Since he knew about Mrs. Delois, Cora had to choose another destination. Brussels, perhaps. One of her relatives lived there. She hadn't seen a cousin in years, but she was desperate. While she was ready to accept Ethan's help, she wouldn't impose on him or put him in danger.

"Try to understand." She took David's hand. "Lord Stark has his own problems and people to take care of. We're like strangers to him and we have a plan. As soon as I'm better, we're going to leave. We can't hide here forever." What she offered was a difficult, uncertain life. Not much for a thirteen-year-old boy.

David nodded but lacked confidence.

She could protect him from bullets. She couldn't protect him from the harsh reality of their future.

thirteen

E THAN HAD MEANT to take a quick nap, but the moment he'd laid his head down in the guest bedroom, he'd collapsed into a deep sleep.

The sun shone low on the horizon when he woke up. After he washed and changed, he headed to Cora's bedroom. She slept soundly, her breathing regular, but he checked her pulse, nevertheless. Steady and strong. Her temperature was normal. He would wait to take another look at the wound. The empty tray showed she'd eaten. He covered her properly and made sure the stove was hot before tiptoeing out of the room. He had barely time to exit before his housekeeper ambushed him in the corridor.

"My lord, may I talk to you for a moment? It's urgent," Mrs. Parker whispered, wringing her hands.

Ethan closed the door behind him gently. "What is it?"

The moment he shut the door, Mrs. Parker came close to him, almost invading his personal space. "I didn't want to disturb you, my lord, since you were tired. I let you sleep. But I must speak my mind. It's the boy. David."

Not what he expected. David was so well-mannered and quiet.

He couldn't be a problem. "What about him? Did he cause trouble?"

"Yes. No. Yes." She huffed.

"Mrs. Parker." He kept his tone low and calm. "What happened?"

"The boy asked me if he could help me do chores after breakfast. He was agitated and eager to help. I thought it was because a boy his age needs to keep himself busy. Lots of energy. I told him he could help with the dishes, and he did a good job, so he did."

"Great," Ethan said, not following.

"Then he scrubbed the floor and cleaned the windows. After that, he scrubbed the stairs and helped the maid with the laundry. I told him to stop, but he didn't listen. He kept going." She waved a hand to gesture at the whole house. "He hasn't stopped since this morning, and now he's polishing the silverware downstairs. The maids are worried you want to replace them with him. He didn't eat. He didn't take his afternoon tea. He did nothing but work."

"Thank you, Mrs. Parker. I'll have a word with him." Although he wasn't sure what he was supposed to say or why David had a burst of desire for house chores.

Mrs. Parker nodded solemnly. "I'll draw a hot bath for him, my lord, should you convince him to stop. He'll need one."

"Please have my and David's dinner served in my personal dining room."

She curtsied. "Yes, my lord."

He found David working furiously on the silver spoons in the strong room. Sweat damped his reddened face, and a feverish light gleamed in his amber gaze. Ethan had seen that look in men caught by the frenzy of the battle.

"David," Ethan said. A chill went down his back. The room didn't have a stove. The boy must be cold.

David stood at attention, dropping the spoon on the table. "Sir."

"What are you doing?"

"Cleaning the silverware."

Ethan took David's clammy hands. Fresh cuts and bruises covered them. "Why are you doing all these chores? Mrs. Parker told me you didn't stop working for the whole day."

"You don't have to worry about my mother and me." David brushed his matted hair from his sweaty forehead. His shirtsleeves were rolled up to his shoulders, showing a few more marks and scratches. "I can earn my keep and do my mother's work as well. I can do anything you want. Any chore you ask me. I won't complain. Mama will rest, and I'll work." He picked up a spoon and showed it to him. "I'm a hard worker." He said all that speech in one breath, shaking from head to toe.

A silent shock went through Ethan. How could he reassure this boy and make him feel safe and welcome without overwhelming him or offending him? He started to talk only to stop. He knew nothing of children. Dammit.

"May I continue, sir?" David asked.

"No, David." He paused. "We need to talk."

David nodded several times, but tears welled in his eyes as he sucked his teeth. Damn. Tears. Ethan had barely spoken, but he'd already said something wrong.

Ethan held up a hand. "You've done nothing wrong. You have nothing to fear from me." Perhaps the tears had nothing to do with fear of him but of something else. "And you and your mother are welcome here. You don't have to do any chores."

David pressed his lips hard, doing a poor job at suppressing his sobs. "We can't stay here without repaying you. We're a burden for you. You'll throw us out."

"No, I will not do such a thing. Who told you that you're a burden? It's ridiculous."

"My mama said we're like strangers to you."

Bugger it. He was terrible at this conversation. He needed to think. "Listen." He set aside the shiny silverware. "I want you to do something for me."

David nodded again. Unshed tears hung on the tips of his eyelashes. "Anything."

"Go to Mrs. Parker and get a warm bath and a change of clothes. Then you'll join me in my personal dining room, and we'll have dinner together and talk man-to-man. Can you do that for me?"

"Yes, sir." David wiped his eyes quickly.

"Good. Go then." He stopped him when David reached out for the damn silverware. "Leave it. Don't worry about it. You need to wash and change. That shirt is soaked, and you're sweaty. You might catch a cold."

With another, "Yes, sir," David left the room.

Ethan placed his hands on the table and hunched his shoulders. The bicarbonate paste used to clean silver was spread everywhere, a testament to David's hard work. He was the last person who could help a thirteen-year-old boy understand he and his mother were safe with him, but somehow he had to. He retired to his room and inhaled the smell of gravy and spices. He mentally thanked his cook.

David arrived in a set of fresh clothes too big for him. Ethan would have to provide something better for the boy.

"Sit." Ethan gestured at the chair in front of him.

David perched on it, his gaze roaming the plates of food on the table.

"You must be starving. We'll eat first and talk later, all right?"

David nodded. He did that a lot.

Ethan kept an eye on the boy as he wolfed down his portion of cured meat, bread, and roasted vegetables. Somehow, David's appetite hurt. Ethan had slept all day while David had done chores, exhausting himself for no reason. Ethan couldn't even enjoy his dinner. Never had he felt so... guilty although he couldn't tell about what.

By the time David polished his plate and leant back in the chair with a satisfied exhale, Ethan hadn't decided on a proper strategy yet.

"David." Ethan hoped he didn't sound too intimidating. "You and your mother are my guests and under my protection. I feel responsible for both of you. Not to mention that your mother is currently my patient. You don't have to earn your keep, do chores, or do anything to prove to me you're a hard worker to stay here. Is that clear?"

David fiddled with his hands covered by the too-long sleeves. "But why would you keep us here, let us eat your food, and use your coal, if we don't pay for anything?"

"As I said, you're under my protection, and it's my duty and pleasure to take care of you."

David's expression changed in a moment. Gone was the frightened boy. Now he was an angry man. His lines hardened, showing what promised to become a hard jaw. "And what does my mother have to do to have your protection? I may be thirteen, but I'm no child. I know what powerful men do to women who don't have money to pay for food and a roof over their heads."

The dinner stirred in Ethan's stomach. "If you don't want to be treated like a child, then I won't hold my tongue," he said, controlling his voice. He reminded himself that Roxbury wasn't the best example of masculinity and that David didn't know Ethan would never, ever take advantage of someone in difficulty. "Your mother doesn't have to do anything to receive my protection, food, or shelter. I will not touch your mother inappropriately under any circumstances. I would never do that. I'm not that type of man. I won't disrespect you or your mother with such disgraceful behaviour. I don't know about your father, but I *am* a gentleman."

"Do you promise you won't touch my mother, I mean, aside from treating her wound?" David didn't cower in front of Ethan's hard stare. The boy had courage and a fierce desire to protect his mother.

Ethan gave him his hand to shake. "I swear it on my honour

and that of my ancestors of the House of Stark that I will be nothing but a gentleman."

David shook his hand. "Thank you, sir."

Ethan held his hand. "You must promise me you'll stop doing chores."

David looked taken aback. "What do you want me to do then?"

"What I want you to do here is take care of your studies."

"Studies?" The hardened expression was gone. He was a boy once again. "What studies?"

Ethan sipped his wine. "What did your tutor teach you? What about your future?"

He traced the pattern of the tablecloth with a finger. "I'm not a good student."

"I wasn't a good student at thirteen either. What would you like to do?"

"I like studying languages." David didn't gaze up and kept staring at the tablecloth.

"Languages. We'll have to find a tutor for the role then. Why languages?"

He shrugged. "I like different languages and talking with different people. People who speak another language have the most interesting stories."

Ethan couldn't help but ruffle David's hair. "Interpreter. Excellent choice."

David didn't brighten up. "But it's impossible."

"Why would you say that? You're young and clever. You can learn languages if you want to." He waited for David to talk, but the boy shifted on the chair and fiddled with the fork without saying anything. "What is it? You can tell me anything."

"I can't read well," David whispered like a confession. "Lord Roxbury says I'm too stupid to read. If I can't read, how can I study and become an interpreter?"

Ethan had always wanted to punch the daylights out of

David's father but never as much as at that moment. Anger soured his mouth, ruining the excellent work of his cook. How dared Roxbury call this boy stupid and crush his dream?

He had to push down his temper not to scare David. "Listen to me very carefully." He leant closer to David and dipped his head to catch the boy's gaze. "You are not stupid. I don't give a damn about what your father says or doesn't say. I'll find you a good tutor who knows languages, and you'll become whoever you want to be, and to hell with Lord Roxbury." He wouldn't apologise for cussing.

David's bottom lip quivered. This child deserved a better father and desperately needed one. David hung his head, his shoulders shaking with silent sobs. Ethan could bet Roxbury had ordered his son not to cry out loud for any reason.

"David." Ethan scraped his chair closer to the boy, not sure about what to do. If he hugged David, would the boy accept the hug or recoil? When he'd been thirteen, he'd hated hugs and kisses. "I know he hurt you, but the things he said aren't true. You aren't stupid. You're a clever, brave boy, and I'm proud of you. I wish I had a son like you." He put a tentative hand on David's shoulder.

David didn't smile as much as Ethan had hoped. "I don't want to return home to him," he whispered with broken words. "I don't want to see him again."

"Then you won't. I promise you that together we'll do everything to keep you and your mother away from him." Ethan wasn't prepared for the sudden, fast hug from the boy.

David threw himself off the chair and wrapped his arms around Ethan's neck, sobbing in earnest now. His slim body shook with the power of his outpouring. Ethan returned the hug, and the moment he did that, David clung to him like a vine, desperate and exhausted. Ethan held him, letting him vent his anger and sadness. Too much sadness for a boy so young. The boy's pain hurt him. He vowed to keep David and Cora safe, no matter what.

He caressed David's curls. "You're going to be all right. No one can force you to stay with Lord Roxbury."

When David's sobs died down, he sagged against Ethan. "I hate him," he said. "I hate my own father."

Ethan couldn't imagine hating his own father. For David, it had to be devastating. "With time, the hate will quench and won't hurt anymore." He took David's face and wiped his tears. "You need to sleep now, and no more chores, all right?"

David's face reddened from the crying.

"I'm not going to throw you out for any reason."

"All right," David said with a small voice.

They went upstairs together. David leant against Ethan, seeking comfort, which was likely the scariest thing that had ever happened to Ethan. He'd rather face pirates and highwaymen than worry about doing or saying the wrong thing and hurting David. He could protect people from physical threats, but emotional ones were another matter, and he wasn't the best person to comfort others. The visceral need to protect David and Cora was undeniable though. He might not have the right words for every situation, but he would do his best.

Ethan led David to his bedroom. "You must be exhausted."

"A little." David climbed onto his bed with sluggish movements, his eyelids drooping. "May I leave the oil lamp on?"

"Of course you may." Ethan tucked the boy in the bed. It was amazing how David could go from being a child to being a man in a moment. Now he was just a boy, terrified and confused.

David took Ethan's hand. "Will you stay here until I fall asleep, please?"

Another surge of affection swelled in Ethan's chest. He might burst out crying too.

He sat on the chair next to the bed. "I won't leave you."

As he watched David fall asleep and his chest rising and falling slowly, he wondered if he was doing the right thing. Not that he didn't want to help David, but he wondered if he could keep his promises. He ought to make a decision between taking full responsibility for David and Cora or simply helping them escape from Roxbury. He hadn't expected the fast, deep attachment to the boy, or the possessive urge to protect Cora. But here he was. And he was frightened.

As David fell asleep, his hand slipped out of Ethan's, and a quick shot of panic sliced through Ethan as if he were about to lose David.

Yes, Ethan, the soldier who had been awarded a Victoria Cross for bravery, was more scared than he'd never been.

fourteen

CORA WINCED AS she sat upright in the bed. Her shoulder burned, her arm throbbed, and a funny taste lingered in her mouth. Not to mention the constant worry gnawing at her. She expected Jacob to barge into the bedroom and drag her away. His silence bothered her. Either he was halfway to the grave, or he was plotting. Both options were terrifying.

She probed the tight bandage. Ethan had done an excellent job. Without him and his blood, she would be dead, but she couldn't allow herself to lower her guard. Jacob would soon search for her and David, and she wouldn't let Jacob hurt David again. Never.

She had to ask Ethan for a higher sum if she wanted to leave. She ought to be quick, especially since Jacob was aware of her connection with Mrs. Delois. Once she and David were in Brussels, she'd find somewhere safe to stay, a place where Jacob wouldn't find them.

All her pounds, painfully stashed aside, had been for nothing. The idea of asking yet another favour of Ethan didn't thrill her. Dash it, he'd given her his own blood. What more could she ask of him? If she stayed at Ethan's house, she would bring only trouble to his door. He didn't deserve that. Maybe it was the shock of having been shot at or the exhaustion that had never left her since the transfusion, but thinking was difficult.

The firm knock on the door could come only from Ethan. "Cora? May I come in?"

She pulled the blanket up although there was nothing of her he hadn't already seen. "Come in."

His figure filled the doorframe, and when he approached the bed, he towered over her. Again she wondered why his broad shoulders and massive body didn't threaten her. She could trust him, certainly on medical matters and on keeping David and her safe. But as for other affairs, she wasn't ready to trust any man, no matter how kind and gentle he was. She'd made that mistake, and it'd almost cost her life. She wouldn't make it again. Her instinct told her Ethan was different, but her instinct had been wrong before.

He carried a tray of potions and bandages. "How do you feel today?" He placed the tray on the nightstand, pushing aside the bottles of drugs and disinfectant.

The smell of carbolic acid would probably be lodged in her nostrils forever, but Ethan's hearty scent reached her senses all the same.

She sagged on the pillows. "I feel sore. Tired. The shoulder burns as well, more than yesterday."

"Let me check your temperature." He touched her forehead.

His rough skin chafed hers a little, but in a pleasant fashion if it made sense. Their gazes met and locked like two pieces of a puzzle. Hot turmoil swirled in the depths of his eyes, but she couldn't understand what type. A stirring started in her chest the longer he stared at her. He broke eye contact before she could examine her reaction more closely.

"No fever. Excellent," he said, touching the sides of her neck. There was something soothing in the way he cradled her head. "I have a light potion of morphia that will help with the pain, but you must eat before taking it and never take it more than twice a day."

"I won't."

He shifted his weight, avoiding gazing at her. His uneasiness gave him away. She knew what was coming. The usual change of the bandages. She wondered if the practice was more embarrassing for him than for her. He was the first man who had seen her naked aside from Jacob, but he had also treated her with respect, and that made the whole difference. As for her, she couldn't deny she felt self-conscious, but her body didn't matter to her right now.

He coughed politely but didn't say anything. She ought to put him out of his misery.

"You may proceed," she said, fighting the odd urge to stroke his rough knuckles. "I understand it's important to keep the wound clean."

He kept his gaze on the floor. "Mrs. Parker refuses to deal with blood and wounds. I'm afraid she'll faint before doing anything useful. I don't trust any of the maids to do a good job. None of them is experienced. But I can find a nurse who won't betray us."

"Ethan." She straightened as much as the bandages allowed. "It's all right. I don't mind." She was beyond caring for her modesty. Jacob had used her body when he'd wanted to, and Ethan had proven to be a gentleman.

Ethan scratched the back of his neck. "Very well."

She started undoing the buttons of her nightgown, but the movement sent a shot of pain down her body. A muffled whimper escaped from her. "Yes, I'm definitely worse than yesterday. I'm afraid you'll have to do the undressing."

His eyes widened in shock, but he recovered his composure in a moment. "Right."

He unfastened the remaining buttons and helped her pull her arms out of the sleeves. He lowered the nightgown to her waist. The bandages crossed her chest and covered her shoulder and breasts but left her neck bare, thank goodness. He gently unravelled the bandages, frowning in concentration.

She couldn't avert her gaze from him. The lines of his face tightened in a harsh expression enhancing his green eyes. She searched for something, a slight twitch of his muscles that might betray his thoughts and waited for a lewd remark, but he never did or said anything. He remained stoic and serious. He lowered his gaze again when the bandage was gone and she sat half-naked in front of him, her full breasts on display. Now a hint of self-doubt caused her cheeks to flame. Since she'd breastfed David, her breasts had grown heavy and lost their firmness. Oddly enough, she'd never cared about that until now. He soaked a cloth in carbolic acid. She braced herself for the sting.

"I diluted it," he said, "since there isn't any sign of infection. It shouldn't sting as much as before."

She pressed her lips, ready for the pain. He dabbed the wound gently without applying too much pressure. Yes, the potion didn't burn as much as yesterday, but she had to draw in a deep breath to ease the tension. The wound was right over her nipple, and the skin was particularly sensitive there. He cleaned the wound on her back, the hole from where the bullet had exited. She still had to decide which side hurt the most. He was so close that his warmth caressed her skin. She couldn't remember the last time a man had treated her with such kindness.

"Please lie down," he said, wiping his hands.

"Gladly." She exhaled when she reclined on the pillow.

"May I examine you?" Again, he didn't look at her.

"Please."

He touched her, starting with her arm on the side of the wound. The pads of his fingers pressed and probed her stiff muscles. "You're very tense. Is it me or the pain?"

"The pain, mostly." Although she couldn't say his touch was painful. Quite the opposite. In a way, it relaxed her and embarrassed her a little.

He went up to her sore shoulder and probed her collarbone. She couldn't suppress a whimper.

He eased the pressure of his fingers. "Sorry. There's a swelling here. The skin appears redder. I believe it's from the brunt of the impact. You'll grow a deep bruise."

"I can feel the skin tender there."

His frown deepened when he touched the stitches. "The skin is a little warm here. There might be the beginning of an infection." He finally raised his gaze to her. "I apologise."

A shiver slithered down her spine as he touched her breast. Her left one was tender and more swollen than the other, but if she was going to be honest with herself, it wasn't pain or revulsion stirring in her belly at his examination.

"Does it hurt?" he asked.

"A little."

His kind touch soothed her nerves and reduced the pain. He checked the second wound.

"The swelling is normal especially when the bullet hits such a soft, delicate area." He rummaged through the bottles and pots of potions and herbs. "As a precaution, I'll apply a mixture of herbs to the wound to prevent an infection and reduce the swelling." He crushed dried herbs in a mortar, adding drops of scented oil to the mixture. "Let me feel your neck glands."

Saying, "Yes," and regretting it happened at the same time.

The cold sensation of feeling his strong fingers around her neck overcame the fresh shot of pain shuddering through her at the examination. She couldn't help it. She recoiled and scurried away from him when he closed a hand around her throat.

His expression tightened further as if she'd slapped him. "What did he do to you?"

Oh, he knew. He understood. Her nakedness triggered a flame of shame throughout her. He saw through her, too close to her soul for her liking. She pulled the blanket up to cover herself and bent her knees. It was her turn to avoid making eye contact. She put a hand on her neck. Her own touch caused a tightness in her chest.

Ethan didn't prompt her. He sat still and waited. Even his breathing sounded slow and controlled.

"Would you like me to leave?" he said. "I may return later to bandage the wound."

"No, don't leave." She kept her knees bent even though the position was uncomfortable and strained her muscles.

He stroked her hand, drawing soothing circles with his thumb over her knuckles. He'd done the same when they'd been trapped under the altar. Maybe she'd never left that oppressive nook. Maybe she was still buried underneath the rubble. And he was next to her as he'd been then. It pained her that it'd taken a bullet into her flesh to realise that. Yes, she'd planned to leave Jacob and had set aside the money to move to France, but she carried her own cage with her.

"It's hard," Ethan said in his deep, calm baritone. "But you're a strong, amazing woman. You can overcome whatever he did to you."

His kindness broke the walls around her heart, and her loneliness poured through the cracks. She couldn't share everything with David although he knew better than anyone what living with Jacob meant. She wanted to be strong for him not to show how miserable she was. She hadn't realised how desperately she needed to talk with someone and unburden herself until Ethan paid her the most beautiful compliment she'd ever received. Did she feel strong and amazing? Not at all. But he thought she was, and for now she could borrow his strength.

"He likes to choke me," she whispered, ashamed of... she wasn't sure what.

Ethan let out a deep noise from his throat like a low growl. "Did he beat you as well?" His words were all but a snarl.

"No, not really." She laced her fingers through his, needing the contact. "When I met him for the first time, he swept me off my feet. He courted me with determination, brought me flowers and presents every day, and was simply charming. He would send me many messages throughout the day and become angry if I didn't reply quickly." She chuckled bitterly. "I thought his anger was a sign he cared about me. I found his interest endearing. We always laughed when we were together. He listened to everything I said, let me talk for hours, and understood me so well. I was so in love. Even my parents were utterly charmed by him, especially because he gave me many expensive presents and made grand gestures to show me his love. Once, he hired an entire orchestra to play a serenade under my window. When I think about how I enjoyed those moments, I feel like a fool."

"You shouldn't." He put his other hand over hers. "He deceived you. His strategy was to overwhelm you with false kindness."

"I haven't understood why yet." She rested her cheek on his big hand, and her pulse quickened as he stroked it.

"I've met men like him. They see people as objects to collect, and all they want is to be adored and worshipped. He loves only himself."

Pity it'd taken her too long to realise that. "When he proposed, I said yes immediately. The fact my dowry was meagre didn't seem to bother him." She paused, remembering the flutter in her belly at Jacob's utter devotion. The way he made her feel special, beautiful, and unique. "After we got married and my parents died, everything changed, not immediately though. The first year was wonderful although he grew increasingly demanding and possessive, but after I became pregnant, he told me he found me unattractive and lost interest in me. I think he found a mistress. He barely paid any attention to me."

"He didn't beat you?" he asked again, caressing her jaw.

"Not really. He became cold and detached, cruel and dismissive. He didn't raise his hand at me, but he raised his voice. His mood always changed. I went mad trying to understand how to behave, not to trigger his temper, and became dependent on those rare, sweet moments when everything seemed perfect. Those moments hurt more than his bouts of bad temper because they were proof he could be kind."

"Hell, Cora." He pressed his forehead to hers. The tips of their noses touched in a suddenly intimate gesture. "I want to kill him." His tone didn't leave room for doubt. He meant every word.

At this point, she couldn't stop talking until she told him everything. "His cruel words and indifference hurt me deeply. He made me feel worthless, called me names, and despised me. When David was born, Jacob's interest in me diminished further. He hated that I spent time with David. He ignored him. He said he wished David had never been born." Her voice broke with the hurt those words still inflicted on her. "David and I didn't exist for him. He didn't usually spend time with his son, but when he did, he mocked David and told him how stupid he was." She put a hand over her throat. "He never visited my bed again, saying I repulsed him. But he enjoys touching me roughly. Yes, there have been slaps. But sometimes he would..." Goodness. She changed her mind. She couldn't go on.

"If it's too difficult to talk, you don't have to." He kissed her hand. "Although I know from experience that talking can heal." He waited patiently for her to talk again, rubbing her hand.

"He would catch me by surprise, close his hands around my neck, and squeeze while touching me." Her voice cracked. "He would tell me that with a little pressure, he'd get rid of me, that he enjoyed controlling the life flowing through me. It happened a few times, enough to scare me to death." Another sob cracked out of her. "On those occasions, he found his release when he was choking me."

Ethan sat so still she wondered if she'd shocked him into silence. "I'm going to kill him." It wasn't a promise or a menace. He sounded as if he'd taken an oath.

She had to admit a dark side of her enjoyed the thought of

Jacob dying and getting what he deserved, but no. She didn't care if he lived or died. She just wanted to be free from him and to keep David safe. "Don't kill him, please. For David and me. Don't do it."

He clenched his jaw. A tendon in his neck beat a fast tempo.

"I don't want you to become a killer for me," she said.

"I've killed before. I've killed men less despicable than Roxbury."

Goodness. The way his gaze darkened chilled her. She caught a glimpse of the ruthless warrior inside him. He had to be terrifying on a battlefield.

She leant against his touch, now careful and gentle. But it wasn't difficult to believe those strong fingers could deliver a merciless death. "I don't care about him. I only want to move on with my life with David."

His wrath thickened the air between them to the point it pressed against her skin like the humidity in summer. She had no doubt he would kill Jacob and leave no trace of the murder. He would never be accused of the crime if he wanted to. But revenge had little meaning for her. She wanted freedom. Everything else didn't matter.

A hint of warmth spilt into his hard gaze. "Let me bandage your wound. I won't touch your neck."

Except that after the moment of truth they'd shared, she found uncovering herself difficult. "I…"

He hunched his shoulders. "I'll do it later if you feel so inclined."

If she were bolder, she would hug him. "Thank you for understanding."

He closed his eyes. "I'll keep my eyes closed and help you put your nightgown on. Without the bandage, you'll have to pay attention to how you move your arm. You might open the wound again."

She dropped the blanket and guided his hands over the neckline of her nightgown. She grimaced as she slid her arms into the sleeves. Yes, the lack of bandage made her arm heavier and caused the tender flesh around the wound to pull.

She tugged at the lapels until her chest was covered. "You can open your eyes."

"May I?" He pointed at the front of her nightgown.

"Please."

He made short work of buttoning the nightgown. Something had changed between them, and she wondered if she would regret sharing her most vulnerable part of herself with him.

"Mama?" David's voice shot a burst of energy into her.

"Darling, come in."

Ethan rose from the bed and gathered his medical supplies. His hard and cold expression softened only when David entered the room. An understanding passed between them, a secret pact Cora couldn't decipher. The connection between Ethan and David seemed a partnership. Or maybe a solemn promise.

"Mama." David hugged her gently, and the tension in her body eased as she held him with one arm. "Lord Stark and I talked."

"About what?" She tried to fix his wayward curls. She could bet he hadn't combed them in days.

Excitement brightened David's face. "Lord Stark will find a tutor for me to teach me languages. He said I can learn to read well with practice."

His happiness was contagious, but she couldn't deny the flare of concern. Ethan shouldn't make promises he couldn't keep.

She kissed David's cheek. "I've always told you that you can read, darling."

"I'm going to read every day." He beamed at Ethan, who smiled back.

"My library is at your disposal." Ethan pointed a finger upstairs. "You can choose whatever you want. I have books in French and Spanish as well."

"Thank you, sir." He jumped off the bed and hugged Ethan in

a surprisingly familiar fashion. What had happened between them while she'd been unconscious?

Ethan held him back. Only tenderness transpired from their hug, but that meant David would suffer twice when they left.

"I have to go." David kissed her cheek before rushing out of the room.

The moment Cora was alone with Ethan, she turned towards him. "Ethan, I must speak my mind," she said in a bitterer tone than she intended.

He paused rolling up a long bandage. "Yes?"

"You can't make promises to David." She tried to keep her voice down. "My first rule with him is to never, ever make promises I can't keep."

He narrowed his gaze. "I mean to keep my promise and find him a tutor. I don't give my word lightly."

"And after you find him a tutor, then what? We can't stay here forever and pretend nothing happened. What about Jacob? He's still my husband and David's father. The law is on his side. He can send the police here and force me back to his house."

"He shot you. I seriously doubt a judge would defend him."

No, she didn't have any faith in the justice system, not when an earl was concerned. "You showed David a future he can't ever have."

"I want to help him." His eyebrows lowered. "He went through a lot for a boy his age."

"Exactly for that reason, I always tell him the truth." Her shoulder hurt. Tarnation. The bandage did make a difference. "Please promise me that you're going to tell him he won't have a tutor. David and I will leave as soon as I recover."

"I won't do such a thing." His chest heaved. "And leave to go where?"

"France was my idea, but Jacob knows about my contact in Paris. I might go to Brussels. A cousin of mine lives there," she added in a whisper.

The clinking of glass stopped when he finished organising his bottles and tools to focus on her. "Cora—"

"I understand if you don't want to have anything to do with me after this mess," she hurried to say when he exhaled.

"Bugger me." He pinched the bridge of his nose. "I'll give you everything you need, but you have other options."

"Like what?" She reclined on the pillow as her arm bothered her.

He rushed to add another cushion to make her more comfortable. She didn't even ask how he understood she needed another pillow. He was attuned to her needs, which started a flutter in her belly. More than a flutter. His kindness was breaking all her defences. Blazes. She wanted to trap his handsome face in her hands and kiss him.

"You can divorce," he said. "It requires a private bill at the parliament, but it has been done several times in the past years. You can start a new life and be free."

"I don't think the parliament will grant me a divorce."

"Why should you leave?" The bed dipped as he sat next to her. "You did nothing wrong. It's him who should leave and be ashamed. Besides, I can give you the money to move to Brussels or anywhere else and live decently any time you want. But first, you should fight to stay here or at least try."

"I don't trust Jacob. In the unlikely chance the parliament grants me a divorce, he will find a way to make me pay. What if he forces me to return to him? What if an opportunity like this one doesn't repeat itself? No, I want to leave him and never see him again."

He squeezed her hand with sudden desperation. "At least talk with Finn. He'll be here shortly anyway with news about Roxbury. He knows the law. He'll tell you what your chances of getting a divorce are."

A divorce was a ridiculous idea although the number of people who requested and obtained it in parliament grew each year. Many couples of the *ton* had divorced. Could she really get her life back and leave Jacob behind without having to run away like a thief?

Ethan's intense stare searched her soul as usual. He had a good point. She could move to Brussels anytime with his help. Besides, she couldn't go anywhere now.

She nodded. "I'll talk to Mr. Purnell, thank you."

He kissed her hand. "Have hope."

No, she didn't trust hope. Only facts

fifteen

ALTHOUGH MR. PURNELL was a tall man with a set of deep black eyes that seemed bottomless, his presence didn't frighten Cora. Just like when she was with Ethan. She tugged at the lapels of her dressing gown as she sat in Ethan's majestic bed in his room with her arm propped on a pile of cushions. She'd need to ask Ethan to bandage her, or she wouldn't sleep for the pain. She'd meant to meet Mr. Purnell in the sitting room, but she'd overestimated her strength. Her head had spun and her back had burnt the moment she'd stood up. So much for leaving.

Ethan stood next to the fireplace, an elbow on the mantelpiece. He glanced at her arm and face, likely realising how uncomfortable she was.

Mr. Purnell removed his bowler hat. "Your ladyship, I trust you're better in Ethan's care. He's an excellent surgeon."

"Lord Stark is taking very good care of me, thank you." Excellent care.

"What news do you bring us?" Ethan asked.

Mr. Purnell plonked down onto the armchair, his wooden leg stretched out in front of him. "Lord Roxbury has been treated for a severe head concussion by his physician, and he's now recovering at home. His butler found him unconscious in the hallway and gave the alarm. It's a serious injury, or so his physician declared, but not life-threatening. Nothing that won't mend. Officially, he slipped and hit his head."

The wave of relief washing over Cora surprised her. But then again, she didn't care about Jacob, only about David. The last thing David needed was to have killed his father. She sagged against the pillows.

"Do you wish to file a formal complaint against your husband?" Mr. Purnell asked. "I can have him in shackles tonight."

"That will keep him busy for a while," Ethan said.

Tempting. "Will Jacob know where I am if I denounce him?"

Mr. Purnell shook his head. "There's no need for that. As the person who's being accused of a crime, he doesn't have the right to know where you are."

"Then yes. I want him charged with..." She paused, not sure where to start.

"Attempted murder," Mr. Purnell completed, "assault and failing to provide assistance."

"Yes, to all that." The charges should help get a divorce, shouldn't they?

"Any questions about the incident and his missing wife and son? Any gossip?" Ethan asked.

Mr. Purnell shrugged. "Lord Roxbury didn't report his wife's and son's disappearances. He said his wife and son are visiting a relative in the country, which is why he dismissed the servants. I discreetly asked a maid about Lady Roxbury's absence and she confirmed that. Also, no servant knows anything about an altercation or gunshot."

"Why would he stay quiet?" She rubbed her hands as a shiver took hold of her.

Without her saying anything, Ethan wrapped a blanket around her shoulders and stoked the fire in the stove. She got used to being spoiled by him quickly. His attention to her needs made her feel special. Something so simple yet not taken for granted.

Mr. Purnell followed the gesture but didn't comment. "My guess is that Lord Roxbury is well aware of his delicate position and is taking time to think, likely exaggerating his condition. He attempted to kill his son and nearly killed his wife. Not the type of news he wants people to talk about. He shot a harmless woman and a child. His peers won't support him. He may also be waiting to find you before making a decision or to recover completely from his injury. Aside from that, I wouldn't know what his strategy might be, but the charges will provoke a reaction from him. Or they might convince a servant to come forwards. I mean, the hallway had to be stained with blood. The maids must suspect something. And who helped her ladyship pack her luggage if she'd left for a visit? Surely, the servants understand the circumstances are questionable."

No, she doubted Jacob's loyal butler, maids, and footmen would say anything about the way Jacob treated her. But yes, the charges would provoke a reaction. She shivered again, wishing for a nice cuppa.

Ethan poured her a cup of hot tea. Goodness. She didn't need to talk. He could read her mind.

"What about the possibility of obtaining a divorce?" he asked. "Could Cora get a divorce from Lord Roxbury?"

She grabbed the cup with both hands and held her breath for Mr. Purnell's answer.

Mr. Purnell exhaled. "It's not feasible, not to mention expensive."

She shouldn't be surprised, but the disappointment sat heavily on her chest.

"Many people query for a private bill. Only this year, there have been more than forty applications for a divorce," Ethan said. "If it's only a matter of money, I can provide it."

Mr. Purnell shook his head. "Yes, many divorces have been

processed by the parliament recently, but the applicants have been men, and not just men but titled ones."

How silly of Cora to believe only for one moment that the law might help her. She sipped her tea, realising only then she'd hoped to get a divorce more than she'd like to admit.

"If a man wants to divorce his wife, all he has to do is declare she's unfaithful, no evidence required. The parliament will grant him a divorce after the payment of the hefty legal fees, naturally." Mr. Purnell cast an apologetic glance at her. "It is unfair, but you have to understand that a wife's infidelity is taken seriously in parliament because it interferes with the Succession Law. Adultery means that a duke's son might not be the rightful heir to the title. Imagine the chaos if every lord is accused of not having the right to inherit because of his mother's adultery. The parliament won't allow such a thing. Thus an unfaithful wife must be cast aside."

"And what does a woman have to do to get a divorce?" she asked.

He opened his mouth and spread his arms. "It's never been done before."

"Never?" Ethan folded his arms over his chest, muscles bulging.

"Never. Not for lack of trying," Mr. Purnell said. "Several ladies have applied for divorce in the past decade, but their claims have always been rejected. No one cares if a lord has a mistress as long as there's one rightful heir. I'm sorry."

"Naturally." She huffed. Brussels then. It was her only hope.

Somehow, she would find a way to give Ethan something back. As much as she cared for and respected him, she didn't want to depend entirely on a man's generosity. Things out of her control might happen. She'd been at the mercy of a man before, and even though Ethan wasn't Jacob, she preferred independence. She wanted to live a life without having debts with anyone.

"There's more, my lady." Mr. Purnell lowered his voice, rubbing his knee. "In the extraordinary case you manage to get a divorce, you must consider that Lord Roxbury will maintain David's custody."

Her next breath was punched out of her. "No. Never."

"If Lord Roxbury, after the accident, decides to file for divorce, the judge will likely let him keep David," he said. "He's his heir. The judge wouldn't let him stay with you."

"No." Ethan's sharp voice could cut glass. "David's safety is paramount. He doesn't want to live with his father."

"I'm ready to sacrifice anything to stay with David." She kept her voice steady in case David might hear her.

Ethan exchanged a glance with her. "If a divorce isn't an option, what's left?"

"I must leave England." Her voice broke. "That's the only solution."

"My lady." Mr. Purnell scratched his short beard. "If you leave and get caught, since I believe Lord Roxbury will do his level best to find you, you'll lose everything, not simply your status but David as well. No judge will allow you to see your son."

She clenched her fists. "Then I must be careful and don't get caught. If I move now when Jacob is unwell, I'll make it."

"There's another possibility." Mr. Purnell took a moment to answer, drumming his fingers on the armrest. "Perhaps something better than a divorce. An annulment."

"The wedding was perfectly valid," she said. "I wasn't forced into marriage and I was of age. We had a one-year engagement with the banners and all that." One year. And she hadn't understood what a monster Jacob was. The more she thought about that, the angrier she became.

"Yes, but if you prove Lord Roxbury treated you and David with cruelty, shot you, and neglected his duty as husband and father, his behaviour will be grounds for an annulment." Mr. Purnell paused and tilted his head as if to say more or less. "It'll be grounds for an annulment with the right judge. Many judges would just take Lord Roxbury's side, but abuse, cruelty, and neglect will grant you an annulment."

Ethan shifted his position, moving halfway towards her. "What will happen to David if Cora obtains an annulment?"

"If the cause of the annulment is cruelty and neglect, David will stay with his mother as Roxbury will be deemed unfit to be a parent."

Cora didn't allow herself to feel relieved because Mr. Purnell frowned with concern. "What worries you, Mr. Purnell?"

He hesitated. "Getting an annulment is only the first step. My lady, you must think of the consequences after such a drastic act."

"What consequences?" Anger crept into Ethan's tone. "Cora will be free from that monster."

Mr. Purnell held up a hand. "How will the lady sustain herself and her son? And before you say that you can provide for them, think about the consequences in your life. I beg your pardon, my lady, but I must speak freely."

Cora nodded. Better to understand the whole situation.

"Unfortunately, a lady who's divorced or received an annulment isn't held in high esteem in society, and whoever helps her will find himself in a delicate position and become an outcast. Specifically, Ethan, you won't enjoy the support of your peers any longer. You're a celebrated war hero, but your status or title won't protect you from public scorn. Not to mention that some lords are already displeased with you and your unconventional methods. Your centre will be closed as those who sustain you will disappear. Lord Roxbury could take his revenge on the Royal Veterans' Society. The shared ownership is a problem for him, but after being publicly shamed, he'll unleash his wrath on you. And let's not forget that after an annulment, David won't have the chance to inherit Lord Roxbury's money or title. He'll become a... you know what I mean."

A bastard.

Cora focused on her cup of tea. Every way she turned, there was an obstacle. "I don't know what to do."

"An annulment seems a good idea anyway," Ethan said. "Scandals come and go. Your case will be forgotten as soon as a new royal wedding is announced or a duchess is with child. All we have to do is stay quiet, avoid the public eye, and wait." He made it sound so simple, and if it'd been only her own reputation at stake, she would have agreed. But David? She could take society's scorn. He shouldn't. She wouldn't allow it.

"I just want Jacob out of my life."

"But think about this." He sat next to her. There was no escaping his magnetic stare or intense presence. "If we only need the support of our peers, then we can obtain it. It's a matter of publicity and how we present ourselves. We can win this battle."

"How?" Cora and Mr. Purnell said together.

"If people know Cora's story and understand what she and David have been through, society won't shun you." He put a hand over hers. "I've seen this before. People became more caring towards the veterans in the centre once they learnt their stories. I've met some very compassionate people in my work at the centre. I'm sure they won't ignore you if they know how cruel Roxbury is."

That sounded wonderful. A flicker of hope kindled in her chest.

"It's not a terrible strategy. How do you think to carry it out?" Mr. Purnell asked.

"We have a charity ball next week here. Lady Kingsley has the centre's cause at heart, and she's very well-loved. I suspect she doubts Lord Roxbury, especially after what happened at the auction. I trust her, and if we secure Lady Kingsley's approval, the others will follow." Ethan sounded excited. "Besides, Lady Kingsley is the sister of Judge Quigley. I believe he's dealt with annulments before."

"Indeed, and he's a decent fellow." Mr. Purnell cradled his

chin. "Lady Roxbury shouldn't be seen though, nor should David. Officially, they aren't here. The truth must not be shared, not until we understand Lord Roxbury's intentions. My son Harry will keep David's company during the ball. They're the same age." He flashed a proud smile she could relate to.

"What do you say, Cora?" Ethan asked. "It's worth trying it."

"If you trust Lady Kingsley, then I shall talk to her." Jacob had mistreated her and David; there was the chance to build a strong case, and if both she and David would be free of him, the plan was worth a try. As for Lady Kingsley's support, she was hopeful. The lady had seemed conflicted that night at the museum.

"Excellent." Mr. Purnell stood up with the help of his walking stick. "If you need anything else, let me know. I'll inform you of any news after I file your report." He bowed. "I wish you a quick recovery, my lady."

Speaking of which, she desperately needed the bandages. "Thank you, Mr. Purnell." She waved and waited for him to leave before facing Ethan.

"There's hope." He smiled.

"Yes." She winced when she straightened.

He was next to her in a moment. "You're in pain. What can I do?"

It was a simple question, but her heart stuttered at the care he treated her with. She was starving for affection. She hadn't realised how much until Ethan had taken her into his house.

"Would you mind bandaging my shoulder?"

THE CONVERSATION with Finn had kindled Ethan's hope. Cora wouldn't need to leave London, and he would take care of her and David. Everything else could sod off. He wouldn't let a bunch of stuffy barons kick Cora and David out of England.

He prepared the fresh bandages to take care of her wound with a light heart. Finally, some good news.

She grimaced when she put her cup of tea on the nightstand. "I'm sorry, Ethan, but I need help to remove the nightgown."

Ethan wasn't getting any more comfortable removing her clothes. He unbuttoned the front and slid the sleeves off her shoulders. Yes, her injured breast had swollen further due to the weight of her arm. "It has to be sore."

"It is. I feel more comfortable when my shoulder is bandaged and my arm doesn't drag me down."

He took the opportunity to probe the wound again. She didn't whimper as usual and didn't avert her gaze. A sign the wound was healing and that she was getting used to his presence. Her nipple was dark and swollen as the bruise grew underneath it.

He cleared his throat. "Sweet almond oil would help with the bruise. I trust you can apply it yourself."

She flushed so fiercely her lips flamed a deep shade of red. "Yes, thank you."

He carefully wrapped the bandage around her shoulder and breasts. When he rolled the bandage behind her back, she rested her cheek on his chest, leaning against him.

Emotion lodged in his throat. Taking responsibility for the wonderful woman in his arms wasn't something he'd asked for but gladly accepted. It was almost a craving, a visceral need to protect her. It wasn't only Cora. He didn't have children, but David... perhaps it was unfair of him to consider the boy his son. David might not want Ethan's affection in that fashion. But Ethan couldn't command his heart. The feelings growing inside him were out of his control. Cora and David were carving their places into his heart, and he loved every moment of it.

He stroked her hair and coiled an arm around her waist. She closed her eyes, likely exhausted.

"My husband tried to kill me, and he's plotting against me. I'm on the verge of becoming an outcast and risking my position, yet

I've never felt safer as I feel with you." Her breath fanned over the skin of his neck.

He shivered, so powerful was the effect of her words on him. For he wished nothing but to be her protector. He caressed her silky hair again, inhaling her sweet lemon scent.

"Keeping you and David safe is the only thing I want. I swear on my honour I will do anything to protect you."

She tilted her head back, and the amber pools of her eyes, ablaze with life, held him captive. "I can give you nothing back. All your generosity and hospitality, I can't repay them."

"I don't care."

"I'll only bring you trouble and scorn from society."

"It doesn't bother me."

"Even emotionally, I'm afraid I'm as dry as a desert."

He kept stroking her, cursing Roxbury for breathing. "A desert will turn into a garden with proper care."

"Yet you still want to protect me."

"Always." He meant it. He wasn't sure what was happening to him, but he meant it.

She cupped his cheek and caressed it with her thumb. Her lips parted as if she wanted to say something, but no word came out.

"What is it?" He brushed an auburn curl from her forehead. "You know you can tell me anything."

"Ethan, I..." She trapped her bottom lip between her teeth.

"Yes?"

"Would you kiss me? May I kiss you?" she whispered.

A shock of stillness froze him.

She lowered her eyelashes. "Forgive me. I shouldn't have asked. I shocked you."

"Wait." He took her chin when she started to move away from him.

He swallowed past the lump in his throat. Her eyes grew larger as if she begged him to understand her. He dipped his head and waited a breath away from her luscious lips in case she changed her mind. The wave of sensations hitting him when he gently pressed his lips against hers caused him to shiver. He had to force himself not to let his passion overwhelm him. She traced the line of his jaw, and a low growl rumbled in his chest. He ran the tip of his tongue along the seam between her lips and growled when she parted them.

It was with effort he restrained himself as he stroked her velvety tongue lightly with his. He wanted to devour her delectable mouth and ravish it with savage thrusts of his tongue. She took him in deeper, sucking gently on his tongue, and his blood shot south. Instant desire gathered in his groin and tightened his shaft painfully. But he'd endure discomfort ten times stronger than that for her. She pressed her lips harder against his, grazing her teeth on them. Shivers caused his skin to pebble.

When she broke the kiss, he found himself unable to let her go. He held her close to his chest, careful not to hurt her shoulder. He didn't know what the kiss meant for them, but whatever was going to happen, whatever the future stored for them, he would cherish it forever.

"Are you all right?" he asked, brushing his knuckles over her cheek.

"Never been better. I hope you'll kiss me again." A corner of her mouth quirked up, and a delightful peach colour crept over her cheeks.

"Any time you want." His pulse raced.

She tangled her fingers through his hair and paused when she touched his missing ear.

He stiffened. "The skin isn't pleasant to the touch."

"No, it's not that. I was thinking of all the pain you endured."

"The ear healed though." He touched the shoulder under his missing ear. "The blade that cut it off sliced my shoulder. The wound got infected. It still hurts."

"You have all my sympathy."

He laughed and kissed her forehead. "Now you need to rest." He helped her don the nightgown and button it.

She took his hand and kissed it. "Thank you."

His pulse kicked faster than when he sparred on the fighting pitch. She'd been denied so much love and care he wouldn't be able to give her all the love she deserved.

But he'd damn well try.

sixteen

T HE WEEK BEFORE the ball had gone by in a blur for Ethan with his visits to the centre, bills to pay, and listening to every gossip. Yet Lord Roxbury remained silent after having declined the invitation to the ball due to a serious indisposition. No one had seen him. No one talked about Cora. No one knew exactly what Roxbury's injury was. Better that way.

On top of that, Ethan never stopped thinking about his kiss with Cora. He paid the bills, and his lips would tingle, reminding him of her. He sparred with Fraser, and his heart would race just as it'd done when he'd kissed her. He sat in the carriage, going somewhere, and Cora's shy smile and flushed cheeks would invade his thoughts for no particular reason. The red roses in Hyde Park would make him think of her. His obsession with her was both amusing and worrying.

After he made sure everything was ready for the evening, he welcomed Harry, Finn's son, who entered from the rear door as a precaution. The boy was shorter than David but had an air of mischief and carelessness David lacked. Unfortunately.

"Harry. You look quite dashing." Ethan eyed the boy's silk waistcoat and jacket.

"Thank you, sir. My mama insisted even though I told her I wouldn't be seen." Harry searched the room. "I like the mystery of this evening and being a spy."

"This isn't a spy job."

"Where's my new friend?"

"In my parlour. Where's your father?"

"He went to the police station and didn't come back. Work as usual," Harry said.

Ethan had hoped David would find a friend his age. The boy needed it. "Follow me. I believe your father explained to you how important it is to keep David out of sight and not talk about him with anyone." He walked down the hallway.

Harry nodded. "I can keep a secret or many. I don't blabber."

"I trust you with that, but no funny business." Ethan paused at the set of double doors to his parlour.

"Funny business? Me?" Harry pointed a finger at himself. "I don't do funny business."

"No firecrackers in the geranium pots."

"I wouldn't dare." Harry had an air of hurt innocence.

"No frogs on the banquet table."

"That was an unfortunate incident I was barely involved in."

Ethan jabbed a finger at him. "And absolutely no Beecham's pills in the lemonade."

Harry was flustered. "Please. There's no proof it was me. I'm shocked you might think I'm capable of upsetting the bowels of innocent people on purpose."

"I'm sure your shock won't last." Ethan held the door open for him.

Harry chuckled. "Although all those people hurrying to the water closet—"

"Harry," he warned.

The boy held up a hand. "I'll be quiet."

Dressed in a plain brown suit, David stood up, a wary expression on his face. For some reason, the low quality of the boy's clothes irked Ethan, especially since Harry wore a fine suit. David should wear warm, decent clothes, not that worn jacket and trousers twice his size. He should have thought about procuring new clothes for the boy.

"Sir," David said, regarding Harry as if he were a strange creature.

"This is Harry Purnell. Harry meet Mr. David Wiley, Viscount Roxbury."

"I'm happy to meet you... your lordship." Harry showed a lopsided smile that promised more than Beecham's pills. "I'm sure we'll be very good friends." He stretched out his arm.

David hesitated before shaking Harry's hand. "Hullo. Please call me David. I'm just David."

"I'll leave you two to get to know each other," Ethan said. "Remember the rules. No one should see David. Harry, I trust you."

Harry stood at attention and offered him a military salute. "Your trust is well placed, Commander."

"I hope so." Ethan gave David a reassuring pat on the shoulder. "Don't let Harry do anything wild."

"Wild?" David twisted the hem of his jacket with restless fingers.

Harry draped an arm around his shoulders. "Don't worry, David. I have everything under control."

Heaven help them. Ethan exited through the second door opening to a side hallway detached from the main corridor. He went up the service stairs and knocked on Cora's door.

"Come in." Just hearing her voice started the usual butterfly-wing sensation in his belly.

As he stepped inside, he couldn't help but study her with a clinical eye. The healthy colour of her skin pleased him, but she winced as she stood up from the bed.

"Why are you standing up?" He took her elbow. "Don't stand up on my accounts."

"I need to do some activity. My arm is growing lazy, and I've been in this bed for ten days." She leant against him, and an unexpected rush of energy went through him.

"Your arm isn't lazy. It needs time to recover." He helped her to the chair. "I'm speaking as your physician."

She adjusted her blouse. Her gown belonged to Mrs. Parker and didn't fit Cora's body. The fabric hung in places and stretched on others.

"How's David?" she asked.

"I left him with Harry in the parlour. Harry is a nice boy. I'm sure they'll become friends." He sat next to her. "May I check your pulse?"

She gave him her arm and hitched a breath when he pulled the sleeve up and pressed two fingers to her kicking vein. Nice and steady. Good. They hadn't kissed again, and he missed their intimacy. He missed kissing her. Too much. He couldn't deny anymore that what he felt for her was more than a desire to protect her.

"No fever. Excellent." He held her hand, and she gripped his fingers. "What is it?"

"I'm a little scared," she whispered.

When he dipped his head to meet her gaze, he nearly shivered with the darkness in it. "I would be surprised if you weren't." He closed his hand around hers. "I'm here for you. You aren't alone. I'm very fond of you and David." He rubbed her cold knuckles.

"So you like children after all." She didn't withdraw her hand.

"Children are mostly a nuisance, but David is different."

"And what about me? You're risking the support of your peers by hiding me here. And Lady Kingsley might disapprove of what you're doing for me. You need her help." She laced her fingers through his, and he acknowledged the quickening of his pulse.

"Yes, it's in my interest that Roxbury is removed from his

current position as one of the centre's owners. I wouldn't have to deal with him any longer. But I want to help you because I hate what you've been through. The bastard shot you." The idea of killing Roxbury never lost its appeal. "Unforgivable. I've always known he doesn't have honour, but I didn't understand the depths of his depravity. He doesn't deserve his title and status. He doesn't deserve you and David."

"And you don't like injustice."

"No, I don't." He brought her hand up and kissed it, glad to find her temperature normal. "You and David deserve better."

"Every day that passes and he doesn't do anything makes me nervous. I feel this urge to flee. I just want to escape from him."

"Forgive me, but leaving now would be reckless. Your desire to leave comes from your exhaustion because the life you led with him drained you. But we need a good plan. A plan that will help you build a future for you and David. You can always leave if the situation doesn't improve. I'll help you." Letting her go would hurt him though.

She rubbed her forehead with a nervous gesture. "You're right. I'm just worried, and the pain doesn't help."

"First, you must recover. Whatever you decide to do, you need to be strong." He kept stroking her knuckles.

She blushed, looking adorable. "I've missed you in the past few days."

"I missed you too."

"I like it when..." She didn't complete the sentence but moved closer and kissed him without warning or without restraint.

And who was he to complain? With her recovery came strength, and her kiss was less chaste and more aggressive, which he loved. Too much. As she invited his tongue into her mouth, a certain stirring started in his trousers. He blamed the way she sucked his tongue and bit his lips.

Instant combustion.

And he wanted more. So much more. But she was still on the mend, and he wouldn't take advantage of her vulnerability.

She slid a finger under his cravat and stroked his neck. He caressed her inner wrist, holding a breath when she moaned. She brushed her soft lips along his jaw, and he had to close his eyes for a moment.

"Cora," he whispered.

She kissed his cheek and rested her forehead against his, letting out a soft chuckle. "I must apologise."

"You're forgiven. For what, anyway?" He caressed her silky skin.

"I'm not usually so wanton. I feel as if I were sixteen again and eager for new experiences." She giggled, and it was a lovely sound.

"By all means, that's wonderful. I can offer many new experiences."

They laced their fingers together, exploring their hands. The difference between his big, rough hands and her slender, elegant ones was stark.

"I feel different, happier since I've been shot." She laughed. "Bizarre, isn't it?"

"Most definitely. I've been shot many times, and I felt different afterwards each time. Not happier," he quipped.

"We have something in common. A bullet wound."

He huffed, feigning outrage. "Make it plural." He unbuttoned his jacket, waistcoat, and shirt to show her the three bullet wounds on his side. "Finn calls them the Three Sisters." He traced the three perfectly aligned holes. "Three different shots at three different times, but they seem aligned on purpose."

"Goodness." She touched the wounds with gentle fingers, stroking them and sending his heart into turmoil, and the jest stopped being funny.

He let her explore his skin and trace his muscles although desire jolted through him.

"You're all sharp ridges," she said, trailing her hand up to his chest. "Do you have many scars?"

He nodded, not trusting his voice.

"Will you show them to me one day?"

"If you wish." If she wanted to caress all his scars, he could only oblige.

"I do." She slid off the armchair and knelt between his thighs. Before he could understand what was happening, she kissed the three wounds with gentle lips.

Bloody hell. He sucked in a breath.

She ran her hand up over his shoulder. "That's a big scar." She touched the rough, bumpy skin of the wound.

"A tulwar, a type of sword," he said hastily because he didn't want to discuss the pirates' fighting technique now.

She gazed up, her hands on his thighs, and he couldn't remain still. He slid a hand around her nape and kissed her again. But this time the kiss was different. He couldn't contain the flow of his desire. He couldn't restrain his need for her.

He slipped off the armchair as well and deepened the kiss. They'd kissed without real depth so far, but the kiss they shared now was a soul-searching one, a conversation on its own. She matched his passion, stroking his chest and brushing his nipples. And he couldn't take it anymore. He stopped her wandering hand and broke the kiss before he ripped her clothes off.

"We ought to stop." He lowered his eyes because if he saw her lovely face, he would kiss her again and confess his feelings. "Or I won't be able to leave this room without having taken your clothes off."

She flushed a deep crimson while she'd been bold and confident a moment ago. He was repeating himself, but the contrast was adorable.

"Yes, we should stop," she said, a quiver in her voice.

He helped her to her feet as he stood up. "Does the thought of us being together make you uncomfortable?"

"No." She buttoned his shirt. "A little. I mean, I haven't been with a man in a long time."

He finished dressing himself. "There's no hurry."

She stared at her hands in her lap. "I'm confused as well. All these emotions, after years of not feeling anything but anger and fear, are frightening."

"Cora." He kissed her hands. "You think too much. Forgive yourself so you can move on."

She smiled. "On a rational level, I'm fully aware only Jacob is to blame. On an emotional one, I'm quite agitated."

"Time is the best doctor." And love, and he'd give her all the love he could. He released her hands. "I'll ask Lady Kingsley to see you when her absence won't be noticed. Is there anything you need? I have to attend to my guests and keep an eye on David and Harry."

Her smile didn't reach her eyes. "Don't worry about me. I'm well. I have my books and magazines to keep me amused. Go. Take care of your guests. I'll see you later."

He kissed her hand again. He couldn't stop himself. "Stay strong."

She gripped his fingers hard before letting his hand go. "Thank you."

"You don't have to thank me."

A weight settled on his chest after he left her room. Hopefully, after Cora talked with Lady Kingsley, she would be less worried. And so would he.

ETHAN's facial muscles would remain frozen in the shape of a polite smile after he'd greeted all his guests for the charity ball.

There was no way out of the endless 'welcome' and 'thank you' and 'it's lovely to see you here.' He had to personally shake hands, bow, and smile at each of his guests if he wanted to keep their support flowing. Many of them didn't give a damn about scarred soldiers. They wanted to show off their supposed good hearts with a generous donation they would gloat about in fancy sitting rooms. But on the other hand, he didn't give a damn about their motivations. As long as they provided money and support for the centre, he was happy. At the very least, those who didn't contribute financially didn't complain about the centre either.

The downside was he couldn't trust some of them when it came to Cora's secret. A few of these civilised people would jump to his throat at the opportunity to use her to destroy him. He hated that Cora might be used as a weapon in someone else's scheme.

He stiffened when Mrs. Sterling entered the room. Since the charity ball was somewhat informal, he'd invited her but never expected her to be here. She wore her mourning weeds as usual although she could wear violet and blue at this stage of the mourning. The black veil covering her face couldn't contain the rage underneath it. He wasn't surprised. He'd kept sending her money.

He bowed. "Madam. Thank you for being here."

"My lord, I told you I don't want your money," she hissed.

"And I told you it was James's wish." And he would honour it despite the fact James hadn't been a model soldier.

"You'll take the money back, my lord, and that will be the end of this ridiculous charade." She jutted out her chin.

He worked his jaw, fighting to keep his voice down. "Your pride won't help you pay the bills."

She gasped, and the veil couldn't hide her hardened expression. "That's none of your business," she hissed. "I'd rather starve than accept money from the man who caused my husband's death."

Enough. "That's not—" He bit his tongue to stop the truth from coming out. She would despise him further and refuse his help again. "War is complicated," he said in a calmer tone.

"So is being a widow." She spun on her heels in a flutter of black velvet and stormed out of the hall.

Stubborn, proud woman. He fixed his cravat and waited for the next guest. Not many people had noticed the argument with Mrs. Sterling, but the scene hadn't been in his favour.

His smile was genuine when he bowed to the Lady Kingsley because, despite the fact she hadn't defended him the night of the auction, she was sympathetic to the Royal Veterans' Society's cause. "My lady. It's a pleasure to see you here."

The old woman offered a bow of her head. "Dear Lord Stark, thank you for your invitation."

He held her hand for a kiss. "Thank you for coming."

She stared at him with confusion as if he'd asked a tricky question she didn't know how to answer. "After the horrible scene at the museum, I couldn't refuse your invitation." She opened and closed her fan. "I shouldn't have let Lord Roxbury convince me it was a good idea to let you go that night. I regret the manner with which I behaved."

"All water under the bridge." Especially since he needed the lady's help. "Lord Roxbury can be very persuasive when he wants to."

"Indeed. I wanted to have a word with him, but he seemed indisposed, and Lady Roxbury isn't in London." Her grey eyebrows drew together. "I wonder why the sudden departure, especially since her husband isn't well. Shouldn't she stay next to him? Anyway, your cause is a noble one. I believe we shall raise enough funds to keep the centre active for the whole year."

"I hope so." He bowed at a passing lady he didn't remember the name of. "I might need to talk to you in private later on in the evening. It's quite a delicate matter. Something I hope you might help me with."

She regarded him with a hint of curiosity. "Whenever you feel inclined. Now if you don't mind, I shall find a glass of champagne." She moved towards the refreshments, through people bowing at her passage and giving friendly greetings. Everyone smiled and welcomed her with warmth and reverence. Definitely, Ethan needed her support.

After he started the dance with the highest-ranking lady as etiquette demanded, he took advantage of a quiet moment to leave the ballroom.

He went down the stairs and headed to the parlour. Empty. Damn. David and Harry weren't there. Games of cards and jigsaw puzzles lay scattered on the rug in front of the fire. He searched the hidden hallway. Nothing. Not even the servants were around. Where to go? The garden perhaps. Harry wouldn't expose David.

Ethan was heading to the garden when he caught a snippet of a conversation.

"... and that's why no one will see us."

He skidded to a stop upon hearing Harry's voice. It came from a nook at the end of the hallway. He crept towards it and hid behind a Grecian column. There they were. If Harry planned another attack with Beecham's pills, Ethan had to stop him.

Harry yanked a button from his jacket until it broke free and handed it to David. "Hold it."

"What is it for?" David asked.

"Insurance. You'll understand when we need it." Harry waved him closer and pointed at the floor.

What the hell were they doing? Curiosity won, and Ethan stood there to find out Harry's latest mischief. The two boys lay on the floor on their bellies. Harry opened the louvered panel of an air vent on the floor, revealing a view of the ballroom.

"See?" Harry said. "From here we can see all the ladies' ankles without being seen. Look."

What? Ethan slowly lowered himself and peered at the ballroom, following Harry's gaze. Dammit, Harry was right. As the ladies danced and twirled around, their skirts inched up, and from the low spot, Ethan caught glimpses of slender ankles and silk stockings. The flounces of the petticoats played a hide-and-seek game with the ladies' legs that he had to admit had its pleasurable interest. The lovely silk slippers in different colours weren't bad either. Hidden behind the louvered panel in the secluded corridor, no one would ever spot them. Besides, the servants were too busy to pay attention to two naughty boys. Clever.

David clamped a hand over his mouth to stifle a giggle.

Harry elbowed him. "Look at that girl, the one in the blue dress. When she spins, you can see her bloomers."

David laughed. It was the first happy, carefree laugh Ethan had heard from the boy. Somehow, it hurt. That moment of laughter reminded Ethan of how miserable David's life had been so far. He was too young to carry worry and sadness on his small shoulders. He should be like Harry. Well, maybe not exactly like Harry.

"But bloomers are nothing special, you know." Harry clicked his tongue. "Them ladies put bloomers on when they want to hide their drawers."

"I don't know anything about drawers, but I guess the ankles look pretty," David said. "Maybe because we never see them."

"Yes, and I don't understand what the fuss is about. Why all the mystery, cloak and dagger around ankles? I've got them, and there isn't anything special about them. Look at that other lady in pink. She shows her bloomers as well. She must be in search of a husband."

"A husband?" David asked.

Harry nodded sagely as if about to reveal an important truth. "Ladies show their ankles and legs when they're looking for a good match. It's a fact."

"What do legs have to do with marriage?"

Harry scratched the top of his head. "Adults are complicated. But when a lady shows you her ankle, she means business."

"What business?" David asked.

All right. That was enough. Ethan straightened and stomped towards them.

"Lads, I told you to stay in the parlour."

Harry sprang up so fast Ethan worried the boy might pull a

muscle. "Have you found my missing button, David?" He smoothed down his jacket, searching around.

"What? I... yes." David opened his hand to reveal the infamous missing button. "Here."

"Thank you." Harry took it and showed it to Ethan as proof of his innocence. "I lost the little bugger here, and we were searching for it."

"Indeed." Ethan folded his arms over his chest.

David blushed at the roots of his hair. Harry instead didn't flinch, all innocence.

"Go to the kitchen using the servants' stairs. Cook will give you a slice of lemon cake," Ethan said, not wanting to spoil the fun for David. "Use the side corridor, and please don't lose any more buttons." He gave Harry a pointed look the boy pretended not to understand.

"Excellent. Don't worry, sir." Harry took David's arm and led him out of the nook. "What's better than lemon cake? I can't think of anything aside from a nice strawberry cake with whipped cream on top."

David stopped and turned towards Ethan. "Sir, we weren't... I mean, we didn't..."

Ethan ruffled David's hair. "It's all right. You need to have fun with someone your age. You did nothing wrong." Or nothing Ethan hadn't done himself.

Harry punched the air. "That's the right attitude. Then we can—"

"No more, Harry." Ethan jabbed a finger at him. "Behave. You've avoided punishment, but the occasion won't be repeated."

Harry stooped his shoulders. "Spoilsport. Let's go, David. I'm sure the cook will have prepare a cup of cocoa for us to drown our sorrows in."

"Thank you, sir." David nodded and let Harry lead him away.

Ethan watched them disappear downstairs, vowing to make David as happy as he was that night.

seventeen

CORA STOKED THE fire in the stove. The wound was healing well, her shoulder and arm were less swollen, and her appetite had returned. Inactivity was her problem. Not because she didn't want to stay cooped up in Ethan's house and be coddled by him, but because Jacob was plotting in the dark, and the thought made her restless.

Could she really leave Ethan behind? The wooden log shot a fiery spark when she broke it in two with the poker. If leaving Ethan meant keeping David safe, yes, she would leave him behind. David would never, ever have to almost kill his father to protect her, no matter what she had to do. She would sacrifice her... affection? Attraction for Ethan? Whatever it was. No, it was deeper than attraction. Stronger than affection. But David was her priority.

Attraction was easy to handle. Love wasn't. Her feelings had tricked her once. The speed with which she'd developed her affection for Ethan scared her. It'd happened before— a burst of intense emotions that had dazzled her. But Ethan wasn't Jacob. If she was going to be honest, her bond with Ethan had started years ago, under the rubble of a small church in Colchester. Her instinct told her she could trust him. Her mind lagged behind. Her lips and skin tingled after the kiss. So confusing.

The sound of the music came muffled through the door. A part of her would love to be in the ballroom and enjoy herself, maybe dance with Ethan. But the shadows never left her. She jolted when a knock came.

"May I?" Ethan asked.

"Come in." She straightened and smoothed down her skirt.

The door swung inwards and Ethan appeared. His gaze heated the moment he smiled at her, and she couldn't deny the warm flicker in her belly. Good heaven. He made her feel desirable and beautiful with one glance. No wonder she couldn't keep her hands to herself when he was close. Her cheeks were pale; fatigue clouded her eyes; her dress didn't fit; her hair looked like something that had been dragged out of the Thames. Yet when he gazed at her, she felt beautiful.

He strode towards her. "I knocked a few times, but you didn't answer. Are you all right?"

She inhaled to calm her heartbeat. "I didn't hear it."

He frowned. Concern often etched his face. "Lady Kingsley, please come in."

The short woman walked in. Her austere dark gown was lightened by her kind smile. Cora didn't lower her guard though. She did a shallow curtsy, keeping her head up. Talking with Lady Kingsley could be the best or worst idea they had ever had.

"Lady Roxbury has been here for a few days as I told you, my lady," Ethan said.

Lady Kingsley sat on the sofa in a froth of skirts, her expression not exactly warm. "I've met your husband on several occasions, but I don't think I've seen you more than a few times." A way to say: I know your husband better than I know you.

"Jacob always made a point of keeping me home and never letting me attend the same parties as he did. Rarely, he took me with him. The night at the museum was one of those occasions." It was the truth. She didn't try to gain the lady's favour. She sat in front of the lady not to show how her legs trembled.

Lady Kingsley arched her eyebrows. "Lord Stark told me about your situation. I can assure you that I won't utter a word about you, but I reserve the right to offer my full support until I hear your story."

"That's fair." Cora grimaced when she shifted her position too quickly and her back hit the armchair.

"What is it?" Lady Kingsley said.

Cora rubbed her shoulder. "The wound. It's still a bit stiff."

"As I told you, my lady, Lord Roxbury shot the countess," Ethan said.

"Jacob was aiming for David, my thirteen-year-old son. Our son." Cora eased back on the armchair gently. "I protected my son. That's all."

"Why did Lord Roxbury want to hurt his son?" Lady Kingsley placed a trembling hand on her chest.

"Why indeed." Cora would have preferred if Jacob had hated only her and not David. Likely, he punished her through David. "Jacob lost interest in me quickly after our first year of marriage. The beginning of our story was like a fairy tale, too good to be true. Then David was born, and Jacob found the baby annoying to the point he didn't want David to sleep close to his bedroom and didn't want to see him at all. He has always been incredibly harsh to David, expecting him to do everything perfectly. David can't read properly because Jacob did nothing but shout at him every time David made a mistake." She stared at her hands on her lap. "Now David is terrified when he reads, has no friends, and believes himself to be worthless, no matter how many times I tell him he's adorable and clever."

Lady Kingsley listened without interrupting. "Was Roxbury cruel to you as well?"

Cora put a hand around her neck. "He never allowed me to keep money or jewels for fear I might use them to leave him. Before leaving the house, he always checked my body to make sure I didn't hide stolen items, a humiliating practice he inflicted on me with pleasure. And he enjoyed choking me."

Ethan's expression became as feral as the last time they'd talked about Jacob's perverse tastes.

"Heaven," Lady Kingsley whispered. "Did he hit you?"

Always that question. "There has been an occasional slap, but no more than that, thank goodness, but he grabbed my throat and choked me on numerous occasions. His cruelty shows itself in his words, shouts, and actions. I'm not defending him, but I can't lie either. I feel like I'm waking up from a nightmare. Only now do I see things clearly. At first, I thought I was the problem. He's an excellent deceiver, a fine manipulator. He uses his charm to fool people. I don't know how he does it, but his technique is effective." She stopped because she couldn't explain something she didn't understand herself. Jacob had put a spell on her, or a curse, and she'd broken it recently.

Ethan touched her shoulder, a simple gesture that told her he wanted to hold her.

Lady Kingsley remained silent for a long time, making Cora wonder if she believed her. "Cruelty is never easy to explain for those who aren't cruel. I was lucky enough to share a long, happy marriage with my husband. My sister wasn't. Her husband..." She cleared her throat. "My brother is a judge, who deals with private bills regarding divorces and annulments. Something my sister would have obtained had she lived."

Cora let out an exhale. "I'm sorry."

Ethan bowed to the older lady. "I didn't know."

"It happened many years ago." Lady Kingsley remained silent for a few moments. "My brother is currently staying in Borrington in a cottage close to the sea. I believe Lord Stark owns an estate in the same village."

"I do."

"Then I suggest that you and Lady Roxbury pay him a visit,"

Lady Kingsley said. "I'll write to him immediately. I'd daresay Barnaby, my brother, is the most expert judge in matters of marriage law. If he can't solve your quandary, no one can. He's also quite compassionate towards wives in situations like yours because of our sister. You can trust him."

"If you agree, Cora," Ethan said, "the trip would be an opportunity to escape London's close scrutiny and give David a moment of respite. As soon as you're strong enough to travel, of course."

She nodded. "I think we should go and see your brother, my lady."

Lady Kingsley rose. "I wish you good luck. You deserve a better future."

Cora stood up as well. "Thank you."

Lady Kingsley took Cora's hands. "I wish my sister had told me what she'd been through with her husband before it'd been too late. I blame myself for not having understood her sadness. Your courage will be an example to other unfortunate women."

She doubted she could be an example to anyone. "I've made so many mistakes."

The lady gave her a tired smile. "But you're here and your son is with you. That's all that matters. Not to mention you're in excellent hands."

Yes, she was.

"I'll escort Lady Kingsley back to the ballroom." Ethan opened the door.

"Nonsense." Lady Kingsley waved a dismissive hand. "I'm old but in good shape. I'll see you later, Lord Stark."

Cora waited to be alone with him before running to hug him. Running was likely an exaggeration. He caught her and held her without saying a word. The more she rested in his embrace, the more relaxed she felt. His arms were home. His warmth was the best luxury she'd ever experienced.

"You're brave. I admire you deeply," he whispered.

She was about to kiss him when Mr. Purnell barged into the room.

"Lady Roxbury, Ethan." Finn shut the door behind him. "Apologies for the intrusion, but I need a word."

She collected herself, clearing her throat.

Ethan offered him a chair. "Roxbury?"

Mr. Purnell nodded. "My commissioner didn't let me file Lady Roxbury's complaint."

"Why?" she asked.

"Lord Roxbury is an earl with an impeccable reputation. The commissioner didn't think it was a good idea to accuse him of such a serious crime without further proof, so he went to see Lord Roxbury." His chest heaved. "The commissioner decided not to prosecute your husband for now since Lord Roxbury claimed you hurt him first. You attacked him, grabbed David, and left. He denied having shot you. He claimed the gunshot wound was self-inflicted."

"Damn." Ethan paced. "What can we do?"

Mr. Purnell rubbed his forehead. "It's tricky. Lord Roxbury and his wife are accusing each other of attempted murder, Lady Roxbury is officially nowhere to be found, and none of the servants were present at the moment of the incident."

"But Cora has been shot," Ethan said. "That wound can't be self-inflicted."

"And Lord Roxbury had his skull cracked open. Listen, if we press the matter with the commissioner, he'll make a hasty decision, and Lady Roxbury won't be the one he'll favour. We're lucky he didn't force me to reveal where Lady Roxbury is. He's conflicted. He didn't believe Lord Roxbury fully, but he won't cause a scandal either."

"In other words," Ethan said, "the commissioner is waiting for the problem to solve itself."

"I'm sorry," Mr. Purnell said. "I hoped to bring better news."

That was it. She had to leave England for good. She should

have guessed Jacob would have done something to stop her. His lies would cause her to end up in prison.

"When do you think I can travel?" Cora asked Ethan.

"A couple of weeks." His expression hardened.

"Two weeks? It's too much. I'm sure I can endure the trip in a couple of days."

"Trip to where, if I may ask?" Mr. Purnell said.

"Borrington," Ethan said at the same time as Cora said, "Brussels."

"What?" Ethan whipped his head towards her.

"I can't stay here. Not after this." Panic caused her to breathe hard. "Jacob will make sure I'm locked up in prison. Besides, he doesn't know I have a cousin in Brussels. I must leave now while he's indisposed."

"You haven't recovered yet. Hours in a carriage will worsen your condition." He gave her a piercing look.

"I can take some morphia."

"You must be joking. Morphia isn't to be taken lightly. It's a drug with seriously harmful health effects. Not to mention that you'll be sleepy and disordered all the time." The muscles around his mouth tightened. "No, I won't drug you when you can simply wait two weeks to see the judge in Borrington instead of a suicidal trip to Brussels." He turned towards his friend. "Lady Kingsley is arranging a meeting with her brother to see if an annulment is possible. But Cora can't travel at the moment."

"Lady Roxbury," Mr. Purnell said in a too-calm tone. "Ethan is right. We know something about travelling while wounded. It's not easy or simple. Morphia or not, you'll never make it to Dover. Wait two weeks and go see the judge."

She trembled. "Anything can happen in two weeks. Jacob can barge here and drag David and me away. Or the commissioner might change his mind and decide to prosecute me."

Ethan narrowed his gaze. "Have you so little faith in me?

Roxbury doesn't know you're here. If he comes here, I'll be able to keep him out of my own house."

"What if he calls the police?"

"He's the one who should be arrested." Ethan paced.

"He's recovering as you are and doesn't know you're here," Mr. Purnell said. "At the moment, he doesn't leave his bed. But I can spread the rumour that you've been seen heading to Dover. That will keep him busy."

No, no. She had to move now. Pain or not, she wouldn't give Jacob time to set up a plan to trap her again. "Ethan, I thank you for everything you've done for David and me—"

"Cora, don't. I can't leave London at the moment. I can't escort you."

"I can't stay here. I'm leaving tomorrow." She stood up, forcing down the pain. "I won't let Jacob take David."

"It's a mistake." His tone sounded low and cold.

"I have to do something before he has me arrested for his injuries." She panted. "What will happen to David then? Please help me leave England. Please."

Ethan exhaled. "If this is your choice, I'll have a carriage prepared for you tomorrow morning."

"Thank you." Her heart broke when he bowed and left her room with Mr. Purnell.

THE NIGHT DIDN'T BRING any counsel to Cora. She was sore and sleepy in the morning but determined to leave England. Jacob had always held more power than she. If he accused her of having tried to kill him and kidnapping David, she would get arrested immediately, and David would live with Jacob. Unacceptable.

She flinched as she slid on a coat with Mrs. Parker's help in the hallway. Ethan stood silent in a corner, waiting to escort her to the carriage that would take her to the train station.

The housekeeper shook her head. "You're making a mistake, my lady. Dover is far, and the trip is going to be uncomfortable. You can't face such a troublesome journey in your condition."

"I must, Mrs. Parker." Cora kept her gaze down.

"If you wait two weeks, his lordship will come with you," she insisted.

"Cora," Ethan said. "You'll start bleeding again in an hour."

"It'll be painful." She swallowed hard. "But the idea of Jacob taking David is more painful. After all, you told me the way we make decisions is pain versus pain."

"I can protect you here." He must have repeated that a dozen times. "Roxbury expects you to travel to Dover. He might be ready to catch you."

"It's a risk I must take."

David dragged his feet down the stairs. His flat hat fell over his face but couldn't hide his scowl.

"We have to go, David." Cora stretched out her arm.

He took her hand, but when she pulled him towards her, he didn't budge.

"Mama."

"Please, darling." A knot formed in her throat, both from the pain and the sorrow of leaving. "We have no choice."

His expression hardened into that of a man. "I want to stay." His voice sounded as hard as steel.

"Don't make this more difficult." Instead, her voice cracked.

"You aren't well, and for the first time in my life—" David blinked tears away.

"For the first time what?" she asked.

David sucked in a deep breath and wiped his face with his sleeve. "Lord Stark is taking good care of us. He's kind. He never makes fun of me. He promised to teach me to read better. Mrs. Parker prepares hot cocoa for me, and Harry wants to play with me. He says he has fun with me. I have a friend. My first friend. Trust Lord Stark. Please."

Mrs. Parker wept in her handkerchief, muttering something about preparing all the hot cocoa David wanted. Ethan remained quiet, but his eyes were suspiciously shiny.

Cora hugged David, ignoring the sting of pain in her shoulder and chest. Yes, for David, it was the first time he'd enjoyed a normal, happy life without being mocked and insulted. What was she supposed to do? She couldn't deprive him of this happiness. And yes, she trusted Ethan with all her heart.

"Please," he whispered. "Lord Stark will protect us. I'm sure of it."

She caressed his curls, letting his hat fall to the floor. "We'll stay."

eighteen

TWO WEEKS OF absolute rest and good food had done wonders for Cora's wound. She could move her arm without feeling pain, and while the flesh was a bit stiff, there was no sign of infection. Ethan had showered her and David with gifts, refurbishing their wardrobes with new clothes, which had kept her busy and David happy. Also, the modiste and her seamstresses were likely celebrating in the best restaurant in London with the ridiculous sum Ethan had given them to stay quiet about the presence of a countess and her son in his house.

The two weeks hadn't been so generous with her mood. She'd gone from high peaks of optimism to deep pits of despair. She'd kept searching the shadows and dark corners of the street from her window, expecting Jacob to materialise out of nowhere. But he hadn't shown himself. Either his head wound was more serious than she thought, or he'd believed the rumour about her leaving for Dover. Whatever the reason, she was glad he was staying away from her.

David had shown more wisdom than she had because leaving would have been a mistake. And he deserved a moment to be just a child.

She entered the library to pick up another book after having devoured half of Ethan's shelves. David and Ethan sat at the table, surrounded by the warm lights from the gas lamps as dusk crept over London. A blazing log fire crackled in the hearth, spreading a cosy orange glow in the room.

David frowned as he read, shoulders hunched over the table.

"And th... the..." He exhaled and cast a fleeting glance at Ethan, who waited patiently. "The day..." He paused again, his breathing speeding up and his feet beating a tempo against the floor.

She recognised the signs of an upcoming moment of panic. David would freeze and bite back tears, unable to read another word. His speech problem had transferred to his reading. He tried too hard, and his efforts backfired until he blamed himself for the failure. She started to stride towards him and tell him to take a breather when Ethan caressed the top of his head. His big hand covered half of David's curls.

"You're doing an excellent job," he said in his deep, calm voice. "We can stop here for today and start again tomorrow. You must be tired."

David shook his head. "I did a poor job. I couldn't finish a sentence without stammering, pausing, or—" He took in a shaky breath.

"You finished the whole chapter." Ethan flipped through the pages. "I'd be surprised if you weren't tired."

"Did I finish the chapter?" David checked the book.

"Ten pages. And to be honest, I wouldn't be able to read..." Ethan tilted his head. "Ses... quip... e... da... lian without twisting my tongue." He whistled. "Goodness. It can't be a real word."

David beamed. "It's very long and weird."

"And I have no idea what it means," Ethan said, scratching the back of his neck.

"Long-winded." Cora walked over to the table, a weight lifting from her chest. "It fits, doesn't it?"

"Mama." David showed her the book. "I read an entire chapter."

"He was astonishingly good." Ethan nodded, standing up.

A few weeks ago, she wouldn't have believed David would be happy to finish a whole chapter.

David exhaled. "No, I wasn't very good."

Cora squeezed his hand. "I'm very proud of you." She glanced at Ethan, pouring all her gratitude into that look.

He gave her a quick nod before turning back to David. "Are you tired?"

David brushed his curls from his face. "Yes."

"Take a moment of rest, have something to eat," Ethan said. "Cook will be happy."

David scraped his chair back and took the book. "I'll practise some more."

"Don't get too tired," Ethan said after him.

"Thank you," Cora said once she was alone with Ethan. "It means so much to him. It means so much to me, too."

"David is a lovely boy." Ethan sagged his shoulders, gathering pencils and papers. "He doesn't have a good opinion of himself, which is a shame. But with a bit of work, we can make him confident again, and not just about reading."

"I intervened every time Jacob mistreated him, but the damage is done."

"You're a good mother."

She smiled. "I simply love him very much."

He blinked and gazed away. She could have sworn that tears glistened in his eyes.

"The love between David and you reminds me of my mother," he said in a low voice. "I was lucky. My father adored me as well. I can't imagine growing up with a father who despised me. The hurt would be unbearable, the damage permanent, the wound unable to heal. David is incredibly strong. Despite the way he's been treated, he doesn't give in to anger or resentment. Many boys would become aggressive and hateful in his place. Your love prevented him from turning his sense of neglect into violence. Remarkable."

She propped her hip against the table. "He still needs a father figure. He's growing up too quickly, and I can't keep up with all the changes. I wish he'd stay my little boy forever, but at the same time, he already isn't."

"He'll become an honourable man, a man we'll be proud of." He arranged the books in a stack on the table. "Were you looking for something to read?"

"Yes." She strode to the shelves. "And to return this."

She rose on her tiptoes and stretched out her arm to put the book back on the shelf, but she moved too quickly without thinking. A sharp pang seared through her like a red-hot blade. Her arm snapped back on reflex without her consent, sending a new shot of pain down her body.

"Dash it."

"Cora." Ethan was next to her in a moment. He coiled an arm around her waist and held her up against him. "You should have asked me." He folded her arm over her chest and massaged her shoulder.

The library tilted. "I didn't imagine it could be so painful."

"It's healing well, but many muscles, nerves, and tendons have been lacerated. It takes time. You shouldn't move quickly." He gently rubbed her back, arm, and shoulder, easing away the tension.

She leant against his warm, hard body. Safety radiated from him, and she was too tired to pretend she didn't want the comfort he provided. She wanted to feel safe and cared for again, and maybe it was selfish of her, and he deserved a better woman than a runaway wife, who wanted an annulment. He tucked her head under his chin, drawing slow circles on her sore muscles. Stroke after stroke, the pain became a dull throb.

"Better?" he asked.

With her ear on his chest, his voice reverberated inside her with a low rumble. She sighed and placed a hand on his broad chest. So soothing.

He brushed the sweetest of kisses on her forehead. "You can use me, Cora."

"Use you?"

"For anything you need. Comfort, money, connections, safety. I'll provide whatever you want, and if at the end of this dark moment, you decide you don't want to see me again, it'll be all right. I don't expect anything in return as long as you and David are safe and happy."

She worried at her bottom lip. "I don't want to use you. I could never do that. I want to repay your generosity and kindness. But you're right. At the moment, I'm too weak not to be selfish."

"You aren't selfish." He caressed her hair, and it felt too good. "You've been mistreated for a long time. You deserve the love and care Roxbury should have provided. I'm happy to provide them for you for as long as you want them."

She sagged against him, for once overwhelmed by too much kindness, and he took her weight. "Thank you, Ethan. You saved David and me. I shall never forget that."

He held her and true to his words, he didn't ask for anything back. She basked in his warmth and safety until her shoulder didn't hurt anymore. She wondered if the same would happen to her heart. If it'd ever stop aching.

If she was going to be honest, it wasn't only gratitude that made her want to be close to him. He kindled sensations she'd long thought to be dead. She hadn't enjoyed her time in bed with Jacob. He wasn't a generous, kind lover. Unsurprisingly. The emotions and needs of her body had faded into oblivion after a while as Jacob had taken what he'd wanted from her. With Ethan, those emotions surged again. A hunger she hadn't experienced in years.

She slid a hand under his waistcoat to touch those hard

muscles. He sucked in a breath as she undid the buttons of his shirt. They both groaned when she touched his naked chest, which was warm and solid like the rest of him. Everything about him inspired safety and calm.

"Cora," he warned. "Anyone can see us."

"You're right." She led him to the small parlour next door and locked the door. "Now only I can see you."

She finished undoing his shirt. He helped her remove his clothes until he was half-naked in front of her. He was a combination of strength, fine lines, and rough skin. Everything about him fascinated her from the scars left from his battles to the sharp ridges of his muscles, and she couldn't deny the wetness pooling between her legs.

She traced the rough scar on his shoulder. "It's a long scar."

"The wound was deep. I can't spar as much as I used to." His gaze never left her face.

"Do you want this?" she asked in case he was only submitting to her needs. It'd happened to her, and she wouldn't impose her will on him.

He let out a low chuckle. "Hell, yes."

"So do I."

He groaned when she kissed his chest, inhaling his heady scent.

He gently held her by the waist and sat her on the polished oak desk. "Last warning," he all but growled. "If you keep touching and kissing me, I won't be able to stop."

"I don't want you to." She widened her legs to accommodate him as he nestled between them.

He dipped his head to capture her mouth in a long, hard kiss. Her skin came alive with foreign sensations. Not even during those beautiful days with Jacob, she'd felt so desperate with desire. Her nipples hardened, and her toes curled. His tongue conquered her mouth unapologetically. The kiss was firm and dominant, but there was care in the way he stroked her jaw and held her waist, causing her spine to wilt.

She tightened her legs around him and rolled her hips forwards. The buttons of her shirt fell prey to his expert fingers. The bandage was removed with efficiency without her feeling any discomfort. Only then, he paused to admire her. His hungry stare, so different from the clinical one he'd given her in the past days, had made her feel self-conscious. Not anymore. She shuddered when he fondled her breast with infinite tenderness. His thumb rubbed her nipple, sending pleasant shivers down her spine.

She arched her back as much as her sore muscles would allow. He changed the rhythm of his ministration and pinched her nipple harder.

"Yes," she cried out. "Harder please."

He obliged, adding his hot, velvety mouth to her sensitive peak.

Too good. She sank her teeth into her bottom lip and tangled her fingers through his thick hair as he tongued her breast. She shivered again when he drew her nipple into his mouth and sucked on it gently. A long moan escaped her. Every inch of her body tingled with sensations.

He bunched up her skirt and ran a reverent hand over her leg. Wetness damped her between her thighs. A trembling sigh left her as he moved his fingers along the slit of her drawers. No man had ever touched her like that, certainly not Jacob who hadn't shown any interest in pleasuring her.

She hitched a breath. He growled deep in his throat, sinking his fingers inside her. The delightful invasion sent her pulse into a frenzy as his thumb drew circles over her sensitive nub. She gripped his solid shoulders, worried that if she said anything, the pleasure might vanish.

He rubbed her slowly, staring at her face. "Do you like it?"

"Goodness, yes."

He kept stroking her with lazy circles, scattering kisses on her neck. His stubble scratched her delicate skin in the most delightful way. He brushed her nipples with his lips, and she couldn't stop a cry.

She gasped as energy roared within her unexpectedly. It was a heated flare coursing through her. She muffled her scream by burying her face in the crook of his neck. His heady, masculine scent added another ounce of pleasure to the fantastic moment.

He kissed her neck and cheek. "Scream as much as you want."

The release both energised and tired her, but she wanted more. Having taken only a taste wasn't enough. She fumbled with the buttons of his trousers until his erection sprang free. He jolted when she wrapped her fingers around him and moved her hand up and down his length.

"Please, Ethan."

His reply was another savage kiss made of thrusts of his tongue, bites, and grazing teeth. Instant wetness. Her need burst out again as if she hadn't had a release a moment ago.

"Please," she begged and didn't care. She spread her legs as widely as possible while he moved closer to her heat with predatory grace.

"Cora." It sounded like a growl, and she liked it. The blunt tip of his shaft stroked her entrance.

She trembled in anticipation, panting, but he didn't take her.

"Are you sure?" he asked, his breath feathering her skin. "You are sore and delicate."

"It's the only thing I can give you." She urged him closer, but he didn't move. In fact, he stiffened.

"What?" There was an icy note in his voice that broke the spell.

She closed her eyes for a moment, realising too late what she'd said. "I didn't mean..."

"I told you I don't want anything from you," he said in a sharp tone. "Certainly not your body. Is this a payment?" he said the last word with disgust.

"No, no." She put her hands on his chest. "It came out wrong."

"Explain then."

"I want you. I really do. It's that I also think this is the only thing I have to offer you because I have nothing else to give." Heaven. She was making a mess. She blamed all the powerful emotions she'd experienced in the past few weeks. They confused her.

A shadow crossed his face. He buttoned himself up and wrapped the bandage around her chest with his usual speed and efficiency.

"Ethan, I didn't mean to offend you," she whispered.

"I want you, Cora, more than anything, but I won't touch you again unless you really want it too, not because you feel guilty or because you believe that you owe me something. I will not take you under these circumstances. I don't want a tumble in exchange for my help." He paused and stared at her. "You owe me nothing."

She shivered with the intensity of his determination. "I really want this, Ethan. With you. Only you."

He cupped her face and caressed her jaw. "When I told you to use me, I meant it. It would be all right if you used me for a tumble and nothing else. I won't complain if you use me for the pleasure you need. But I do not want or accept any payment from you in any form. I don't want you to feel obliged to kiss me. I won't accept it. I don't want you to have a tumble with me so that you can ease your guilt." He dressed her, focusing on the buttons and avoiding her gaze. "You owe me nothing. I hope I've made myself clear." He kissed her hand before releasing her. He walked backwards to the door and opened it, his stare never leaving her. "If it's a payment, it's not enjoyable." He shut the door behind him before she could say anything.

She remained sitting on the desk, her chest empty. There was some truth in his accusations because the desperate need to do something for him and show him her endless gratitude pulsed strongly. But she did want him as well. She couldn't stop thinking about touching and kissing him, and that had nothing to do with the gratitude she had for him. She'd expressed herself in the wrong manner. Served her right.

She slipped off the desk. She would find a way to show him that her desire was genuine.

nineteen

CORA SHIFTED ON the seat of the carriage where she'd been for hours. Maybe the exclusive town of Borrington, where many members of the *ton* loved to spend the holidays, was the loveliest village in England, but there wasn't a railway that reached it, and the country road leading to it had been built by the Romans and never improved.

No, she couldn't have travelled to Brussels two weeks ago without writhing in unbearable agony. Next to her, David held her hand, although his attention was focused on the view of endless barley fields and gentle hills while Harry kept talking about... something. The boy never stopped talking, jumping from one subject to another without any apparent connection. She didn't mind the chatter, but after a while, she'd stopped listening.

"Take another sip." Ethan handed her a vial of diluted laudanum. As usual, he anticipated her needs.

She brushed his fingers while taking the vial. They stared at each other, but he was the first to break eye contact. Since that evening in the parlour, he'd been polite but rather detached. Busy with getting ready for the trip and making sure no one suspected she and David were in his house, he hadn't spent a lot of time with her, and she hadn't had the opportunity to show him how much she wanted him.

Never mind. Once she recovered from the trip, there would be plenty of occasions. The potion had an immediate effect on her pain, and she eased back on the seat, her eyelids growing heavy. Harry's voice sounded distant. It lulled her to sleep.

"Cora." Ethan's voice jolted her.

She blinked her eyes open to find his emerald gaze on her. She was leaning against him with her head on his shoulder. "I dozed off."

"Good. You were pale and needed the rest. We're at the inn." He helped her out of the carriage. "David and Harry are already inside with Mrs. Parker. Please wear your scarf and hat."

Oh right, her disguise. She pulled her scarf up and her hat down to cover her face as much as possible. A precaution Mr. Purnell had suggested. Even David had hided his hair under a large hat. She doubted anyone in this remote part of the country would recognise her.

Cora's legs trembled when she climbed down the short steps, but Ethan's strong hands comforted and sustained her as always. Even without a sore back and shoulder, she would be exhausted after hours of travelling on a rough road. Ethan had insisted on not travelling for longer than a couple of hours. They'd stopped constantly to give her time to rest. Despite that, she couldn't say she was fond of the trip so far.

"How are you?" Ethan held her, his brow furrowed in concern. He'd asked her that question every ten minutes, and she couldn't help but love his attention.

"Tired, but otherwise well."

"We'll sleep here for tonight."

"We are two hours away from Borrington," she said. "I don't mind travelling."

"It's dusk. We would arrive in Borrington when it's dark. The road is rough in broad daylight. It must be a nightmare at night. I don't want to take risks." He held the door to the inn open. "And my shoulder is sore as well."

Harry was at the counter, talking with the innkeeper, while David gazed around with wide eyes. Not that there was much to see, just the dark wainscoting and the patrons scattered around, but he stared at everything with awe.

"Are you enjoying the trip?" she asked.

"The view of the country was fantastic. So much green, and I'm looking forward to seeing the sea. I've never been to the sea," he said to Ethan. "I didn't know the world was so..." He spread his arms. "... big."

Cora laughed. "Me either."

Harry joined in, his cheeks flushed. "You should see Scotland. Hills everywhere, endlessly. And lakes as big as the sea with monsters."

"Capital." David burst with happiness.

"They aren't real monsters," Mrs Parker said. "And the lack of monsters is the only good thing about Scotland. Everything else is cold and wet and smells of whiskey."

"Still, I'd love to see it," Cora said.

"You're going to love Borrington and its sandy beach." Ethan kept supporting her with his arm coiled around her waist.

David couldn't remain still. "I can't wait. The sea."

"We're going to swim." Harry raised a fist in the air.

Mrs. Parker dabbed her forehead with a handkerchief. "I can't share your enthusiasm, lads. The sand ends up everywhere, the water is cold, and the salt dries the skin."

"But we're going to take a swim, aren't we?" David gazed up at Ethan.

"By all means," Ethan said.

"I'm starving." Harry put a hand on his stomach. "Can we have dinner?"

The warm atmosphere inside the inn and the scent of stew lifted Cora's spirits. David wolfed down two portions of stew under the proud eye of Ethan before she could finish half of hers. Harry, instead, ate slowly only because he kept talking. They all went up the stairs to their bedrooms with heavy feet, exhaustion catching up with them.

She exhaled when she lay down in her bed. David fell asleep next to her in a moment while Harry slept on a separate bed. Mrs. Parker had falls asleep quickly as well in the bed next to Harry. For a boy with endless energy, Harry had fallen asleep faster than she could blink.

The latest book David was reading rested on his chest as he breathed softly. She put the book aside. He'd changed so much in such a short time. He laughed, read, had a friend, and was excited as a boy his age should be. If being shot meant seeing David enjoying life, she would endure the pain time and again.

She'd changed too. Before the incident, she would have never trusted anyone, but Ethan was different. He deserved her trust and much more.

The knock on the door distracted her from her thoughts. "Cora?" Ethan said from the other side.

She slid out of bed and opened the door, clenching the lapels of her dressing gown. "Ethan."

He eyed David with a fondness that touched her heart. "Already asleep, isn't he?"

"All of them. Bursting with energy one moment, and utterly exhausted the next."

"I just wanted to give you this cream." He handed her a pot. "For your sore muscles. It contains camphor. It smells nice and soothes the pain. It'll make the last hours of the trip more comfortable."

She closed her hand around his, taking the pot. His tenderness towards her never failed to make her shudder. "You always think of my well-being."

"Gladly."

She should remove her hand. She was officially a married

woman in her dressing gown with a sleeping chaperone; he was a marquess, standing in the hallway of an inn late at night. Hardly appropriate. His green eyes held her captive, and his fingers were warm and strong under hers. They were a promise of care without any demand. Not many men would have treated her with the respect Ethan had shown her.

The flutter in her chest had nothing to do with the fact he was undeniably handsome or with the heated moments they'd shared. It was his kindness and care that mesmerised her.

They kept holding hands over the pot and staring at each other until Harry stirred in the bed, mumbling something about swimming in his sleep.

They released the pot at the same time as thieves caught red-handed. The pot dropped, but Ethan snatched it before it crashed on the floor.

"Excellent reflexes," she said.

"Yes, well…" He rubbed the back of his neck and handed her the camphor again. "Good night. If you need anything, my room is right next to yours."

"Good night." She closed the door and waited exactly two minutes before leaving her room because she needed something. She needed to apologise.

The hallway was deserted. The lamps cast quivering shadows on the wainscoting, mirroring the quivering in her heart. Now or never. She closed the door behind her and hurried barefoot to Ethan's room. She knocked without hesitation, but when he swept into view, she couldn't say anything. Her tongue knotted. She wasn't sure what she wanted to tell him. How odd.

She fiddled with the sash of her dressing gown, racking her brain for something clever to say, or just something.

"Are you well? Is it David?" He started to go towards her room.

"I'm fine. David is fine, too. I just wanted to…" She exhaled. "Nothing. I'd better go to bed."

"Wait." He took her hand and tugged at it. "Tell me." He gently pulled her into his room and closed the door, and escaping his presence was impossible. "If the wound bothers you, I need to know."

"No, I'm fine." She folded her arms over her chest and unfolded them. "I wanted to apologise for what I said in our last conversation. I didn't mean to offend you, but it seems I did."

He leant against the wall. "It's all right. I understand."

"Do you?"

He nodded. "I'm not angry with you. Not anymore."

"Good. Yes. Well. Then I... actually, I don't understand what you understand. How can you understand when I don't understand? There are so many things I don't understand. I'm so confused." Drat. She wasn't making any sense.

"I'm confused too. But here." He touched his head. "Not here." He placed a hand on his chest, right over his heart.

"Oh." Great. One moment, she vomited words. The next, she was speechless.

A corner of his mouth quirked up. "Cora." His tone suddenly turned serious, and the air between them was charged with tension. "I love you," he said with simplicity and without giving her time to prepare herself for an answer or a reaction.

Her mouth dropped open. She stopped fidgeting. She stopped thinking about apologising. The situation had taken a turn she hadn't expected.

"You don't have to say anything. I'm simply telling you the truth to make you understand why I'd do anything to make you happy, even though you don't feel the same way as I do."

She started fidgeting again. The last thing she wanted was to hurt him. But a storm of emotions burst within her. She'd spent many years without love and affection. She wasn't sure if she could fall in love right now when there were many things out of her control. Or if she should let herself go and enjoy the moment without thinking about the future. But how could she not think about the future?

"Ethan, I don't know what to say." Ouch. Why did she always say the wrong thing? "I'm sorry..."

"Then don't say anything." He chuckled nervously. "I prefer you to stay silent rather than hear all the reasons why you can't love me."

It wasn't that she couldn't love him. It was a matter of time. Time for her emotions, worries, and fears to settle and let her live. And she was still married. She took his hand and held it in hers. "You're the most wonderful man I've ever met."

"Stop right there. I don't want to hear the 'but.'"

"There isn't any but, only time for me to take back my life and make sure David is safe. Only then, I'll let my heart speak loudly."

He kissed her knuckles and put her hand on his chest. "I don't want to put any pressure on you. You have enough of it on your own. And I don't want to give you another reason to worry. But I'm here if you need me. I'll always be for you and David."

She threw her arms around his neck and hugged him, squeezing him as tightly as her recovering strength allowed. He held her, kissing her temple. She didn't know for how long they remained hugging each other, but she released him reluctantly.

She caressed his face and ran her fingers through his hair, feeling the missing ear. "I have to return to David before he wakes up and gets scared by my absence."

"Good night." He stroked her cheek with such devotion she wanted to weep.

"Good night." Although she wasn't sure it'd be a good night.

ETHAN'S EMOTIONS went up and down in a confused state that left him exhausted as the carriage drove closer to Borrington.

Watching Cora sleeping in front of him in the carriage had filled him with sadness. He didn't regret having told her he loved her, but he shouldn't add more worries to her frail shoulders. His timing hadn't been the best. She had too many concerns to deal with.

"The sea." David stuck his head out of the window.

"Yes." Harry squeezed himself out as well.

The boys' enthusiasm made Ethan laugh with sheer happiness.

Cora bolted awake. "What is it?"

"The sea, Mama." David pointed at the blue-grey expanse frothing against the cliff.

She widened her eyes at the view. He helped her move closer to the window.

"Is it the first time you've seen the sea?" he asked, holding her by the waist.

"No, but I haven't seen it in years." She inhaled. "The air smells lovely. No coal or dust."

Mrs. Parker huffed. "When the saltiness of the air withers your eyes, you'll wish for London's air, my lady."

Cora laughed, and the sound captured all his attention.

He held her close as the carriage went downhill. "Almost there."

When the white walls of his house came into view after a turn, the coachman slowed the carriage in front of Ethan's estate.

She squeezed his hand when he helped her out. "Thank you." She tilted her head up. "This is fancier than I expected."

"My parents were fond of this place. We often spent the summer here."

David and Harry rushed past them to the balcony in the garden opening to the cliff. The waves foamed and crushed against the rocks with a soothing sound while seagulls cawed overhead. Perfect for helping Cora recover.

A small army of servants swarmed around them to carry their bags, bow, or curtsy as Mrs. Parker took charge of the introductions. Once inside, David ran from one corner of the entry hallway to another. Harry could barely keep up with him.

"Can we go to the beach?" they asked together, their eyes shining.

"Not alone," Ethan said. "We'll go later, all together. You may ask the groom to show you the ponies."

"Ponies." Harry's eyes widened too much for Ethan's liking. "We can ride them to the beach."

"Only if the groom and two stable hands are with you."

Harry seized David's arm and pulled. "Let's go before he changes his mind."

"Later, Mama." David kissed Cora's cheek and vanished behind Harry in a chaos of voices and laughter.

"Thank you," Cora said, her voice suspiciously low.

"Wait to thank me. David is with Harry. Anything could happen." He offered her his arm. "I'll show you to your room." He dismissed the maid. "You must be tired."

"A bit." She took his arm, and together they went up the sweeping stairs.

Compared to his house in London, this one was airy and sparkling with large windows and hallways wide enough for six people to walk abreast.

He opened the window in her bedroom and let the fresh sea air rush in. "Judge Quigley will see us tomorrow. Do you fancy a swim with the lads later? There's a part of the bay where the water is rather warm."

"Yes. I haven't swum in years."

"I have a bathing machine for you and Mrs. Parker, should you wish to take a swim with us."

"Would love to."

He bowed. "I'll let you rest then. See you later." He didn't make it to the door though.

Cora caught his hand. "Ethan."

The husky tone in which she said his name sent a shudder

through him. The desire in her voice couldn't be only his imagination. Although she was too pale and tired to do more than nap.

She didn't add anything else, and he didn't mind. She wasn't in love with him; that much was clear. But that fact didn't change the way he felt, not one bit. And if she needed the physical pleasure, he was more than happy to give her what she wanted.

"What do you need?" he asked, eager to do her bidding.

"I just wanted to thank you. I was about to make a mistake two weeks ago, and while you pointed it out, you let me do what I wanted, even if it was a mistake. I regret my stubbornness, but I thank you for letting me do what I thought was right." She released his hand. "That's all."

"I would never force my will upon you. Not even when you're wrong."

She smiled, and her cheeks regained a bit of colour. "But I hope you'll always tell me when I'm wrong."

"Always." It was such a meaningful word. It implied they wanted to share the rest of their lives together. He wasn't scared, quite the opposite. He was eager to start the rest of his life with her.

"You know that..." She sagged on the bed. "I only need time. Too many things have happened in a short period."

"Shush." He helped her lie down and removed her boots. "You don't owe me anything, remember? Not even an explanation."

"You're wonderful. I'm not sure I deserve you."

"That's nonsense." He pulled a quilt over her. "Take a nap. Doctor's order."

Her eyelids drooped thanks to the laudanum and the fatigue. He held her hand until she fell asleep. Maybe she would never love him as much as he loved her, but his promise to protect her would last all his life.

twenty

THE BATHING MACHINE jerked along Ethan's private sandy beach towards the quiet waves. Not the most comfortable means of transport, especially since the horse attached to it walked backwards towards the shore. But the excitement of swimming for the first time in the sea dulled the throb in Cora's shoulder. The small window offered only a glimpse of the ocean and a secluded bay. Tall cliffs formed a C-shaped coastline. The warm air left her skin damp with perspiration.

Mrs. Parker sat in front of her on the wooden bench, seemingly unaffected by the beauty of the sea. "Can you swim, my lady?"

"I learnt to swim in a lake in Hertfordshire. This is the first time I've tried the ocean."

"It's going to be cold, no matter the season or what Lord Stark says." She tugged at her swimming suit— a complete set of bloomers, blouse, cap, and belt. "But this should keep us warm."

Yes, Cora had no doubt. When she'd swum in the lake in summer, she'd worn only a tunic. The bloomers and shirt were rather thick, covering her from her chest to her knees, and when wet, they wouldn't let any part of her body be visible. "I wonder why it is this bright red colour."

Mrs. Parker shifted on the seat as the machine jolted to a stop. "If we drown, we'll be visible and easily identifiable."

"Oh." That dampened Cora's enthusiasm a little.

"And it isn't the most flattering garment. We look like a giant strawberries."

Mrs. Parker opened the door, and the lazy sound of the waves reached Cora's ears. The horse snorted, stomping his hooves in the shallow water. The machine allowed the ladies to step into the water without being seen and without crossing the beach in their swimming suits. Not that Cora cared about Ethan glancing at her calves, and his servants were too distant for them to see anything.

She searched the beach for David. He swam not far from her with Ethan and Harry, among tall sprays of water and loud laughter. Ethan would keep the boys safe. She had no doubt. The sunlight shone over them, hitting the drops of water and turning them into little stars. She giggled when she lowered herself into the sea, not as cold as she expected.

"Goodness me." Mrs. Parker splashed around, keeping her head fully out of the water.

"It's easier than swimming in the lake," Cora said, moving her arms slowly. "The water is less heavy."

"If you say so, my lady. I swim only because my physician says it is good for my bones and joints." She wrinkled her nose. "I personally dislike the sand, the salt, and the cold. And the country. Too much fresh air can't possibly be good."

David's laughter carried across the distance. He, Harry, and Ethan were splashing each other, raising tall sprays of water. She caught a glimpse of Ethan's naked chest and his golden skin as he defended himself from the boys' attacks.

"Mama," David shouted and waved his arms.

She waved back. His happiness was mirrored in her own heart. Not even when she and David had spent time alone, had he been as carefree as he was now. He swam towards her, raising splashes and sprays of water. His auburn hair sparked with coppery hues in the sunlight. Ethan followed him closely. Harry kept disappearing in and out of view as he dived into the waves.

"They are coming here." Mrs. Parker sank a few inches, hiding herself. "That's not appropriate."

"They're boys," Cora said.

"Not the marquess."

No, he was not.

"Mama." David threw himself at her, laughing.

She hugged him and kissed his cheek, tasting the salty water. "You're a natural-born swimmer."

"It's Lord Stark who's a great teacher. Look." He brushed his wet hair from his face. "Lord Stark, can we show it to Mother?"

Unbidden, her gaze dipped to Ethan's broad, wet chest. Drops trickled down from his hair and hard jaw to his pectoral muscles and the dark hairs. Water spiked his black eyelashes, enhancing his emerald eyes. He met her gaze, and she focused her attention on a funny-looking cloud. It looked like a dog with an umbrella. How odd.

"I apologise for the intrusion, ladies, but David insisted on coming here," he said.

"Mama, look." David put his hands on Ethan's shoulders.

"Ready?" Ethan asked, dipping into the water.

David nodded, his young face brightening. "As high as you can."

"What are you two doing?" She tried to understand what David was doing with his feet underwater.

"One, two, three..." Ethan shoved David up and tossed him in the air.

Cora gasped. Harry hooted. David rolled back and dived into the sea, raising a wall of water. Then he disappeared.

"David." She shot forwards, but David emerged, smiling so widely he showed all his teeth.

"Did you see it?" he asked.

"I did." She exhaled in relief. "It was incredible."

"Me." Harry did the same, yelling as he flew up in the air.

"Again, again," David and Harry said in chorus.

David jumped in and out of the water, taking turns with Harry. Ethan winced as the muscles around that long, deep scar twitched.

"David, let Lord Stark decide. Don't be too insistent," she said.

David composed himself in a moment. "Sorry, Lord Stark."

"Does your shoulder bother you?" she asked.

"Don't worry." Ethan waved David closer. "It's barely a twinge. I'm more than happy to play."

"Yes." David punched the air and jumped again.

Cora laughed. "It seems rather enjoyable."

"Why don't you try?" David tugged at her hand. "Would you let her try, sir?"

"Good gracious, no," Mrs. Parker muttered, rubbing her forehead.

"Ladies don't have fun, never," Harry said. "Especially in the sea. It's something to do with their nerves. The sea upsets them. They're too delicate." He cheekily grinned at her.

A dare. And Cora wanted to accept it. "Yes, I'd like to try, if Lord Stark doesn't mind."

David elbowed Harry. "I told you my mama isn't scared of anything."

Not quite.

Ethan stared at her for a long, intense moment before he joined his hands to form a step. "You place your foot here and your hands on my shoulders. At the count of three, you push yourself up, and I'll throw you up. Then gravity will do the rest."

"Exciting." She did as she was told, but she hadn't considered the position brought her quite close to him.

"My lady, please," Mrs. Parker whispered.

"Just this once, and there isn't anyone here aside from us." Cora giggled.

"Your wound?" Ethan asked.

"It's fine, and I want to try." Goodness. She was more insistent than the boys.

When she put her hands on his solid shoulders, her smile faltered. His eyes were the same colour as the sea. His wet skin only enhanced his harsh lines. His Adam's apple was particularly prominent, and she wanted to trace it with her fingertips or lick the salty drops from his skin.

"Do you trust me?" he asked.

"Yes." No hesitation because it was true.

"Ready?" He sounded low and husky.

"Yes." Instead, her voice was tiny. She slid her foot into the step formed by his hands. Their bodies brushed against each other. His skin was so warm she felt the heat in her core.

"One." He sucked in a deep breath that raised his chest. She was breathless too. "Two." His gaze dipped to her lips, and she didn't mind. "Three."

He threw her up. It was a mighty push that propelled her into the air, making her feel light and weightless. The world turned upside down as the sky and the sea exchanged places. Then she dived into the water with a big splash. The sounds disappeared. Bubbles tickled her skin. When she emerged, she burst out laughing. It was liberating.

"Mama." David hugged her, and they laughed together. The more she heard him laugh, the harder she laughed.

Another first. She couldn't remember the last time she and David had laughed so hard that their bellies hurt. Every moment they'd spent together, even the most beautiful ones, had been tainted by something Jacob had said, done, or by the thought that Jacob would be home soon, or that they would need to return to London and face his anger again. A constant shadow even on the brightest days.

The wave of sadness caught her by surprise. Not exactly sadness, but the laughter made her too aware of what she'd lost in the past years and how accustomed she'd become to being miserable. Jacob's presence was like a cold blade stabbing her soul without warning. It was odd how she'd grown used to being unhappy and considering her life to be an endless grey series of events out of her control. How different her life looked now.

Ethan would disagree, but she owed this new perspective to him. His expert hands had healed her flesh wound. His love had freed her spirit. His kindness had made David feel safe. And she loved him. Heaven, she did love him. Desperately.

How ignorant she'd been about her own feelings. How silly not to understand immediately what he meant to her. Being with him wasn't another prison. He was freedom itself for David and her.

She held David harder with desperation. He was the only good thing Jacob had given her. Her laughter turned into a sob, which she masked with a cough, not wanting to spoil the day for David. She released him and stared at the water, glad it hid her tears.

"Isn't it wonderful?" David asked.

She nodded and rubbed her eyes. "Very enjoyable."

Ethan frowned at her, likely having understood her change of mood. "We should return home and have dinner."

"May I stay five more minutes?" David asked.

"Tomorrow, we'll stay longer. After we meet Judge Quigley, we'll spend the day on the beach and have a picnic here. What do you say, Mrs. Parker?"

"Words fail me, my lord." Mrs. Parker arched her eyebrows.

Ethan patted David's cheek. "It's important for your mother to rest."

David nodded and started to swim towards the beach with Harry.

"Race you there." Harry sped up, waving his arms furiously.

"Not fair." David chased him.

Mrs. Parker headed to the bathing machine, muttering something about eating sand and sandwiches. Cora went to follow her, but Ethan took her hand.

"Are you all right?" he asked.

"Yes." She blinked her tears away.

"Your shoulder? Was it too much?"

"No, it's fine."

"Then what is it?" He stroked her knuckles.

She lowered her gaze. "It's odd how a moment of intense happiness can remind you of all the moments of sadness in your life. David has never been happier because the rest of his life has been horrible. Today is the first time he's laughed so freely."

He held her hand underwater. "I understand what you mean."

She wanted to say more. She wanted to spend more time with him. She wanted everything about him— his beauty, kindness, and warmth. "Thank you for today, for being so good to David. He needed it, and Ethan I—"

"My lady?" Mrs. Parker called from the bathing machine. "We should go."

Ethan released her hand. "I enjoy spending time with David. He's a lovely boy."

"Will you meet me later? Please? Somewhere quiet where no one will bother us."

He nodded but frowned. "We could meet at the gazebo at the edge of the garden. It's beautiful and private."

"All right." She glanced at him as she swam to Mrs. Parker. He waved, looking like a god just emerged from the sea with the foam around him and his wet hair.

In the bathing machine, Cora removed her soaked swimming suit. Her hand tingled from Ethan's gentle touch. Her heart stuttered from his kindness. Her soul hummed for him. If her situation were different, if her presence in his life wouldn't bring trouble to him, she would love to be officially courted by him. She was certain that Ethan, once he chose a woman, would dedicate himself to her, and she wondered how it would feel. Because he might love her, but she was married and disgraced in the eyes of society.

"He's a decent man, you know, my lady," Mrs. Parker said, removing her cap.

"Pardon?" She towelled herself dry and donned her drawers.

"His Lordship. He isn't like other lords." The housekeeper turned serious. "He might be an unconventional lord, I blame his time spent with the army for that, but he never chases the maids. He's respectful to everyone, and he doesn't go around with women, if you know what I mean."

Yes, she did. "He's an honourable man."

"Yes, aside from his bizarre idea of having a picnic on the sand." Mrs. Parker shook her head. "I've known him since his first wail echoed in the house, and it was such a wail! You could hear it throughout the house. I've been in service of the Starks all my life." Her voice cracked. "When his lordship left to go to war, I feared I'd die of grief. I've never met a gentleman kinder than his lordship. His parents were the best employers a housekeeper could ever want and the most lovely people."

"I easily believe you." Cora brushed sand from her wet hair. "But why are you telling me that? Did I give the impression of not considering him an honourable man?"

"Oh, no, my lady. It's just that..." She sighed. "Forgive me. I spoke too much."

"Please tell me."

The bathing machine stopped with a jolt, and Cora grabbed the edge of the bench not to slip off it.

Mrs. Parker flushed. "He seems quite taken by you if I may say so. You have your personal troubles, but His Lordship isn't a man who gives up easily when it comes to the people he cares about. Once he loves, he loves fiercely."

Yes, Cora easily believed that too.

ETHAN LOOSENED the knot of his cravat, walking along the path in his garden.

Thoughts tormented him, but for once, they were pleasant thoughts. At the beach, he'd caught a glimpse of a family life he might never have. If Cora decided to leave, if she had to, he would lose David too. His chest tightened at the thought of never seeing Cora and David again, of never laughing with them. He hoped Cora didn't want to tell him she wanted to leave.

The garden here was wilder than the one in his London house. Thick hedgerows and tall trees formed a green gallery that protected the house from the strong sea winds. Weeds kept growing at the edge of the path, no matter how hard the gardeners worked. The indomitable nature of the wild plants had an endearing quality he appreciated because they endured the weather and the pruning with stubbornness without wilting, just like Cora.

He headed for the fully enclosed gazebo that had surrendered to the vegetation years ago. He didn't care, quite the opposite. The English ivy and purple bindweed created a fairy-tale-like dome and nearly covered the front gate. More than a gazebo, it was a fancy garden shed, almost a small flat.

He stepped inside, shoving aside the long green stems and closing the door behind him, only to come to an abrupt halt upon seeing Cora. She sat on the wrought-iron bench, every inch a fairy of gold and fire. Her cheeks flushed when she raised her head.

"Ethan." His name, pronounced with such tenderness, started a flutter in his belly.

"Isn't this place beautiful?"

"Yes, it is. So different from the manicured gardens in London." She made room for him on the bench.

He sat next to her. "Are you tired?"

"A little, but I think swimming helped my stiff muscles." She lifted her arm. "No pain at all. The dive didn't bother me."

"I asked Cook to prepare a soup for you with—" He wasn't prepared for her kiss.

Cora took his face and kissed him, a sweet, chaste kiss that ignited the fire of his passion in a moment. She moved her lips over his, giving him little bites.

"Forgive me," she whispered against his lips. "I wanted to kiss you when we were swimming, and I couldn't resist."

He caressed her silky cheek and stroked her bottom lip with his thumb. "Is this why you asked me to see you?"

She ran her tongue over her bottom lip. "Yes."

"I understand you perfectly. I can barely contain myself when I see you. The only thing I can think of is to kiss you."

He inched closer, sharing his breath with her. When their lips met again, he couldn't suppress a growl of pleasure. The scent of lemons teased his nostrils. Underneath her perfume, the aroma of camphor reminded him she was still recovering. He held her by the waist. She climbed onto his lap, straddling him. Not what he expected but wasn't going to complain. The moment of pause was filled by their desire as they stared at each other. The sunlight filtering through the leaves played with her freckles.

"You're so beautiful," he whispered, tracing the line of her jaw.

Her next kiss was sheer passion. He got lost in that kiss, in the warmth of her skin, and in her sweet scent. Each lash of her tongue caused him to shiver with need. She undid his trousers and gripped him as if she needed it, too.

"Cora—" He gasped as she worked his length with her small hand.

"You said you wouldn't touch me unless I wanted it." She rubbed the tip.

"Hell." He forgot what he wanted to say next. He was so hard that it hurt.

Her skirts gathered around them when she rocked her hips over him. Sweet torture. He groaned as she guided him closer to the slit of her drawers. He could feel her heat and wetness over him.

"I want you, Ethan," she said, brushing her lips over his neck. "I really do. Don't doubt me."

He'd give her whatever she needed. He didn't care if it was only a physical affair for her. He didn't care if she didn't feel what he felt. As long as she wanted him not because she meant to repay him.

She rolled her hips and sheathed him inside her, inch by inch. She paused to kiss him hard and deep. She was a tight velvet fist, clenching him. He reclined his head and sank his fingers into her supple bottom cheeks. She slowly moved down, sheathing him with her softness. They both groaned when he was buried deep inside her.

"It's been so long..." She breathed on his neck. "You feel wonderful."

"Bloody hell, Cora. You too." He was about to explode with pleasure and need.

Before she started moving, he unbuttoned her shirt and tugged at the bandages until he bared her spectacular breasts. He tongued and pinched her nipples, tearing a delicious moan out of her.

With his hands on her hips, he helped her find a rhythm, moving her up and down. Her inner muscles gripped him hard, bringing him to the verge of a cliff. Her breasts bounced when she moved, and he paused to kiss them again. She placed her hands on his shoulders and went faster. He stared at her face, savouring every little movement of her hips and every blush on her cheeks. He wouldn't last long. His body was already on fire.

He slid a hand between them and rubbed her, smiling as she moaned louder. She found her release with a cry, digging her fingers into his shoulders. Her inner muscles squeezed him tightly with little spasms. He couldn't contain himself any longer.

Before spilling, he lifted her and held her against his chest as they both shivered in each other's arms. They remained wrapped one around the other, their chests touching with each breath. It was perfect. Thinking he might lose it all was a dark blade twisting in his soul.

She brushed her lips against his ear. "I love you, Ethan. It scares me to death, but I do."

He hugged her more tightly, hardly believing her words. He hadn't dared to hope she would reciprocate his feelings. A rush of energy coursed through him, bringing a tightness to his chest from too much happiness.

"It'll be my goal to dispel your fears and show you how happy we can be."

"You've already shown me that. That's why I fell in love with you. I was only scared to admit it."

He pulled her head down for another long kiss. But he wanted more. He wanted to hear her scream of ecstasy again. He swapped their places and knelt between her open legs, putting his hands on her knees. She stared at him with wide eyes, her chest rising and falling quickly. He pulled her thighs further apart and took a moment to admire her glistening pink beauty.

"You don't have to," she whispered, her cheeks crimson.

"I want to." He stroked her intimately, caressing her silky skin. She shivered. "Have you ever experienced that?"

She shook her head. "Jacob has never... He doesn't think..."

"It'll be my pleasure then to be the first." He dipped his head and kissed her deeply, enjoying her gasp and her hips jolting.

He lapped at her and stroked her nub with his tongue, adding his fingers to her tightness. Her thigh muscles closed in on him in a lemon-scented hug as he dug his tongue deeper. The scent of her arousal drove him crazy with need and hardened him in a second.

She screamed again, louder than the first time, gripping the edge of the bench. Her fingers seized his hair as she pushed her hips towards him. He didn't stop kissing her until the little pulses finished and she fell silent. She was a vision. Her eyes were clouded with pleasure, her lips reddened and kiss-swollen, and her nipples hard and puckering.

When she sagged, panting, he adjusted her skirts and cleaned her with his handkerchief. "Next time, I want you in my bed for an entire night."

She smiled and snuggled closer to him. "Next time, my love."

twenty-one

A T DINNER, CORA couldn't remain still after what happened in the gazebo. She hadn't had an enjoyable tumble in a decade, as her deliciously sore, intimate parts proved it. It was as if Ethan was still inside her, and she loved it. Ethan sitting next to her didn't make the situation lighter. Her face flamed every time their gazes met, and a pulse started between her legs. When his leg brushed hers, she had to suppress a moan. When his hand touched hers under the table, she wanted to kiss him.

"Did I show you how to turn a fork into a catapult?" Harry asked David.

"No. How?" David said at the same time as Ethan said, "Don't try, Harry."

"I'll show you tomorrow when we are alone." Harry winked at David.

Tomorrow. They would meet Judge Quigley. Her stomach churned with worry. Ethan held her hand. As usual, he sensed the shifts in her mood.

Mrs. Parker strode into the dining room. Her chatelain swung from her belt, clinking with each step. "My lord, an urgent message from London." She placed the folded piece of paper on the table.

His fingers tensed over Cora's hand as he read.

"What is it?" she asked.

"A message from my solicitor about Lord Roxbury."

At hearing the name, David fell silent and stopped eating. "Did he find us?"

Ethan shook his head. "He started a motion of no confidence against me to have me removed from the ownership of the land of the Royal Veterans' Society."

"His revenge." Cora's voice shook with anger. "He knows about David and me. He knows we're with you. This is his way of forcing us out." She glanced at the door, nearly expecting Jacob to barge inside.

"Sooner or later, he was bound to do something like that anyway." Ethan folded the message, his jaw muscle bunching. "Lady Kingsley will support me."

David pushed his plate aside. "I don't want to see him ever again, but I don't want to leave either."

"Your mother and I will protect you." Ethan patted David's shoulder from across the table.

"Trust my father," Harry said, stealing a piece of roasted potato from David's plate. "He's a good copper. He'll get Lord Roxbury arrested."

"If you'll excuse me. I have to write to my solicitor." Ethan rose and stopped Harry from taking another piece of David's dinner. "Harry, ask for a second helping. Don't take David's food."

"Yes, sir," Harry muttered.

"I've lost my appetite anyway." David pushed his plate towards Harry.

"You need to eat, darling. Please." Cora had to admit her appetite was gone as well.

"I'll see you later." Ethan bowed to Cora before leaving the dining room.

They finished eating in silence. The fact that Harry encouraged David to eat and didn't joke was a testament to the heavy atmosphere.

After dinner, Cora knocked on the door to Ethan's study, finding him at his desk. A deep frown marred his brow as he wrote.

"I won't take up your time." She hesitated on the threshold. If Jacob had been at that desk, he would have yelled at her to leave him alone. "I just wanted to see you for a moment. I'll leave you to your work."

"A moment isn't enough. It'll never be." Ethan opened his arms, and she ran to him.

She sat on his lap and snuggled closer to his warmth. His heartbeat quickened as she rested her cheek on his chest.

"You should never fear coming to me." The deep rumble of his voice reverberated inside her. "I always want you by my side."

Always. Could they have always? They loved each other, but her situation was complicated at best and uncertain at worst. He was a marquess, who would need to marry and produce an heir one day. She couldn't give anything to him aside from her heart.

"I'm sorry. If I hadn't asked for your help, Jacob would have never attacked you." She wrapped her arm around his neck.

"No, he would have. He's never approved of my management of the centre. He doesn't scare me. This battle with him has nothing to do with yours. We'll win, and he'll remain alone and forgotten with his bitterness."

She pulled away from him, needing to see his face. "What if I can't get an annulment? What will happen to us?"

He ran a finger over the curve of her jaw. "No matter what Quigley says, no matter what Roxbury does, no matter what the entire world thinks, we'll be together. And if you can't get an annulment or you'll be forced to leave England, I'll come with you." A shadow crossed his face.

"But you can't leave England. Your life and responsibilities are here."

He pressed his lips in a grim line.

She caressed his cleft chin. "I understand. I can't ask you to sacrifice your life for me. I don't want you to."

"I'd gladly do it."

"No." She gripped the lapel of his jacket. "If I'm forced to leave England, the law will be against me. A countess can't leave her husband, an earl, taking his son and heir with her. David will be the next Earl of Roxbury, even if Jacob doesn't like it. He won't simply let him go." A chill crept down her back.

"I will never, ever let Roxbury take David." A hard glint flashed in his gaze. "David will stay with you. Legally or otherwise. If you must leave, I'll provide for you and David and visit you every time I can."

Gosh, it sounded like an uncertain future made of stolen moments of happiness and the constant threat of Jacob finding them.

"I know how the prospect sounds." He kissed her temple. "But we both agree that David is our priority. His safety is our first concern."

"Yes, it's—" She jolted as a loud thud came from the hallway. She gripped his arm. "What is it?"

"Ha! I hit you." Harry's voice thundered.

"You cheated." That was David.

Another thud came, followed by Mrs. Parker's scream and her inaudible words.

Ethan exhaled and pitched the bridge of his nose. "I think that answers your question."

ETHAN WALKED with Cora by his arm, heading to Judge Quigley's house after the short drive on the carriage. The emotions of the past few days had turned his life upside down, both in a good and bad fashion.

As he held Cora's hand, he knew no other woman would ever take her place in his heart. But her fear was justified. The law would be against her if an annulment wasn't possible. She might escape Roxbury's clutches, but she would remain his wife and live with the constant fear of being found and dragged to him or in prison. And David would be caught in the middle of the war between his parents.

Too many things could go wrong. Too many lives could be destroyed. Including those of the soldiers at his centre because Roxbury would take his revenge against whatever he saw fit. Cora remained silent. Since last night, a little crease wrinkled the space between her eyebrows.

He wanted to smooth her worry lines with his lips and forget their happiness was at stake. "Is your shoulder painful? I hope the swim didn't cause any stress."

"Only a sting, but I'm fine. Really. I don't need the bandage anymore."

"Good." He ignored the worry clenching his stomach.

A nagging feeling bothered him. Or maybe he cared too much about her and David, and no bad omen was on the horizon.

Judge Quigley's white cottage rose from the top of a hill, surrounded by trees and wisteria. With the sea in the background and the puffy clouds overhead, the view was breathtaking, but it did nothing to soothe Ethan's inner turmoil. He'd been afraid for his life before at the edge of a battle, but losing Cora was a new type of fear. More visceral. More intimate.

"Lord Stark, Lady Roxbury." The judge himself opened the door.

Short and with soft features, the judge had a paternal expression that eased some of the tension in Ethan's chest.

"Welcome." Judge Quigley shook Ethan's hand and bowed to Cora. "My sister sent me a letter regarding your visit. She thinks I might be of help. Please come in and tell me everything." He showed them to a small study with a diamond window opening to the sea.

No carriages rattling by, no street vendors yelling their prices, and no chatting crowd. Only the seagulls and the rhythmic slosh of the waves against the rocks. Ethan could get used to the peace and quiet. He, Cora, and David would spend a few weeks here in summer... if everything went well.

He held out a chair for Cora and sat next to her while she told Judge Quigley everything about her life with Roxbury. The romantic courtship, her husband's possessiveness turned into indifference, and his cruelty towards her and David. Hearing her story for the second time didn't make it easier to endure. Every time Ethan thought about what Roxbury had done to her, his blood boiled and he wanted to smash something. Possibly Roxbury's face.

Judge Quigley nodded and took notes in his notebook without interrupting Cora, his pince-nez glasses perched on his nose.

When Cora told him about the night of the shooting, Judge Quigley stopped taking notes. "Lord Roxbury tried to shoot his own son?"

Cora nodded. "He said he didn't mean to kill him but only to teach him a lesson."

"It doesn't lessen the gravity of what he did." Judge Quigley scowled. "He hit you instead."

"I can show you the wound from the gunshot," Cora said. "It's healed recently, but the scar is visible."

"That won't be necessary, my lady," Judge Quigley said. "I believe you."

"Is an annulment possible?" Ethan asked when the judge didn't add anything.

"Well." Judge Quigley removed his glasses. "I believe everything Lady Roxbury told me, and Lord Roxbury clearly neglected her and his son, not to mention the attempted murder and the cruelty, but that unfortunately isn't the point. The point is what we can prove. We have Lady Roxbury's word against Lord Roxbury's word."

"But there's the wound from Lord Roxbury's gun," Ethan said.

Judge Quigley held up a hand. "Yes, but Lady Roxbury didn't go to the police or the hospital after the incident. She went to you. If she'd gone to the police, they would have investigated the matter further, inspected the room where the shooting happened, questioned Lord Roxbury, and above all, Lady Roxbury's injury would have been recorded by the doctors of the hospital. As of now, the gunshot wound could come from any incident with a gun, and Lord Roxbury's testimony on the event contradicts Lady Roxbury's. After I received my sister's letter, I did some research and discovered that Commissioner North, Detective Inspector Purnell's superior, refused to file Lady Roxbury's complaint for attempted murder." He spread his arms. "Instead, Lord Roxbury's head injury has been recorded by the physician Lord Roxbury's butler called. After the incident, Lord Roxbury went straight to the hospital although he hasn't officially denounced his wife as of yet. He told Commissioner North that his wife attacked him while spreading the rumour that his wife had left London to visit some relatives. Likely, to avoid gossip, but it's quite confusing. He can easily accuse his wife of having tried to kill him before fleeing, and Lady Roxbury could have staged the shooting."

"David would confirm what happened," Cora said.

"My lady, David is a thirteen-year-old boy and your son." Judge Quigley shook his head. "I'm afraid his word doesn't carry the legal weight we need for an annulment case, which is taken very seriously by the parliament."

Ethan clenched his fist in a futile attempt to calm himself down. "There must be something we can do."

"It depends," Judge Quigley said. "If you can provide another witness, an adult who isn't related to Lady Roxbury, someone who can testify to Lord Roxbury's abuse, then, yes, there's grounds for an annulment."

"I could testify," Ethan said.

"Now, now, Lord Stark." Judge Quigley pinched the bridge of his nose. "Any jury will understand you're speaking only to protect the lady. You have never witnessed any arguments between Lord and Lady Roxbury or acts of violence, have you?"

Damn. "No."

"Also, how are you going to explain the fact Lady Roxbury came to you instead of going to the hospital?" The judge lifted his shoulders. "The court will come to the conclusion that Lady Roxbury and you see each other regularly, which won't help our case. Your association with Lady Roxbury rules you out as a witness, and if we present this case in court, we want to make sure our defence is impeccable and beyond criticism. Our witness must be someone *super partes*, impartial."

"Cora?" Ethan turned towards her. "Can you think of anyone? Someone who has been with you in the past years? Your maid, perhaps."

"A physician?" Judge Quigley suggested.

"My maid would never say a word against my husband. There's Mrs. Marshall," Cora said. "She was my midwife and our governess for years. She helped me with David when he was a baby. My husband sent her away when she questioned him about the way he treated David."

Judge Quigley scribbled in his notebook. "Can she attest to the neglect Lord Roxbury showed towards his own son and the cruelty towards you?"

"Certainly. I haven't been close to any other member of the household. But Mrs. Marshall left our house years ago. I don't know where she lives now."

"Finn will find her," Ethan said, pausing for a moment. "If the annulment is successful, what will happen to David?"

Judge Quigley exhaled, lowering his pen. "David will become

an out-of-marriage child. He'll lose his right to the title or any inheritance from his father. An annulment is very different from a divorce from this point of view. After a divorce, paternity isn't questioned, but the annulment effectively revokes it. Unfortunately, the father has the last word on the children's custody, especially for male children. Lord Roxbury might decide he wants David by his side despite everything."

"Succession law," Ethan said grimly.

Judge Quigley nodded. "Without David, Lord Roxbury would have no heir, and that poses a problem in terms of inheritance. No court would let a succession war start over Lord Roxbury's estate in case his long-lost uncle or third-removed cousin came forwards to claim the title and money. It would be better if David remained the heir."

"But I don't care about Lord Roxbury's money." Cora closed her fists on her lap. "All I ask is for David to be free and to stay with me. My husband can do whatever he wants with his land and money."

"My lady." Judge Quigley put his glasses back on to peer at her. "How do you expect to sustain your son and yourself? I believe you don't have any close relatives. If David remains the heir, Lord Roxbury will be required to provide you with an allowance as his heir's mother while David will live with his father. If David is removed from the inheritance line and hence disowned, he and you won't receive a penny. Your dowry might be returned to you, but it won't last long. How will you survive?"

Ethan couldn't stay silent. "I'll provide for her and David. Gladly." He turned towards Judge Quigley. "What can we do to remove David from Lord Roxbury's line?"

The judge scribbled again in his notebook. "If you can prove Lord Roxbury's cruelty towards his son with a witness, I'll file the procedure and do my best to have the court consider it in a timely fashion."

It sounded easy, but Cora's paleness worried Ethan.

"We'll find Mrs. Marshall," he said. "We can win this case."

FROM THE WINDOW of her room, Cora watched David playing cricket with Harry in the garden. Seeing him carefree and happy, enjoying life as a thirteen-year-old boy should, broke her heart because his present happiness was at risk. She wasn't deluded. Jacob would fight tooth and nail to get David's custody if only to spite her.

He didn't care about David or an heir. He'd often expressed his poor opinion of his son. But he would fight for David only as a last act of cruelty. And what would she do then?

She had to decide if the conversation with Judge Quigley had stoked her hope or quenched it. Even if they found Mrs. Marshall, she might not want to testify against Jacob, and even if she did, her testimony might not be strong enough to grant an annulment. On top of that, Jacob would do his level best to terrify the woman and ridicule her. Too many things could go wrong, and she didn't like it. David shouldn't become a pawn in Jacob's schemes.

"Cora." Ethan's deep voice was like a caress.

She turned around and found him close to her. Concern furrowed his brow.

"How are you?" He leant against the wall next to her, regarding her from underneath his long eyelashes.

"Too many dark thoughts. I don't want to lose David." She wrapped her arms around herself.

"Roxbury will not have him. You have my word."

She pressed two fingers to her temples. "When you said you wanted to provide for us—"

He stepped closer. "You and David won't lack anything."

She appreciated his offer; she really did. But... "I know you expect nothing from me."

He stiffened. "But?"

"I've been at Jacob's mercy, or lack thereof, most of my adult life. I know you aren't him, but I don't want to be at the mercy of a man again." Goodness, it came out harsher than she thought. "What I mean," she hurried to say when he tensed, "is that my independence, both legal and financial, is of extreme importance to me. I want to accept your help, but at the same time, I want to provide for myself. My dowry wasn't large. It won't support me. I want to be able to protect my son. What will happen if you can't provide for us any longer? If you're forced to cut off my allowance because of a legal situation? Or if you find a wife—"

"Cora," he warned.

"We must think of all the possible outcomes. You're a marquess. You're expected to marry and produce an heir. I'll be your dirty secret anyone could use against you."

He pressed his lips in a flat line. "I am a man of my word. If I promise I'll provide for you and David, that's exactly what I'm going to do. It is a matter of trust. I do hope you trust me."

"I do, Ethan, with all my heart. Then you should understand why it's important for me to be independent. Life is unpredictable. Things can change in a moment. I want to have a job that will allow me to provide for David myself. And I told you. I will accept your money for as long as you'll provide it."

He lowered his gaze. His dark eyelashes fanned over his cheeks. "Tell me how I can help you achieve the life you want, and I'll do my best."

Once again, he proved to her how wonderful he was. Yes, he was an honourable man but a dominant one as well. Yet here he was, ready to support her. If she didn't already love him, she would fall in love with him right then.

On sheer impulse, she threw herself at him and hugged him with all the strength she could muster. His reply was immediate. He wrapped his arms around her and pulled her closer to his warmth. She needed a hug. She needed him.

He wouldn't take advantage of his position of power over her, she was certain of that, but she had to find her independence for herself and David. Maybe he found it hard to contemplate a terrible scenario in which everything went wrong, but she had to do it.

He caressed her cheek and brushed the softest of kisses on her forehead. A burning tingle started at the base of her neck and slithered down her back.

"I'm here for you and David," he whispered against her skin. "Whatever you need, I'll do my best to provide."

She tilted her head back to see his face. "You're the best gentleman I've ever met, and I love and trust you with all my heart."

He dipped his gaze to her lips, causing them to itch a little. She darted out her tongue and ran it over her bottom lip. Pure hunger ignited his stare as he watched the gesture with predatory intent. He inched closer and paused a breath away from her lips. His whole body tensed as he waited for her permission. She rose on her tiptoes and pressed her lips against his. A low growl rumbled from his chest. He kissed her back, cradling her body as if it were the most precious thing he'd ever touched.

She parted her lips and stroked his with the tip of her tongue. Another growl came out of him as he opened his mouth to devour hers. She welcomed him into hers, and the moment their tongues touched, something broke in her chest. All her need for love and care burst out of her. Not only that. She wanted to give him love and care too.

She gripped his head and tangled her fingers through his thick hair. His passion exploded too as he thrust his tongue into her mouth and conquered it with dominant lashes. He gently pushed her against the wall, caging her with his body and arms. Desperate for more closeness, she shoved aside his jacket and ran her hands over his chest. She wanted to feel his warm skin under her palms and his firm lips on her neck.

He kissed her deeper, trailing a hand up her waist to her breast. "Cora, I want you in my bed."

"I want to be in your bed, too."

"I want to wake up next to you every morning and—"

Whatever he meant to say was cut off by the sound of angry steps stomping towards them.

"No," David shouted, his face reddening. "You promised. You're a liar." He lunged and tackled Ethan hard enough to force him to step back from Cora. "You lied." He shoved Ethan with his clenched fists.

"David, stop." She tried to pull him back, but he didn't budge.

"He gave me his word that he wouldn't touch you." He pointed an accusatory finger at Ethan. "That he wouldn't expect you to... to..."

"David, it's not what you think." Cora grabbed his arm, but he shrugged her off.

"How could you!" David shook with rage.

Ethan shook his head. "I didn't break my promise. I didn't touch her against her will."

"I trusted you." David's voice quivered. "I thought you were different."

"I swear it," Ethan said, his voice cracking as well. "I didn't force her."

"Liar." David's eyes ignited. He obviously wasn't listening.

Enough. Cora stepped in front of his son and took his shoulders, forcing him to stare at her. "Ethan didn't do anything wrong. He didn't force me. You misunderstood what happened. He would never hurt me."

Tears hung on David's eyelashes. "He was all over you."

"And I wanted it." She cupped his heated face. "Ethan is an honourable gentleman. He kept his promise. I'm not completely inept. If I hadn't wanted to be kissed by him, I would have fought him. Did you see me fighting him and screaming? You know I can do that. You've seen me countless times screaming at your father."

"I would never touch her inappropriately," Ethan said. The hurt in his expression upset her. "I care deeply about you and your mother."

"Is it true?" David asked. "He didn't force you?"

"He didn't. I'm telling the truth. I would never lie to you, sweetheart."

"I'm sorry." David rushed out of the room. His footsteps echoed from the hallway and died down.

Ethan ran a hand over his face. "I'm sorry."

"Don't apologise. You did nothing wrong."

"I should have talked to him."

She loved how David had the courage to stand up against Ethan to protect her, but he'd misunderstood what had happened.

"I'll talk to him." She started to go after David, but Ethan stopped her.

"I'll speak with him. Let me. He and I had a pact, and he feels betrayed by me. I must set it right. I love him too." He brushed his knuckles against her cheeks before going after David.

twenty-two

ETHAN HAD FACED many battles and intense conversations, but the one he was about to have with David bothered him. David's hurt and his angry words had been a dagger to Ethan's heart. He hated that David had felt betrayed. David had been let down by his own father. Ethan had to do better if he wanted to take care of him.

"David?" He knocked on David's ajar door. Through the crack, he caught a glimpse of David lying on the bed, his face buried in the pillow. "May I come in?"

David didn't answer or move.

Ethan stepped inside tentatively. "I'm sorry for what happened."

No answer. David didn't even stir.

"But I assure you, I swear on my honour that I hold your mother in high esteem, and I didn't break my promise to you." He sat on the edge of the bed. "I admire her, adore her. She's an amazing woman. My intentions towards her are noble. I would never force my attentions on her. I'm lucky enough that she reciprocates and returns my affection."

David propped himself up. His eyes were red and swollen. He

wiped the tears quickly with the back of his hands. "Do you want to marry her?"

Ethan couldn't understand if David hoped for a yes or if the thought horrified him. The boy's tone was flat with a hint of sadness.

"If she would have me, yes." He meant it. "I want to marry her. I want her to share the rest of my life with her."

The best way to take care of Cora was to marry her and secure a future for her and David. But that wasn't the reason he wanted to marry her. She was indeed an amazing woman, strong and compassionate, beautiful and clever. He couldn't imagine anyone better to share his life with.

"I thought you were..." David traced the pattern on the quilt with a finger.

"I wasn't. I wouldn't lie to you." He put a hand on his chest. "Our deal is still standing."

"I apologise, sir," David whispered.

"Apologies accepted." Ethan stroked David's shoulder. "But I understand. You were protecting your mother. You were brave. I admire your courage."

The boy's face didn't brighten. "If you marry my mama, we'll become a family. Does it mean you..." He sucked in a shaky breath. "You want me in your life as part of your family?" The question was barely a whisper but carried so much fear to give Ethan the chills.

"There's nothing I want more than to take care of you and have you by my side. I love you, David. You're already part of my family." He moved at the same time as David did.

They hugged each other. David hid his face in Ethan's chest, shaking.

Ethan rubbed his back. "Of course I want you in my life if you want me in yours. And if your mother doesn't want to marry me, I'll take care of you all the same, and we'll find a way to see each other. Our bond won't break. No matter what."

A sob left David, and Ethan kissed the top of his head. He expected David to refuse the hugs and kisses; that was what Ethan would have done at David's age. Many times he'd slipped free of his father's embrace or rolled his eyes at his mother's kisses. He'd endured kisses and hugs for the sake of his parents but had voiced his complaints. But David was different. He needed all the affection his father had denied him.

Ethan regretted having kept his parents' affection at a distance. Only now he understood how much his father and mother must have wanted to hug and kiss him.

He held David until the boy stopped shaking. "Do I have your blessing for courting your mother?"

David wiped his face. "I hope she says yes."

He handed David a handkerchief. "I don't want to give you false hopes, though. First, she must obtain an annulment, and it's a rather complicated affair. Then she has to agree to marry me."

"If Mother gets an annulment, does it mean I won't be Lord Roxbury's son anymore?" Too much hope gleamed in his eyes.

Ethan hated to break the boy's heart. "We can't change the fact Lord Roxbury is your father, but we can fight for your right to choose with whom you want to live."

David nodded solemnly. "I'll do anything you ask."

It was better to prepare him for what was coming. "If the request for an annulment fails, your mother wants to leave England with you. Are you ready for that?"

"If it can help Mama get away from Lord Roxbury, yes, but I would miss you terribly."

"So would I. You are brave indeed." He caressed David's hair.

"If everything goes wrong, if we can't leave, what are we going to do?" David twisted the handkerchief. Like Cora, he was preparing himself for the worst possible situation. "I don't want to return to Lord Roxbury's house. I want to stay here with you."

Heartbreaking. Now Ethan understood why Cora had told him not to make promises he couldn't keep. If everything went wrong, he was ready to flee with Cora and David, which meant a life away from England. But he couldn't promise David he would leave with them. Not yet. "We must fight for the annulment first. Then we'll see."

"I'll fight back." David clenched his fists. "If Lord Roxbury wants me back, I'll fight him. Harry promised to help me. He knows many tricks to repel an opponent. He'll teach me how to use a slingshot and fighting techniques from the far east in case Lord Roxbury wants to shoot me again. Harry couldn't believe me when I told him Lord Roxbury had tried to shoot me. He said that nothing so exciting had ever happened to him."

Oh, boy. "Let's use Harry as the last resort, shall we?"

A corner of David's mouth quirked up. "He showed me how to make firecrackers from pine cones and resin."

"Lovely. Mrs. Parker must be beside herself with happiness."

David chuckled.

"Take what Harry says and does with caution."

David laughed. "He's funny though, and he's my friend. I don't want to leave him too."

As they hugged each other again, Ethan made a decision then and there. Yes, if Cora didn't get an annulment, he would flee with her and David.

THE TRIP back to London was a silent one. Cora wished time would speed so she'd learn what would happen to her. Ethan's tense expression showed his concern. Even Harry sat in silence, staring at the view of green fields and hills, dozing off now and then. David slept with his head on her shoulder, gripping her hand with surprising strength. Mrs. Parker dozed off, her head hanging over her chest.

"I sent a wire to Finn yesterday," Ethan said. "Hopefully, when we're back, we should receive an answer about Mrs. Marshall."

She wrung her hands, hoping that Mrs. Marshall wasn't dead or refused to help her.

"Stop worrying," Ethan whispered, seemingly reading her mind.

"How do you know what I was thinking?" She pouted.

"It was written all over your face. I've seen that dark expression on the faces of many soldiers before a battle. The truth is that we don't know what will happen, thus despairing is pointless."

"Thinking about the worst possible outcome prepares me for it."

"No. It only poisons your mind with failure." He kissed her knuckles. "You've been with Roxbury for too long, and now you find it hard to believe a better future is possible. Your first fight against him is to free yourself from the shackles of despair he restrained you with. Learn to hope. You'll be surprised by how powerful hope is."

It was a beautiful speech, but worry gripped her all the same. The option of leaving England had lost its appeal. Until a while ago, it'd been her dream. Now it was a nightmare because leaving Ethan would crush her. Because she wanted everything. She wanted to be rid of Jacob, to be free to love Ethan, and to live happily with her new family.

She focused on the beautiful image of herself, Ethan, and David swimming together and laughing. That was the future she wanted. That was the future she would fight for.

THE BOISTEROUS VOICES coming from downstairs in the inn didn't let Cora sleep. Her shoulder was fine, but the trip still exhausted her. Hence their stop. Mrs. Parker, David, and Harry didn't share her predicament since they'd fallen asleep the moment they'd touched their pillows.

Although it might be the worry more than the patrons' voices to trouble her. She pushed the quilt aside and tiptoed out of the room. The smell of roasted chicken and ale wafted from the stairs at the bottom of the corridor. She wrapped the shawl around her shoulders and stared at the darkness through the window in the empty corridor. Good gracious. Not a street lamp lit the road. Only the moonlight glowed over the treetops. She had to decide if she preferred the darkness of the country or the constant light of London's nights.

She felt Ethan's presence before he spoke.

He stood behind her. "Are you unwell?"

Of course he'd ask that. She turned around and leant against him. "No. Only nervous."

He hugged her, taking her weight. "You are barefoot."

She wiggled her toes. "My feet are a bit cold."

"I can't allow that." He lifted her by the waist and gathered her in his arms.

She didn't protest, quite the opposite. His scent enveloped her when he carried her to his bedroom and laid her on his bed.

"Is David all right?" He rubbed her foot.

"Asleep. Everyone fell asleep immediately." She breathed faster as he massaged her toes and ankles. "I'm tired but couldn't sleep."

"You're too tense." He slid his hand up her calf, kneading the muscle.

"Yes, perhaps I am." Her pulse quickened although he wasn't doing anything inappropriate. But seeing him kneel in front of her with his hands up her skirt conjured up all sorts of delicious visions.

He pushed her legs apart and made room for his bulk between them. His stare struck a chord deep inside her. He closed his eyes and inhaled deeply. "Your scent is driving me mad."

"My scent?"

He shoved her nightgown and dressing gown up her legs, baring them. After he pushed her thighs further apart, he inhaled again. "Here it's so strong." He trailed his fingers along her inner thighs.

She trembled with each delicate touch of his fingertips. A jolt of desire went through her when he brushed his lips against her skin. The light stubble on his jaw enhanced the sensation, tearing a moan out of her. He brought her legs over his shoulders until she was sprawled in front of him, her legs wrapped around his neck. He shot her a predatory glare before dipping his head. The first lash of his tongue sent a shudder through her body and caused her toes to curl. She gripped the bedsheet as he took his time to kiss her deeply, pushing his tongue inside her and teasing her nub with his lips. His thumb stroked her now and then, slipping inside her gently.

The pleasure was so intense she couldn't speak, only moan. As he drew slow circles with the tip of his tongue, the onslaught of pleasure caught her by surprise. The release was almost painful, going through her body like a bolt of lightning. An incoherent sound came out of her. Her back arched of its own accord. She fell limp on the bed, enjoying every last ounce of her release. He grazed her inner thigh lightly and kissed his way up to her breasts.

"You're too sweet. I can't resist." He shoved aside her garments and latched his mouth around her nipple.

Crying out in pleasure, she wrapped her arms and legs around him. He followed her, never stopping tonguing her nipple. She writhed and rolled her hips, desperate to touch more of his skin.

"Take me, Ethan. Please." She tangled her fingers through his thick hair and pulled his head up for a savage kiss.

He stretched out on top of her without hurting her though. A green fire set his eyes ablaze with hunger. His chest heaved as he sheathed himself inside her with one smooth thrust. The sensation of being filled and stretched made her jerk her hips up to meet him and feel him deeper. He cursed under his breath before kissing her lips. His features were contorted with desire as he thrust in and out of her.

"I love you, Cora," he said.

His dark husky voice and the possessiveness in his gaze were a stark contrast with the tender, slow movements he made in and out of her. He contained his strength for her sake. His restraint was the most romantic gesture she'd ever received, more romantic than Jacob's serenade or flowers.

They laced their fingers together, staring at each other, joined by their bodies and souls, sharing their breath.

"I love you, Ethan," she whispered as he pumped into her.

They found their release at the same time, lost in each other's gaze. He pulled out of her at the last moment but kept holding her hands and breathing with her as she trembled underneath him. He rolled off her and gathered her in his arms, forming a protective shell around her.

"Nothing will harm you as long as I live," he said, kissing her neck.

She'd been wrong to lose hope. She'd been wrong to poison her moments with him with dark thoughts. Their love would never be crushed by whatever happened to them.

She squeezed him tightly. He stroked her hair and back until she fell asleep in the safety of his embrace.

twenty-three

GOING THROUGH THE mail had never been so nerve-wracking for Cora. She and Ethan had barely time to step into his house in London before they rushed upstairs to his study and went through all the letters, bills, and messages he'd received. The amount was twice bigger than what Jacob received. Despite Ethan employed a secretary, the amount he had to check himself was impressive. She removed her gloves and tossed them on a chair while he searched for Finn's letter.

He drew in a long breath. "It's this one." He showed the message to her before skimming it. "Finn found Mrs. Marshall. Damn. She works in Mrs. Sterling's house," he said the lady's name with a strained note.

"Is that a problem?"

"Mrs. Sterling isn't exactly fond of me." He sat on the chair next to her. "Her husband, James, was one of my lieutenants. We fought together against the Thorne Pirates. A good man but never followed my orders. He disobeyed me and died when the pirates blew up a warehouse. I've never told Mrs. Sterling the truth about why James died. She considers me responsible for his death because I didn't protect him. She keeps refusing the allowance that would allow her and her daughter to live decently. That's how much she hates me."

"If James had followed your orders, would he be alive today?"

"I can't answer that for certain. Surely, he wouldn't have died that day, but there had been other battles. But Mrs. Sterling is a wife who lost her beloved husband. She can say whatever she wants. She can blame me or insult me. I would never complain or judge her. If blaming me helps her carry on, I'm all right with that. But she might influence Mrs. Marshall and forbid her to testify."

She exhaled, releasing her frustration. Everywhere they turned, there was something against them. "We should talk to Mrs. Marshall and hope she wants to get involved in my legal quandary. And if she refuses, we'll find another way." She leant back in the chair. "I'll send a message to Mrs. Marshall immediately."

He smiled. "You're being more optimistic."

"A little step towards the light."

"There's something else I must tell you." His serious tone caused her to sit upright.

"Yes?"

He took her hand, a light tremor going through him. "I asked David permission to court you."

A quiver went down her back. "Really?"

"He asked me if I wanted to marry you and build a family with you and him, and I replied in earnest. When you get an annulment, I want to marry you and live with you and David by my side."

A dream. A riot of emotions roared within her. The more she wanted that future, the more frightened of losing it she was. "I want that too."

He caressed her cheek. "I know what you're thinking. Mrs. Marshall could refuse to testify, and even if she does, Roxbury could fight the annulment, or insist on taking David."

She chuckled bitterly. "You know me too well. Is David happy about the possibility of you marrying me?"

"Very much although he's aware of the difficulties. He understands."

Her voice shook with emotion. "If I don't get the annulment, he'll be devastated."

"We'll all be devastated, and both David and I love you very much. And I do want to marry you." His deep, calm voice worked wonders on her inner turmoil. Being hopeful and optimistic required more effort than worry. He cupped her face. "More than anything. I want to be your husband and take care of you. I want to give you all the love you were denied. Having dreams isn't wrong. You can't be miserable, waiting for a grim future that might never be."

"You're right." She leant against his touch. His words of hope relieved and frightened her in equal measure. "I have more to lose now than before."

He kissed her. "You don't have to do everything alone. We're together. David included."

"What about your soldiers? Are you ready to sacrifice the Royal Veterans' Society for me? Is it even right to do so?"

A muscle in his jaw bunched. "I'll find a solution for my men. Now that Lady Kingsley is on my side, I'm more hopeful. You..." He kissed her hand. "You're irreplaceable."

She hadn't expected that. "Ethan."

"Roxbury made you believe nothing good could possibly happen to your life. But it's a lie. I know from experience that despairing doesn't make you stronger. It makes you miserable."

She hugged him, feeding on his strength and hope. "You're like a warm fireplace after a long, cold walk in the dark."

"That's how love should feel."

~

MRS. MARSHALL HADN'T CHANGED MUCH since the last time Cora had seen her, except for one important detail. The air of constant sadness, caused by her frequent arguments with Jacob, was gone from her face, replaced by a serene smile and a bright gaze. The sunlight going through the leafy trees in Ethan's garden exalted her complexion. She'd looked older when at Jacob's employment.

Her motherly hug brought happy tears to Cora's eyes. "My lady. What a pleasure seeing you again."

Cora returned the hug, her heartbeat stuttering with nostalgia. "Mrs. Marshall. I've missed you."

Ethan loomed behind them, silent and protective like a gargoyle, as Cora and Mrs. Marshall exchanged greetings and memories.

"What did you want to talk to me about?" Mrs. Marshall sat on a bench under a weeping willow tree. So fitting.

"I need your help in regard to a very delicate matter." Cora told again the whole story about Jacob trying to kill David and ending up shooting at her.

The shock of that night never failed to cause her to hitch a breath or to feel the sting of the bullet in her chest. Mrs. Marshall's expression tightened in a familiar manner as Cora told her that the shot would have killed David.

When she finished explaining about the annulment, she closed her hand around Mrs. Marshall's. "I need your testimony to prove that Jacob behaved cruelly to David and me. Your testimony will be crucial to granting David and me our freedom. Please."

Mrs. Marshall exhaled. Sadness darkened her expression. "See, Lord Roxbury met with Mrs. Sterling the other week."

"What?" Cora and Ethan said together.

Mrs. Marshall nodded. "I don't know what they talked about, but after the meeting, Mrs. Sterling summoned me. She forbade me from getting involved in Lord Roxbury's business. She actually forbade me from meeting you, but when I read your message, I couldn't ignore it. Rumours about Lady Roxbury having nearly killed her husband have circulated for weeks. Knowing how Lord Roxbury behaved with you, I worried you might have done something reckless. No one knew where you were. No one heard your version of the incident. That's why I wanted to see you. But if I don't obey Mrs. Sterling, I'll lose my job, and I'm too old to find employment elsewhere. Also..." She shot a fleeting glance at Ethan. "Rumour has it that you're Lord Stark's mistress."

Ethan didn't flinch, but then again, they couldn't expect to keep their relationship secret for long.

Cora mentally scolded herself. They'd assumed Jacob had been quiet in the past few weeks. Quite the opposite. He was one step ahead of them. He'd known he needed to stop Mrs. Marshall from cooperating with Cora before Cora herself knew she needed the former governess's testimony. She had to respond in kind.

"I wish to speak to Mrs. Sterling. Alone," she added before Ethan could say anything. "Can we go to see her, please?"

"Mrs. Sterling won't see you and will give me the sack," Mrs. Marshall said.

"If you lose your job," Ethan said, "I'll employ you."

Cora couldn't help but smile at him.

Mrs. Marshall didn't look relieved. "Thank you, Lord Stark, but I'm fond of Mrs. Sterling and her daughter. I've been with her since well before her tragedy. It's not simply my job. I don't want to give her another cause of pain."

"I'll take full responsibility." Cora ignored the little sting Mrs. Marshall's words gave her. The governess showed more loyalty towards Mrs. Sterling than towards her former employer. Maybe it was understandable, but Mrs. Sterling didn't risk losing everything, including her daughter. "Please. Jacob shot me. What will happen if David and I are forced to be with him again? What if Jacob finally kills one of us? Do you want David's death on your conscience?" She was playing dirty, but for David, she would do anything.

Mrs. Marshall paled but nodded. "I'll take you to her."

THE DRIVE to Mrs. Sterling's townhouse was both long and short. Cora wanted to conclude the meeting as quickly as possible, but at the same time, she doubted her negotiation skills, wishing for more time to prepare a convincing speech.

She took a deep breath, watching Mrs. Sterling's door from Ethan's carriage. The dark walls of the modest but decent town-house lacked any decorations. No pots of flowers, bright curtains, or statues. If the widow was anything like her house, Cora would face a rather austere woman.

Ethan sat next to her in the carriage. "It's better if I don't show myself unless you want me to come with you."

"Thank you, but I want to see her alone."

Ethan held the door open as Cora and Mrs. Marshall exited the carriage and entered the gloomy townhouse.

"I'll take all the blame for this encounter," Cora said, stepping into the hallway. "Mrs. Sterling won't punish you."

"Thank you." Mrs. Marshall showed her to the sitting room. "Please try to understand, my lady. I'm very fond of you and David. But Mrs. Sterling lost her husband, and her daughter is having trouble recovering from the loss. They're going through a dark moment. If it weren't for her little daughter, Mrs. Sterling wouldn't carry on."

"You don't owe me an explanation. Really." If she lost Ethan, she would go through a dark moment too. But she was fighting for her family. If she needed to be a hag, she would be.

"I'll call Mrs. Sterling." Mrs. Marshall bowed in her way out.

Left alone in the sitting room, Cora paced on the oriental carpet, thinking about not ruining her chance. Was she making promises she couldn't keep? No, Ethan was right. She had to be hopeful and not despair. She had to be as strong as he was. She paused when loud voices came from upstairs. She couldn't understand the words, but one came loud and clear: betrayal. Footfalls echoed. A door slammed, causing the paintings on the wall to shake. She swallowed hard.

The door was flung open. "What is the meaning of this?"

Cora jutted out her chin. She'd faced Jacob countless times. She could win this battle.

Mrs. Sterling cut a striking figure, dressed in her widow's weeds. The dark fabric made her young face look older but enhanced her pointed chin and clever eyes. Cora's chest tightened for the woman who must have known an unbearable pain too soon. If she was going to be honest, being a widow had never been a terrifying possibility for her. But Ethan was another matter.

"Lady Roxbury." She didn't offer a seat to Cora as she strode into the room, her fury palpable. "I don't understand why you're here. And Mrs. Marshall shouldn't have allowed you to come. I don't want you in my house."

Cora held up a hand. "I'm the only one to be blamed. I didn't give Mrs. Marshall any choice. I forced her to take me here. I used our friendship to push her to do me this favour, for I must speak to you."

Mrs. Sterling pressed her pale lips in a white slash. Cora wondered when the last time the woman had enjoyed a proper meal and a good night's sleep had been.

"About what?" she asked.

"I need Mrs. Marshall's help to get an annulment from Lord Roxbury." Straight to the point. "And I need you to let her help me."

"I will not change my mind," Mrs. Sterling said, closing her bony hands. "I have no quarrel against you, my lady, and I'm sorry for your troubles, but I'm aware of your association with Lord

Stark and the fact he's fond of you. Whatever displeases Lord Stark pleases me."

"I won't discuss your personal dislike of Lord Stark. You have your reasons." Unfounded, but she wouldn't speak ill of Mrs. Sterling's husband.

Mrs. Sterling huffed. "I bet he told you not so charming things about me. Did he call me a hag?"

How little did she know about Ethan.

Cora shook her head. "Actually, Lord Stark defended you when I pointed out that your judgement of him was unfair. He's never spoken a single ill word about you."

The lady arched her brow. "He defended me?"

"He said that after your loss, you had the right to say whatever you wanted, even to insult him, and he wouldn't judge you or complain." Her defence of Ethan wasn't a strategy to win the widow's help. No one could accuse Ethan of being dishonourable in front of her.

A moment of thick silence followed. Only the ticking of the clock on the mantelpiece filled it.

"Why would he say such a thing?" Mrs. Sterling sounded genuinely curious.

"Lord Stark knows what love is. He knows how painful losing someone can be. He has nothing but respect for you and your loss, and he sincerely wishes to take care of you and your daughter. Trust me, he'll never stop offering his help for any reason. No matter how many times you reject him."

Mrs. Sterling's pale cheeks flamed red, hard to say if in anger or another emotion. "Why should I help you?"

"Because you shouldn't trust a word my husband said." Cora lifted her chin. "I won't tell you all my story, but I'll show you." She unbuttoned her shirt and uncovered the rounded scar on her breast. "Jacob shot me. I nearly bled to death. Lord Stark saved my life in more ways than once. He stitched the wound and gave me his blood without expecting anything from me."

Mrs. Sterling moved closer with tentative steps and examined the wound. "Lord Roxbury said you tried to kill him and then you fled with David to hide in your lover's house, Lord Stark's house."

She shook her head. "He tried to shoot David. I stepped in front of my son to protect him, and the bullet hit me. My son David carried me to Lord Stark's house, and he's proven to be nothing but a gentleman."

"Why would Lord Roxbury shoot his own son?" Mrs. Sterling gripped the back of a chair as if needing support.

"Jacob has despised David from the moment he was born, regarding him as too stupid to be a Roxbury. My son isn't allowed to call Jacob father, and in a way, I'm glad of that. Because a father shouldn't humiliate his son whenever he makes a mistake, shouldn't tell him he's a worthless rat. No man behaving like that deserves to be called a father." From Mrs. Sterling's stern face, Cora couldn't understand if her words had the desired effect. "Jacob hates me too. When we first met, he lured me in with flowers, poems, and romantic words only to discard me once we were married." She took a step closer. "Mrs. Sterling, you understand my position. I can't return to Jacob's house. I have nothing. No money, no position, no husband deserving of that name, and no protection. No means to keep my son safe. My only wish is to regain freedom for my son and me. I beg you. My future is in your hands. Let Mrs. Marshall testify. Let her tell the truth. Jacob is a coward who must face his sins. Only you can bring me the justice my son and I desperately need and deserve. Please." She wouldn't cry in front of the widow lest Mrs. Sterling believe Cora tried to manipulate her.

Mrs. Sterling lowered her gaze, shivering. "I have a daughter," she said after a long pause. "Annette. Without James, she's the only thing keeping me alive. She's my reason to leave the bed in the morning. She's the reason I keep eating. I would do anything to protect her." She raised her gaze to Cora, showing the ardent flames in it. "From one mother to another, I will help you, my lady."

Cora exhaled. "Thank you."

"And..." Mrs. Sterling straightened. Her cheeks regained a bit of colour. "Please tell Lord Stark that I accept the allowance."

twenty-four

IT WAS CURIOUS how to invalidate one single certificate, a person had to produce a hundred different certificates supplied by a hundred different officers, solicitors, and clerks.

For three weeks, Cora had done nothing but sign and fill out forms and documents, write letters to solicitors, and have interviews with several members of the House of Lords. She was tired of recounting the story of her marriage, especially since she didn't understand if her words fell on sympathetic ears or not. As true politicians, the lords she'd spoken with had remained unfathomable. At least Mrs. Sterling had shown some compassion.

Judge Quigley seemed to conjure up new documents to read and sign and forms to fill out of thin air with the unapologetic ease only bureaucrats possessed, and poor Mrs. Marshall had written pages upon pages to describe what she'd seen while at Jacob's service on top of having to repeat her testimony no less than twenty-seven times. David couldn't escape the interviews either. He'd been questioned and examined as much as Cora and Mrs. Marshall, never contradicting himself. But then again, when one told the truth, there was no need to remember anything. In all that chaos, Ethan's legal problem with his centre had been neglected. But Ethan had told her his solicitors were handling the case, whatever that meant.

After all the frenetic activity of documents and interviews, it was a matter of waiting for answers while cooped up in Ethan's house as a precaution in case Jacob got ideas. He'd shot her once. He could shoot her twice.

Not that Cora could complain about the inactivity, but if she could take a walk in the park, the waiting would be less consuming. Not even the books and the library helped speed up the time. She reclined on the Chesterfield sofa, opening and closing the book without reading a word, too worried to do anything.

Ethan walked inside with David. "Cora, fancy a walk? You've been in the house for too long."

Goodness. He truly could read her mind. "What about Jacob? What if he hurts us?"

David tilted his head. "You're right, sir. Mama always thinks the worst."

"But... well..." No point in ending her protest. He was right.

"Judge Quigley believes that at this point in the case, there's no need not to go out. Finn will come with us. Since the annulment has been filed with the court, he says Roxbury can't force you to do anything until we hear the verdict, and he won't be stupid enough to shoot you in a public place."

"Please, Mama?" David asked, shifting his weight from one foot to another. "Harry wants to play cricket with me."

"Let's go." She couldn't leave the library fast enough.

Warm sunlight caressed Cora's cheeks like a promise of a happy future. A light breeze blew from the north, carrying a prelude to autumn, and the smell of freshly mowed grass filled her lungs. With her arm hooked through Ethan's, she watched Finn, David, and Harry hitting the ball with a cricket bat while Mrs. Parker complained about too much fresh air. The warm day and the two boys enjoying themselves lifted a weight from her chest.

She would live this moment fully. She would enjoy Ethan, David, and the sunlight without poisoning her happiness with fear. It'd taken a long time to learn that lesson, but better late than never.

Sitting under the shade of a tall birch in the park, she snuggled closer to Ethan.

He tugged at her hand. "Do you know what birches symbolise?"

"No idea."

He shifted his position to kiss her hand. "New beginnings."

"I like new beginnings."

The boys' happy voices broke the spell. She laughed as Harry improvised a victory dance after a particularly good delivery. David accused him of cheating. Another normal Tuesday.

Ethan lent closer to whisper in her ear, "Promise me you won't be angry."

She faced him. "About what?"

"Just promise me."

She narrowed her gaze. "Your request is suspicious, but I promise not to be angry. Or try to."

He took out a small velvet box from his pocket. "This is for you." He opened the lid, revealing a beautiful golden band with a gemstone the colour of amber.

Her breath caught in her chest. "Ethan..."

"Don't say it's too early and that we don't know if the annulment will be successful and that the world will end, and we're all doomed, and whatever other disaster you can think of. Please. This once, be optimistic and make me the happiest man in the world."

She pointed a finger at him. "You're making fun of me."

"I wouldn't dare." He smiled. "The stone is an amber sapphire. I didn't know they existed. I chose it because it matches your eyes, and I hope to see it on your finger every day for the rest of our lives."

"It's beautiful." She stretched out her hand, giggling with happiness.

Ethan's chest expanded as he slid the ring onto her finger. "I guess that means you agree to be my wife."

She pouted. "I don't remember you asking."

He barked out a laugh. "Let me make amends." He kissed her hand. "My lovely Cora, would you do me the great honour of being my—"

"Yes." She wrapped her arms around his neck. "Yes, yes, yes." She scattered kisses on his face as he hugged her and laughed.

"Your lordship, your ladyship, please." Mrs. Parker dabbed her forehead with a handkerchief. "Congratulations, by the way, but please."

"You're right, Mrs. Parker," Cora said.

"We'll be happy. I promise," he whispered, moving away from Cora.

"I believe you." Her heart burst with joy.

"What a charismatic scene." A shadow crept over Cora.

She hadn't heard Jacob's voice in weeks, but hearing it now brought her back in time in a moment. Visions of the dark days with him flashed across her mind. Shivers danced on her skin. Cold gripped her stomach, and her knees threatened to buckle. She released Ethan and gazed up, and here he was, standing like a crow in front of her, obscuring the sunlight.

Ethan shot up before she could draw her next breath. "Leave."

Jacob didn't spare a glance at him. He kept his stare on Cora. "Believe me, I have no intention of enduring your company more than necessary. I simply wanted to deliver a quick message to *my* wife." He glared at the ring.

Cora stood up on trembling legs. Ethan wrapped an arm around her waist, holding her up. "Then speak and leave, for I have no intention of enduring your company either."

David, Harry, and Finn had stopped playing. David held

Finn's hand, and Harry stood in front of him, shielding him from Jacob with his cricket bat at the ready.

"It would be in your interest to drop your absurd request for an annulment." Jacob didn't spare the slightest bit of attention to David. "If you push, I'll push back." Without any further words, he pivoted and left. His black coat billowed behind him like a dark banner.

Cora snuggled closer to Ethan, needing his strength. "What did he mean?" she asked.

"Nothing we weren't prepared to hear," Ethan said.

THE MOMENT ETHAN had given Cora the ring should have been one to rejoice and commit to memory. The symbol of a new beginning for them. Roxbury had tainted it with his poison. For once, Ethan's optimism had been shaken.

He sat in the chair in his study with Cora curled up on his lap. She hadn't smiled once since the encounter with Roxbury, and he hated that Roxbury had robbed them of their joy.

He stroked her back and kissed the top of her head. "Whatever he unleashes against us, we'll fight it together. We're a family. He's a lonely, pathetic man who doesn't have anyone. He can't possibly be stronger than we are."

"I agree, but Jacob is also ruthless and cruel. We wouldn't do certain things because we're decent. He isn't. He won't have any scruples about bribing, manipulating, or using other people to get what he wants. I don't trust him. I've seen him furious, but he was beyond that. We provoked him, and he'll lash back."

"Let him. We'll fight back. I'm not afraid of him."

She rested her head on his chest. "And I'm tired of him in my life."

"Ethan, your ladyship." Finn barged inside, shoving the door hard enough to make it hit the wall. He nearly lost his balance on his wooden leg as he rushed to give them a folder. "It's arrived from the court."

He froze. Cora remained still.

"Open it," Ethan said, holding Cora tightly.

So far, he'd been confident about their future, but he couldn't deny a hint of concern as he watched the innocent-looking folder that might make him the happiest man in the empire.

"Why me? Oh, bother." Finn ripped the envelope and skimmed the document. His happiness burst out. "It's done. You won. You've got the annulment. You aren't married anymore." He waved the documents as if they were one of those flags people used to greet the queen on the street.

It took a moment for Ethan to understand he didn't need to be worried anymore. They won. Roxbury's cruelty had lost. Cora and David were free.

"Thank heavens." Ethan sagged in the armchair, squeezing Cora against him. No one would take her away from him. She would be his wife. They would share their lives. He had a family.

Cora raised her fists as David would do.

Finn stuck his head out of the door and yelled, "We won. Everyone. We won."

David rushed into the room and leapt into Ethan's arms, climbing over his mother and making a mess of limbs, kisses, and clothes.

"Mama."

Ethan scattered kisses on Cora's cheeks and David's face, laughing and shouting at the same time. His family was in his arms.

Mrs. Parker cried in her handkerchief, and Harry ran around, hooting and shooting small firecrackers in the room. One porcelain vase fell prey to Harry's enthusiasm. Red sparks flew towards the ceiling as the loud bangs covered the noise of London's traffic, Mrs. Parker's protests, and Finn chasing his son.

But this time, Ethan didn't scold him.

twenty-five

ETHAN COULDN'T THINK of a better place to celebrate their legal victory than the Royal Veterans' Society. Finn, Harry, Lady Kingsley, her brother, and all the people who worked with him were gathered in the main hall. One large gathering of all the people he cared about. Lady Kingsley had sided with Ethan against Roxbury's motion. The chances Roxbury could win that case were rather slim. Cora looked ecstatic. The permanent flush on her cheeks exalted her lovely freckles. David didn't stop smiling or laughing.

Ethan lost count of how many congratulations and toasts he'd received and exchanged with his friends. The main hall of the centre had been adorned with festoons and flowers. Cakes and sandwiches competed for space on the long table. A simple feast, but the love he felt for his family was powerful.

"Is it true you're engaged to be married, Commander?" Fraser asked.

"May I see what's under the eye patch, Mr. Fraser?" Harry asked.

Ethan kissed Cora's cheek, glad he didn't have to hide his feelings anymore. "Will you show them?"

She giggled and raised her hand. "My engagement ring." She showed her amber sapphire to everyone with a proud look.

Lady Kingsley smiled at Ethan and raised her glass to them. "Well done, my lady."

"We'll have a wedding reception as soon as possible." Ethan kissed Cora again, lingering more than it was polite, but he pretended not to hear the lady's gasp.

"A wedding." Harry fished out a firecracker and a match from his pockets. "Let's celebrate."

His father stopped him. "No firecrackers here."

Harry stooped his shoulders. "Only one?"

"No, the noise will upset our friends," Finn said in a low tone.

Mrs. Parker pushed a trolley where a tall cake rested on the top. Cherry flowers and whipped cream adorned the last layer. "A celebration isn't a celebration without a cake. Cook had to be quick, but I can assure you the result is delicious."

Ethan clapped his hands and cheered with everyone. He fed dollops of cream to Cora, smearing the tip of her nose in the process. She laughed so hard she sagged against him. Until she stopped laughing and turned serious, staring at a point behind him.

"What is it?" He cupped her face.

She paled. "He's here."

Roxbury entered the hall, clicking the heels of his tall boots against the wooden floor. Silence dropped. Only the sound of Roxbury's footfalls echoed in the high ceiling. David rushed towards Ethan, breathing hard.

Roxbury stopped in the middle of the room, hands over the pommel of his walking stick. "I'm sorry to interrupt this merry party."

A couple of blue-uniformed constables stood behind him. They shifted their weights nervously.

Ethan wrapped one arm around David and the other around Cora. "What do you want?"

Roxbury pointed a finger at David. "The rat is still my son. The marriage might have been annulled, but David is my son. He'll come with me now."

"You have no right to take him," Ethan said. "Cora is David's sole guardian."

"No." David gripped Ethan's arm with both hands.

"Over my dead body," Cora said, straightening.

Roxbury tilted his head. "That can be arranged."

Ethan held David closer. "David doesn't want to come with you. He stays here with his mother. He had no obligation to live with you, and if you disagree, we'll see you in court."

"I don't give a damn about what David wants. He's my heir, for now. He must return home with me." Roxbury jabbed a finger in the direction of the police. "The law is on my side."

"Lord Roxbury." Judge Quigley came forward. "I must speak. You don't have any authority over the child. The marriage has been annulled. Our motion about Lady Cora being the sole guardian was approved. Before you lay any claims on the child, you must legally recognise him as your heir, but after that, the mother will have the last word either way."

"Which will be no," Cora said.

"I knew you would say that." Roxbury scratched his chin. "But we have a problem because unless David comes with me, the police will kick out your crazy soldiers. I'm still one of the owners of this piece of land, despite the fact Lady Kingsley showed her support to Stark, and you know, my solicitor found something irregular about Lord Stark's late father's documents."

Ethan froze, trying to remain calm.

"What irregularity?" Judge Quigley asked.

Hell.

"Apparently, this building isn't supposed to be used as a medical facility but only for residential purposes," Roxbury said in a fake apologetic tone.

Judge Quigley's eyebrows hit his hairline. "Goodness. So this establishment isn't legal."

Ethan shook with anger. Mutters spread. Cora slid his hand into his.

"And did Detective Inspector Purnell know that?" Judge Quigley asked Finn. "Margaret?" He turned towards his sister.

Finn opened his mouth, but Ethan cut him off. "No. I kept the information secret while my solicitor studied the case to find a solution. Finn had no idea. Even Lady Kingsley didn't know it."

Lady Kingsley put a hand on her rising chest. "Barnaby, you know me. I don't understand property law."

Judge Quigley was about to say something, but Roxbury scoffed.

"Excellent." Roxbury clapped his hands. "Now that we've established how ridiculous you people all are, we can move on from this drama. Here's my proposition. I will help you with this little legal problem and let your soldiers stay here if David comes with me. If you refuse…" He sighed. "Then I'll have your guests kicked out of this building right now. Judge Quigley knows I have every right to do so. Your choice, Stark."

Unfortunately, Roxbury was right, but he wouldn't hand him David. "The boy stays here where he belongs with his family."

"No, the boy will come with me while I file the documents for his custody," Roxbury said.

"That's utmost irregular." Judge Quigley shook a fist. "David stays here."

Roxbury shrugged. "Have it your way then. The police will take your soldiers."

"You'll have to go through me," Ethan said, closing his fists.

"We'll leave, Commander," one of the soldiers said. "You've been kind to us, but we can't allow you to make such a horrible choice."

"We're used to being kicked out," another one said. "This place was too good to be true."

Cora hugged David. "It's not fair. How are you going to live out of here?" she asked the soldiers.

"Since you can't choose between your soldiers and David, I'll take both." Roxbury waved towards the officers. "Gentlemen."

"No, wait." David shrugged free from Cora's grip. "Leave them alone. I'll come with you."

"David, no," Cora said at the same time as Ethan said, "Don't do this."

"Finally, some sense." Roxbury turned around. "Come, rat. Say goodbye to your mother, or should I say, farewell?"

Tears welling in his eyes, David hugged Cora. "Mama."

"No, no." She squeezed him hard. "You aren't leaving me."

"It's my choice." He disentangled himself from her grip. "You and Lord Stark have been brave. It's my turn."

Cora turned towards Ethan. "I have to go with him."

No, no, no. What the hell was happening? Ethan needed to think. With a bit of time, he would manage to find a legal solution. But he hated leaving Cora and David with Roxbury for one single second.

Roxbury smirked. "Good. A proper family reunion. Come, Cora. We have to talk about many things."

David took Ethan's hand. "Thank you for what you have done for me." He wrapped his arms around him. "Thank you, Papa," he whispered. "For me, you're my only papa."

That was the moment Ethan's heart broke. He held David back, feeling the boy's body quivering. No, Ethan wouldn't let him go. Never. "You're my son, David, and I made a promise. I won't let anything happen to you, and I won't let Roxbury take you. Ever." He released David and gently pushed him towards Cora. "I have a proposition," he said.

Roxbury exhaled. "You aren't in the position—"

"I challenge you to a fight." Ethan's voice boomed in the hall.

Roxbury stomped his walking stick on the floor. "I'm not going to fight with you."

"Ethan," Finn said in a low voice. "Lord Roxbury has always kicked your arse. He cheats. What are you doing?"

"The right thing." Ethan stepped towards Roxbury. "Your son doesn't want you as his father. Your wife left you. They both prefer my company because you're a weak, pathetic man who can't fight without cheating. You left the army because you were a coward, hiding behind your father's title and power."

"Shut up." Roxbury twitched his hand over the pommel.

Ethan raised his voice so everyone in the hall would hear his official challenge. "I, Ethan Alexander Hertford , Marquess of Stark, challenge Jacob Wiley, Earl of Roxbury, to a fight." Everyone fell silent and turned towards them. "The prize is David and this building. If I win, you'll leave David alone and sell your part to me." He faced Roxbury. "If you have a shred of honour left, you'll accept the challenge."

"He's always been a coward," Finn said. "Born a coward, die a coward. He might be a good fighter in the ring, but outside? A chicken."

"We went to war," Fraser said, "while he hid behind his father to stay safe at home."

Roxbury's eyes showed too much white as anger transformed his features.

"I'm so disappointed by you, Lord Roxbury." Lady Kingsley shook her head. "I thought you were a gentleman. Instead, you're a fraud. You use your charm to trick people. Shame on you."

"At least your father was a man of his word," Judge Quigley said. "Everyone revered him. The same can't be said about you."

Roxbury's nostrils flared. Good. Ethan's confidence grew. For a vain man like him, who put himself in the centre of the world and who loved only himself as Narcissus had, being confronted with society's scorn and disdain hurt.

"Leave him be, Ethan." Finn lifted his glass. "Lord Roxbury is a spineless worm, good at threatening people weaker than he is. He doesn't have an ounce of courage. His father was a better man. David is a better man than Lord Roxbury."

"I've never liked his eyes," Mrs. Parker said. "Too cold and close to each other."

"He's a chicken." Harry stepped in front of David. "He knows Lord Stark will knock him out with one punch." He went around the room, imitating a chicken. "Nobody likes you, Lord Roxbury."

If Ethan hadn't been so tense, he would have laughed.

"Enough." Roxbury beat his walking stick against the floor. The veins in his neck throbbed. "I accept the challenge."

Ethan's pulse beat a fast rhythm in his temples. Finally.

Finn pulled out his notebook. "Excellent. Let's finalise the legal terms. Judge Quigley, if you will assist me, please. After that, may the best man win." He winked at Ethan and raised a closed fist in encouragement.

"Ethan." Cora cupped his face. The gold band of her ring was warm from her skin. "Are you sure?"

He kissed her inner wrist. "Very much."

Harry tugged at his sleeve. "I can drop some marbles on the floor and make him slip."

"Why don't I have these ideas?" David sounded disappointed.

Ethan patted Harry's shoulder. "There's no need for that." He removed his shirt and boots.

"Bets are on, ladies and gentlemen," Harry said with his usual cheek. "Who will win? The ugly lord with the courage of a chicken, or the former soldier who got a Victoria Cross and gutted pirates?"

David sat in a corner, his expression grave. Papa. The word echoed in Ethan's mind and gave him the strength to face the challenge.

"It's done." Finn asked Ethan and Roxbury to sign a hastily prepared document.

The others made space, pushing the chairs and the table to the edges of the room. Then it was time to start.

"He'll hit your shoulder," Finn whispered. "Anticipate his moves."

Anger rose to the fore the moment Ethan stepped onto the improvised fighting pitch. Too much angry energy coursed through him. He ought to calm himself or the anger would become a disadvantage. He threw shadow punches while Roxbury stripped to his breeches and tossed an impatient glance towards Ethan.

Cora and David held each other. The sight was nothing new. Ethan had seen them hugging countless times in the past weeks. But both of them had a different meaning in his life. They were his family. His wife and his son. The word family filled him with pride and love.

Finn raised a hand. "Let's start."

Everyone spread around, forming a circle. Mrs. Parker paled to the point of looking about to faint. Lady Kingsley watched the scene through her fingers. Judge Quigley read the document again.

Ethan brought up his fists. Roxbury did the same.

"David will never be yours," Ethan said with confidence. David's future depended on his fighting skills.

"You're going to make a fool out of yourself, Stark."

Ethan lunged, aiming at Roxbury's head. But Roxbury was a quick bastard, fast on his feet and coordinated. Ethan would give him that. And obviously, the blow to the head hadn't been as serious as he'd claimed it to be.

"You're quick," he said as Roxbury smirked. "But then again, all cowards are fast. They need the speed to run from danger."

Roxbury's smirk vanished. He threw a punch that hit Ethan's stomach. Dammit. He had to admit that Roxbury was a good boxer too. Ethan squeezed his eyes shut for a moment. The pain caused him to bend over, and Roxbury took advantage of the vulnerable position to punch Ethan's shoulder. Immediate agony burst through his body. His muscles locked in reaction to the blow.

"It's too easy." Roxbury didn't breathe hard. Not a drop of sweat glistened on his skin. "I'll take everything from you, Stark. Although Cora and David have never been yours to start with. They are and always will be mine."

No. They were Ethan's family now. They belonged to Ethan, and Ethan belonged to them. Roxbury's taunting only fed Ethan's wrath further. He was so angry that the searing pain coursing through him became a dull throb.

He spun on his feet and caught Roxbury under the jaw with an uppercut. The impact hurt his own knuckles and burned his shoulder. He poured all his anger and hate into the punch. Roxbury spun on his feet in an elegant pirouette and dropped to the floor with a soft thud.

Ethan remained tense and ready, waiting for Roxbury to stand up. But he remained on the floor.

Finn rushed to the unmoving earl with his uneven gait and crouched.

"Is he dead?" Harry asked with too much excitement. "I bet a shilling on that."

Finn rolled Roxbury onto his back and touched his neck. "Knocked out." He staggered to his feet and raised Ethan's arm. "Lord Stark wins."

Then cheers exploded. Cora and David threw themselves at him. He hugged and kissed them among their tears and sobs. His shoulder hurt like the devil, and his legs trembled, but he'd never felt stronger.

CORA DIDN'T WANT to cry. She'd promised herself she wouldn't. But as she sat at the banquet table in her wedding gown after her wedding ceremony, she couldn't stop tears of joy from welling in her eyes.

Next to her, Ethan looked handsome in his dark groom suit. His friends and soldiers filled the garden in a chaos of rising glasses and loud chatter. After Ethan had defeated Jacob, Judge Quigley had done nothing but complain about the legal situation of the centre and the poor management on Ethan's part. Ethan had listened at the accusations without complaining. The judge had put money, resources, and effort into making the centre legal, likely because his sister was involved. But never mind. The Royal Veterans' Society would stay where it was. No one would be kicked out. Jacob had lost the favour of London's peers, opting to move to Bath. He wasn't going to win the award for the most likable earl any time soon.

David never left Ethan's side. Every time he called Ethan Papa, a burst of love made her happy. Ethan said it was the first time he'd been called Papa, but it was the first time for Cora and David as well. Never would she have thought her life could be so full of love and joy. It wasn't just her wedding with Ethan that made her happy, but David. Watching him laugh, smile, and be a happy boy was the best thing that had ever happened to her.

Ethan wiped her tears with his thumb. "There's something I want to ask you."

"Yes, to whatever you want." Her voice sounded tiny although joy roared within her chest.

He laughed. "I'm afraid you'll have to listen first because I need your approval."

"What is it?" She jolted when Harry caused something to explode. It looked like a pine cone.

"I want to adopt David." A little crease appeared between his eyebrows. "I want him to be legally and officially my son."

"You're his guardian. Do you really want to adopt him?"

"Absolutely. If he agrees."

She couldn't have imagined her joy could be greater. "That would be wonderful."

She rested her head on her husband's shoulder. He gazed down at her and kissed her hand.

"I've found my family," he said, wrapping an arm around David as well.

"We both have."

THE END

about the author

Love stories have always captured my imagination. What's better than two people falling in love with each other? I write steamy romance, usually with a paranormal twist in an historical setting. Add a touch of suspense and mystery and a pinch of darkness. I love stories with  strong, sexy heroes and mischievous heroines who pull no punches.

I live in the City of Sails, New Zealand, drinking tea (coffee gives me anxiety) and devouring books.

Join my newsletter for exclusive content and the chance to receive an ARC copy of my books. Just copy and paste this link into your browser:

<u>Barbara's Newsletter</u>

also by barbara russell

If you love steamy paranormal romance set in Victorian London, my
Royal Occult Bureau series is for you:

<u>The Royal Occult Bureau Series</u>

Are you into shape-shifter romance? Check out my da Vinci's Beasts
series, set in WW2:

<u>da Vinci's Beasts Series</u>

For more Victorian paranormal romance with witches and sexy warriors,
see the Knights of the White Blade series:

<u>The White Order Series</u>

Love steampunk? Check out my Auckland Steampunk series:

<u>Auckland Steampunk Series</u>